# Curiosities at
## *Christmastime*

A Modern Day Pride & Prejudice Reimagining

#2
Seasonal
Situations

# NEY MITCH

# DEDICATION & AUTHOR'S NOTE

Happy holidays readers, or happy any day that you pick up this tale. Welcome to Book II of the series. This time, I managed to do the impossible: keep a series down to three books rather than being my traditionally long-winded self. When the book ends, there will be an Afterword to explain the choices that I made in this chapter
of the trilogy.

This book picks up the precise moment that the first book ended, so, we all can delve into the situation at hand. Friends, into the season, we go!

I do hope you enjoy this chapter of the series, lay back and have fun with it, and are having a great Christmas, Hannukah, Kwanzaa, Winter Solstice, or happy holidays.

Once more, I dedicate this book to my family, whom I love, and any friends who have picked up this tale. Special thanks to my publisher and anyone who helped me make this series possible.

A special thanks to A. K. Madison, who saved my life by giving her insight on Alexandria and letting me pick her brain whenever I needed it, and also to Helyn Roberts-Vickers who has been constant company of mine these three years at least.

Ney Mitch

# ONE
## OVERCOME

There Mr. Darcy stood.

There, I was, crouched on the cold ground, all my spirit disturbed, and I was overcome at the sudden turn of events that shook the foundation of my current state.

Here at the beginning of all things…

Here at the end of the evening.

Here at the beginning of the Halloween festivities.

And here, at the end of my composure.

And I could not believe where I was, and where I had been.

An hour ago, I was happy, carefree, and feeling as if all my life was coming together, was forming, and shaping in the proper way.

And now, in the present, all had been overturned. I liked a man, was in the way of falling in love with him, and for me to be entirely wrong was one thing.

To be able to run off, suffer in silence, and run away from the eyes of the world, was another thing.

But for my grief to have an observer, it is mortifying.

And for the observer to be the one man who you never wanted to see you cry, was the undoing of everything.

In the darkness, on the evening of mischief and mishaps, I saw his face clearly. He was standing across the street, behind a car that must've been his.

Walking around it, he moved slowly, taking in my expression.

Our eyes locked. I felt all the embarrassment, the humiliation, and pain swell in my face, and it was as if he had read everything out loud and had seen the agonies in my very soul.

I didn't want him to see me like this. For indeed, it was the last thing that I had ever wanted to happen.

"Elizabeth?" he asked, still moving slowly. To my surprise, his tone was filled with concern.

I didn't want him to see me like this and was not going to allow it to happen.

Standing up, I took a step back.

"Please," I declared, desperately and with much anxiety.

That was the only word that I could get out, but there was something about my tone that halted Darcy. He sensed that I did not want him to come closer, and that I meant what I implied.

"Please," I repeated, lower and with my emotions stirred. My heartbreak was in my tone, and he perceived. "You must understand…that I did not want you to see me this way."

We did not speak.

Rather, through the darkness, we stared at each other. Our eyes said much, but also saying so little.

With him, it was confusion, astonishment, and uncertainty of what to do next.

With me, it was alarm, shock, and feeling an added pain to an already painful evening. Not only was I betrayed, but there was a spectator for the aftermath.

Still looking at him, I stood up slowly. I felt as if there was a weight to my limbs, holding them down to the earth, and binding me to an inferno of burdens. Telling my feet to move, and my arms to defy them being too heavy to swing in the air, I turned around and began to attempt to walk back to the school.

After taking three slow and heavy steps, Darcy called out to me.

"Elizabeth," he exclaimed, "I don't understand. Can't I do anything?"

I stopped.

His words were kind. His words were honestly *kind*, and if it had come from any other direction, I would have asked them to walk me back to the school.

But it was too late.

Everything was too late.

Gathering my courage, I turned right back to him.

I'm sure that I must have looked so heartbroken to him, and that rendered him speechless again. His tall and handsome frame had a mysteriousness to it, especially under the cover of night. But his face was like stone, except for his eyes. They did say something, but I didn't know what that was.

"You must know something," I began, no matter how strange I sounded when I spoke, "that no matter what happened, I would never do this one thing in front of you."

He did not speak, but still only looked at me.

"I would never let you see me cry," I uttered, simply and slowly. "No matter what, I would never let you see me cry."

When hearing that, he blinked, and I detected a quiet, but present surprise.

But I did not waste time trying to find out. I had no curiosity about the matter.

I only had one instinct: get out of there. By all that was safe and secure in me, retreat was the only thing on my mind.

No longer did my limbs feel like weights. The boulder that was 'suffering' had been lifted off my shoulders, and I got the use of my legs back.

Turning again, I ran away, placing as much distance between myself and the phantom of my past.

———

And yet, how quickly I had forgotten that there were two ghosts from my history in the area.

While I had just run from the phantom of my past, there was a phantom of the present, still in the school's **walls.**

Once I got close to the front doors, I stood there. If Wickham had been wise, he would have already left. But wisdom does not often coincide with worthless pieces of cheating horse crap. And that's precisely what he was.

I was afraid to face him again—but that fear lasted for no more than ten seconds.

Instead, it was replaced by anger, wrath, and an instinctive desire for revenge in some way. Knowing that he was within the school walls would not keep me outside. Oh no! I had come here to do a job, and he must go. Not I!

Wiping the emotion from my eyes, I told myself to look happy. Going back into the school, I joined everyone and began to hand out candy.

There was only one issue: Jane was Jane.

And as a result, she was able to detect that something was wrong with me.

"What is it? Are you alright?" she whispered to me.

"Nothing," I rushed out, too eagerly, with a smile plastered on my face and my eyes lit up perhaps a little too much. "Just taken away by the moment."

"First, you disappeared for more than you usually take when you go to the bathroom. And second, with you, I know when there is a real smile versus a fake one. It's forced. What's wrong?"

Still smiling, I handed out some food to some of the last students who were in the lineup.

"I can't tell you," I said, barely moving my mouth. "Because, if I do tell you, then I might just break down. I cannot do that. Not in public. I refuse to do that. All that I can tell you is that something terrible has happened. Give me the right to not cause a scene. Because, under the circumstances, I can forget myself and do just that."

Jane looked alarmed for a moment, but she replaced her look with a mask of fake nonchalance.

"Okay. Got it."

We continued to hand out the last of the candy until all the students were done and were filing into people's vans, where they would travel around in shifts.

Once the last child left, Jane leaned into me.

"Whatever is going on, you don't have to hand out candy to trick or treaters."

"No," I rushed out. "I know that you want to take Josie and Killian out. I don't want to be that person who makes you stay inside and take my place. It's fine," I stressed. "I'll still be at home. I've got enough composure to hand out candy."

Jane gave me a sympathetic look.

"Once I get done taking the children trick or treating," she said, "we can talk all you want about whatever is going on."

"You've gotta have an ear that will put up with a long story."

She tapped her ear. "Earlobes for days."

———

Jane drove us home, parked the car, she and the kids got out and immediately went trick or treating, while I manned my station. That meant that I was going to sit in the living room, keeping an eye out for children coming by for candy.

When I went inside, I was met by hearing the song 'Jack's Lament' from the movie 'Nightmare Before Christmas', and I was met with a rather anachronistic sight. In the living room, Kitty was wearing a sexy sorceress costume, Lieutenant Fitzwilliam was dressed as Sherlock Holmes, and they were slow dancing to the song. Since the music was very loud, they didn't hear me come in, and for a second, I halted.

Standing there, I could not help but watch them as they slowly danced to a song that didn't match their romantic mood—but it also did. There was something about them both that were so wrapped up in each other, there was blatant comfort between the two, and I was not watching a forced romantic moment.

No. They fit.

Kitty's eyes were closed as she pressed her face under Richard's neck. He rested his head over hers, and there was a desire for them to touch the other. To be one with the other.

Kitty really did love Richard Fitzwilliam.

And he loved her.

It was real. Everything about it was so real.

For a second, I wondered about it. It was as if I was floating out of my own grief and realized that a person actually could find happiness in another person, and it could be a long-lasting sensation.

Did Wickham ever look at me that way?

Wickham!

His face returned to me, and so did the deception, the cheating, and the fact that I clearly meant nothing to him. All the pangs of being lied to had rendered me blind. Did I willfully not notice all the signs that were there?

This was just another moment where I felt the proverbial rug being pulled out from my inner security, and I felt as if I never knew myself.

So close we humans come to discovering who we are, and then for that discovery to never have been a discovery at all. Rather, it was just another bump along the road that unravels to a great unwinding.

And I was undone.

Taking my eyes away from Kitty and Fitzwilliam, I tiptoed up the stairs, went into my bedroom, and found the comfort of solitude.

With my door closed, having shut out the entire world, in my belongings, I belonged. I sunk down to the floor, pressed my knees against my chest, wrapped my head around them, and placed my face on my knees.

Then I gave way fully. I wept. Truly, I could not recall if tears came or not, but it signified nothing. My body shook as the shock had gone away, and it gave way to the after-effects of heartbreak.

Downstairs, Halloween songs blasted, and it led to me being able to drown out my grief, and the world was given a break from the racket that I had made.

How could I have been so blind? So completely taken in, as it were. I mean, I knew that Wickham and I had only just started dating, and that we had never actually said that we were monogamous. In a world of people living off implications, time has taught us that people must communicate everything, and spell everything out, for it to become cemented in stone.

Simply put, if you want to be in an exclusive relationship, you must tell the person that you are wholly committed and that you don't want an open relationship. That you want it to be a one-on-one sort of thing.

Wickham and I never actually spoke about it, so maybe he was unsure of—

What was I doing?

Was I about to justify this? At first, I wondered if I had completely forgotten my pride, but I didn't. I was merely trying to justify Wickham's betrayal, because it would alleviate my pain. I could explain away the embarrassment that I felt at being deceived. But you know what? I needed to confront this. I needed to call this what it was. Wickham knew that we were together, and I felt that way about him. He had betrayed me, and even could be described as cheating on me, if it had gone on further. And if we had dated longer, it would have been cheating. After all, it was evident that Wickham was going to continue seeing this other woman while he was with me. They were clearly attached and heavy about it.

No, it was better to know now and face the music.

It was better to feel this pain, rather than for it to get even worse, and I would want to kill him. Or for my dad to find out, and then he would kill Wickham instead.

But I was safe now, in the sanctuary that was my room. After the weeping subsided, I removed my clothes, threw on my pajamas, went to bed and did everything in my power to resist playing sad music to match my mood. In truth, I was very tempted to put on the song 'King of Sorrow' by Sade, but I managed to resist the impulse.

At first, I remembered that I had to wait at the door for trick-or-treaters, but luckily, Kitty and Richard were clearly staying home. That left me the freedom to pass my job down to them, and they could man the door.

My eyelids grew heavy, and I was willing to let the matter rest, and decided to think about it tomorrow morning.

And so, it was.

So, it would be.

Tomorrow would bring me the strength to confront it all and know what to do next.

Finally, I fell asleep and let the world fade away.

# TWO
# WHAT DREAMS MAKE YOU CONFRONT

F ade away, the world did.
...    When I opened my eyes again, I was standing on the front steps to the University of Louisville's Library.

The sky was an indication of it being just before dawn, as it was a deep blue, but the sun was nowhere to be seen. Surely the library could not be open. When I looked up at the building, I had a sudden flashback of all the times I studied in there, back when I was an undergrad.

But I suspected otherwise. Going up the steps, I opened the door and, sure enough, it was not locked. When I entered, the library had the familiar welcome coziness that you get when you go into a quiet place.

I walked past the counter that had the new releases, the art displays at the very beginning, the shelves that contained the movies and shows that you were able to rent and watch in a smaller room that had the DVD and blue-ray player. There was even a VCR from older movies and documentaries that they still had the VHS tapes from.

I had grown used to that collection because it had documentaries of Henry VIII's wives, and that sad part of history always drew me in. We often think that we're living in the worst of times, but when you dig into history, you see just how much there was no such thing as the 'golden age', but times were always barbaric

—after all, humanity is humanity, and it can never be fully auto-corrected. All we can do is point out when we are wrong, but wrong is eternal.

As I moved around the film and tv collection, I walked to the end of the library, where there were some very lovely steps that led to the second floor. It had been a favorite place for me to go, so I walked up them to the second floor.

And then I felt a familiar presence.

Walking among the desks and chairs, I came upon the back of a man who was sitting at a cubby, reading. At first, I just studied him, then I felt comfortable enough to speak.

"Is it a good read?"

He raised the book, and it was 'The Great Gatsby'.

"It never gets old," Darcy answered, "no matter how many times I read it."

"I suppose it's because its story never stops being relevant," I analyzed. "The pursuit of wealth to obtain the happy moment from your past. To get that love that you thought was real love, but it was never real to begin with. And to be surrounded by people who have nothing true about them, and the only one who dies, is the one who actually did care. It's always the careless ones who get the caring ones killed."

"Precisely." Darcy lowered the book and looked at me. "That happens in the social world, the political world, and the romantic one. It makes it hard to put yourself out there, doesn't it?"

"Yes. That's why the worst thing that you could do was to put your heart on your sleeve."

"And you did not do that," he said, closing the book, "until now."

My body shook again, and my face gave way to surprise at being forced to face the matter so quickly.

"Lizzy, I know that you met me. And you know that I know it."

"And it was in the worst way," I furthered, "of all the times to see you again, it had to be like that."

"When your heart was on your sleeve."

"That's the last way that I wanted you to see me," I declared, exasperated.

"Part of that was on you," he said, standing up, "you could have avoided this if you had chosen to meet me earlier. You could have controlled it then, and this would not have happened."

Suddenly, I got angry.

"If you're about to do that thing where I am the one to blame," I declared, "I don't need to put up with this."

I turned and walked away, around the bookshelves. I quickened my pace as Darcy followed me.

"But you have to, and you know it," he continued. "It's the only way for you to make sense of things. When you put off something, you are only delaying the situation, and now it caught up with you."

I moved around another bookshelf, and he followed me.

"I had my reasons," I said over my shoulder.

"Yes, you did. But look what happened. What was it like seeing me again?"

"You know what it was like. It was agony."

"You make seeing me seem worse than what Wickham did."

I stopped, turned, and looked at him. He stopped in his place, and we were facing each other from across a study table.

"That's not true," I said simply.

"Is it?" he asked, his brow furrowed. "He hurt you, and what was the first thought that you had afterwards, was that you never wanted me to see you cry?"

"Of course, I never wanted you to see me like that."

"Why not?"

"Because it was all that I had left!" I roared. The silence between us became deafening, and no longer did I have to worry about us being overheard, because no one was in the library. Especially since we were not even there to begin with. I lowered my voice, to add emphasis to what I had meant. After all, if you shout too much for too long, when does anyone ever take you seriously? "What you have to understand is that looking strong is important to me. Hell, I never met anyone who it was not important to. And I'm no different; I simply am aware of the fact."

"But now it's different," Darcy interjected, "Now you have met me. And now you have to ask yourself, what do you do next?"

Confusion etched over my face and clearly across my mind. I honestly did not know what to do or what was the next step to take.

"I don't think that I'm ready to tell you," I determined, then I turned, and I walked away.

Darcy followed me, so I picked up my pace.

He walked quickly after me.

So, I sped up, moving around bookshelves, creating a winding path for Darcy to follow. He continued to relentlessly pursue me.

"What do you plan to do next?" He continued to call after me. Sometimes his voice felt so close, as if he was whispering through my ear. Other times it felt like it was coming from a great distance, as if he was shouting at me from across a field. The volume was variable and pounded against my ears. "What do you plan to do next?"

Past many books we raced, row upon row of book titles that would never be opened, because they were worthy to read, but who ever has enough time? No one ever has enough time.

Eventually Darcy caught up to me when we reached a section of the library that had an exhibit on Regency writers. Seeing that there was nowhere else to go, I turned around.

"I was not lying to you, when I said that I don't know," I answered. "I truly don't know. I know how this is going to end, and I know that I will eventually overcome this, and that I will fight to beat myself. And that I will win. But as for what to do next, for the next step, no I don't know where to go."

"Then meet me," Darcy stressed. "Get to know the man that I am now. Start there."

"I will let things unfold as they will," I said, "but that's it. I'm not going to seek you out. And I don't want you to come to me. I'll let things happen organically. I am not going to force anything. I'm done forcing things to happen that are not meant to happen in the first place."

Darcy rubbed his lip and then placed his hand in his pockets.

"I'm sorry about what happened between you and Wickham."
I sighed.

"Thank you. That means a lot, believe me."

"I'd say that this is going to go away eventually, but I don't know," he said. "It's hard to be betrayed. But if it helps, it's not your fault. Do not do that thing where you wonder what you could have done to have prevented that. That's just the way that some people are. You did not deserve what he put you through."

"Thank you and don't worry," I assured him, "I blamed myself for two seconds, then the third second kicked in, and I came to my senses. Give me a few months, and I'll find a way to laugh myself out of this. But for right now, I am upset, and perhaps I need to be. Perhaps I need to feel this now."

Darcy took a book from the shelf and tossed it to me.

"Sometimes, nothing helps a person recover than understanding that misery loves company. Just remember, the lead character from that book got over it. And so will you."

Having caught the book, I read the title and author:

It Takes a Witch
Heather Blake

I grinned. I recognized that title before…

# THREE
## THE MORNING AFTER

I woke up the next morning to the familiar noises that come with a full house.

"Lizzy?" Jane called to me, as I rubbed my eyes, "are you awake?"

"Barely!" I croaked, rising out of my bed, with my dream from the night before still gnawing away at my consciousness.

"Oh, sorry! Kitty! Are you awake?"

"Just got out of the shower. But Mary is almost dressed."

"Mary!" Jane called. "Are you decent?"

"Coming!" Mary called downstairs. "Need help with breakfast?"

"Oh yeah."

"Roger that."

I overheard Mary walking downstairs, as I stood up and put on my bathrobe. As I tied it around my waist, I clutched my head, because I felt an intense ache.

As I passed the mirror, I looked at my reflection. Even though beauty sleep always leads to someone looking like an ogre, there was nothing out of the ordinary.

A part of me was glad of it, but it was also provocative. Our outsides never match our insides. Internally, I was falling apart and felt the anxiety of being so thoroughly heartbroken. I felt the ugliness of being in agony, as if I had aged fifty years, and did not want the world to see my face. Even though they would understand the grotesque aspect of a heartbroken person, you don't want them to see it—but you also do. They would empathize, or ridicule, and you don't know on what face the coin will fall.

All that you know is that you have to face the music and live. Laugh, live, and overcome.

Welcome to the morning after, Lizzy!

———

As I left my bedroom, I bumped into Richard Fitzwilliam, who had nothing else but a towel around his waist.

"Whoa," I asserted, determined to sound natural, "hello, birthday suit."

"Sorry," Richard Fitzwilliam said. "Never was sold on the whole 'man's got to get a bathrobe' sort of thing. I'm bringing primal back."

He walked to Kitty's bedroom, and they immediately talked about Thanksgiving.

From one holiday to the next. After all, we were now in November.

I went into the bathroom, removed my clothes, and then I turned on the shower.

I could not explain it, but the sound of the running water triggered something within me. Flashes of Wickham and I raced across my thoughts together.

I liked him.

Everything about him was perfect.

Almost too perfect.

Maybe that was the problem. I had met an ideal and realized that there was no such thing as an ideal. And Wickham did think highly of himself. When you date someone who has a sense of superiority, that might be a bad thing. People have limits and limitations, and the more they are aware of it, the better.

I stepped into the shower, letting the water run all over me.

Thank the gods of sanitation that showers were invented. As the water fell all over me and the pressure push along my skin, I felt the baptism of being born anew. For nothing helps a woman or man become what they once were, like a shower to help them return to their best state.

Then I remember Wickham kissing that woman the night before.

The horrible scene. I felt it pang against my heart, which beat quicker. My stomach lurched out, as if it had been wounded and I clutched my chest, kneeling over. I slid to the shower floor, and I wept again. With the waterdrops falling all over my face, it was impossible to tell where my grief began and waterdrops ended. I was glad about it.

Giving into my heartbreak, I moved into a fetal position, holding my knees to my chest, and I wept even more violently. I wanted to bang my hands against the bathroom walls, tear down the tiles, and break something. Anything to release the agony that had now transitioned to anger.

That was the second stage.

I had never indulged denial as the first stage of this sort of situation, but it had been replaced by sorrow, embarrassment, and now it was turning to rage.

I had a right to be angry. So angry, I would be.

But the pain in my stomach was still there, and it would be there for quite some time longer. That was the natural way of things.

Eventually I knew that there was nothing for it but to collect myself, I stood up, and I turned off the water.

I had bathed long enough.

One day, I would be myself again.

I just needed to fall apart for a little while. There was no point in denying it.

———

When I exited the bathroom, Mama had come out of her bedroom, fully dressed.

She looked refreshed and pleasant. She smiled at me, which was quite a surprise.

"Morning," I greeted her.

"Good morning," she said, her tone as easygoing as her expression.

"You look cheery," I said, "have a good time last night?"

"I went to a Halloween party with the girls," she said, referring to her friends. "We had a great time, and my costume was a hit."

"What did you go as?"

"Hera, Queen of the Greek Gods."

I chuckled, even though I didn't really want to socialize very much right now. In fact, I still wanted to keep the world at a distance. Yet since mama was being pleasant, I wanted to take advantage of the opportunity.

"That must've been a great costume. Why didn't you give me a chance to see it?"

"Don't worry, I got pictures from the party. We had such a great time. I felt like I was fifteen and we were at a high school dance again. When I was growing up, I came from a different generation, where the guys had no problem asking us girls to dance."

"Well, that was different. In your generation there were actual dance moves and routines. In ours, it was just 'get up and hope for the best' without us having any rhythm. Besides, many guys were interested in dancing at Sante Fe High. They just didn't want to dance with me, that's all."

"That was their problem," she replied, boldly. "They were all royal buttholes. You were as gorgeous as the rest of them."

She called all my bullies 'royal buttholes'. I was filled with joy at her maternal desire to protect me. She was finally being overprotective, and I found a profound joy in it. Feeling the compliment of her motherly vulgar tones, I smiled and then began to burst into tears.

"Oh, thank you, mom," I said with a sob.

When seeing me so meek and appreciative of her concern for

me, mom's face softened, and she shifted from pleasantness to a burst of maternal affection.

"Oh," she replied, hugging me. All my strength gave way and I let her hold me as I collapsed into her embrace. "What's this about? Mind you, I like it, but is something wrong?"

She didn't know. How could she? My reaction was not just from the memory of the ghosts from my wonder years, but it was also in response to the night before.

A flash of Wickham kissing the other woman had come to mind again, and I needed her to hold me, as she was doing now.

When looking into her eyes, I could not tell her. I didn't want to tell anyone just yet, for I was still embarrassed.

"It's fine," I rushed out, "I just needed that."

"You're hiding something," she replied, "but fine, keep your secrets. I know that you will tell me when you are ready. It's just that…"

"What?"

"You never open up to me about things. So, when you get around to it, that would be nice."

"I…"

She swiped the air, dismissively.

"Don't worry, I won't prod anymore."

I smiled sadly.

"Thanks."

As I went back to my bedroom, she called out to me.

"Your father's going to arrive in the next few days, isn't he?" she asked.

"Yeah," I replied, "by next week."

"Fine. Tell him that his guestroom is waiting for him."

I squinted.

"You're not angry at the idea of seeing him," I said, "despite everything that's going on?"

"It just occurred to me that it's good that your father is coming. It's good for Mary to see him. Whatever is going on between us should not affect how we ought to be there for you all."

"Now that's the right way of looking at things," I said, proud of her. Then I had another thought. She was being very empathetic right now—which meant, there was more to this story. "Mom?"

She turned to me, her face lovely from a natural illumination.

"You're glowing," I realized. Then it was like a light had turned on in my head. "You met someone!"

Mom blushed and she covered her mouth, looking at the floor.

"You've met a guy, haven't you?" I asked, folding my arms over my chest. "I knew it!"

"Well, if your father can do it—"

"I'm not judging you," I said, "in fact, I think this might be good for you. Is it just a two-week sort of thing? Or are we going to meet this guy at a family dinner?"

Mom blushed, and scratched her chin, looking a little bashful.

"I would like to bring him to a family dinner, but not to meet you all. Because you already know him."

"We do?" I asked, with an arched eyebrow.

"Yes."

"Well," I said, a little impatient that she was waiting so long, "who is the guy?"

"William Lucas."

If I had been holding something, I would drop it.

"Mr. Lucas?" I asked, scarcely able to believe my ears. "Did I hear you right?"

"Yes," she said, drawing the word out slowly.

"Charlotte Lucas's dad?" I shrieked.

"Keep your voice down. I still haven't told your sisters yet. I didn't want to tell you, but I figured that I should start doing it."

"Yeah, you think?" I was so flabbergasted. "And you both really like each other?"

"Yeah, we do. And don't look at me that way. He's been a widower for three years now. He's finally ready to start dating again."

"And what about Charlotte? Has he told her?"

"Not yet. We're waiting for the right time."

I rubbed my eyes, frustrated.

"Mom, I got news for you."

"What?"

"With these sorts of situations, there's no such thing as the right time. It's like a Band-Aid that has to come off before it comes off naturally. It's gonna hurt, but it will be better to get it over with." My breath was ragged. "Would it help if I told Charlotte?"

Mom was quick to accept my offer and confirmed that I was the best person to deliver the news. Once she gave me her permission, it was all set to go. I asked her if she also wanted me to tell my sisters for her, but she realized that she had to break the news herself. In that way, she would do right by us.

———

When I went back to my room, I realized just how much I was the bearer of shocking news. But that was the way that it often was with me. I was used to being the one to break news to people. Maybe I was giving into that role a little too much. Because if I did that, then that would keep people from learning how to communicate with other people independently.

Looking in the mirror, I began to brush my hair. As I looked at myself, I wondered about how my life was turning out—again.

But it was so alarming. My dad was dating my mom's cousin.

My mom was dating my friend's widowed father.

What was going on?

I know that life is complicated, but this was a lot to take in. While I was not in the mood to get in the way of my parents living a little, and grabbing life by the proverbial horns, I still was a little worried. Either this all could end really well, or there was drama up ahead.

Well, we shall see.

But, regarding coupling, there was another set of pictures that could not be done away with.

Kitty had Richard Fitzwilliam.

Jane had Bingley.

Mom was dating William Lucas.

Dad was dating Anna Gardiner.

20

And Lydia has—Denny, who was dating everyone.

Everyone was happy…and then there was me.

I looked at my phone.

Wickham had not called or texted.

I wanted him to, but also did not want him to. At all.

Whatever excuse he would give would change nothing. But that's the problem when you like someone who cheats on you. You hate them, but you are still attracted to them. You are angry that they have not explained themselves, but there is nothing to explain.

But I knew what was going to happen.

Wickham would never call or text me again.

And I would never call him.

I still liked him but would never call him.

I would regret that we would never be together.

But I would never call him.

And I still did not have a big love of my life, as everyone else had by my age.

Maybe I was not meant for it.

Oh well.

———

When I went downstairs, fully dressed, Josie and Killian had just finished eating and Jane was taking them to school.

"Lizzy," Jane said, "are you feeling better this morning?"

"I am," I lied. "Sorry that I pulled a running man on you the night before. But I'm better now."

"Good. We gotta go," she said, getting Josie to put her coat on, "and don't forget that we have rehearsal tonight for the play."

I breathed in heavily. I had to go back to George-Mason so soon after the incident that turned my life upside down. But since Wickham knew about the rehearsals, I knew that I would not see him there. I think I was safe from having to see that walking piece of 'vomit'. Maybe I should pour soup all over his car. I think I liked that idea.

"Right," I said, getting some bacon and eggs from out of the fridge. "I'll be home in time for you to take us."

"Good. And are you ready to tell me what's bothering you?"

"I just found out something, that's all. Give me a couple months, and then I will tell you everything."

"Okay," Jane replied, "keep your secrets. For now."

"Lizzy," Kitty said as she was pouring some orange juice for Richard, who had just fondly smacked her bum and kissed her cheek, "movie night is coming up, and we've settled on the 'Dragonheart' films. But since there are five of them, we can't choose which one to watch. We've all got our choices, and you have to break the vote. I want to watch the Third 'Dragonheart' movie."

"Which one was that one again?" I asked.

"The Sorcerer's Curse'."

"Oh, yeah, I like that one."

"But I like the first one best," Richard countered, as Kitty pinched his chest. "What's better than Sean Connery's dragon, Draco?"

"Josie and I want to watch the second movie," Killian said as they were headed to the front door. "It's got kung-fu in it."

"I like the fifth one though," I said, trying to maintain my fake, but valiant, optimistic attitude. "'Dragonheart: Vengeance' is so underrated that it's not even funny."

"Well," Mary said, "I like the fourth movie because—"

Her face distorted, and she clutched her stomach.

"Mary?" I asked, "you okay?"

Quickly, she ran to the trash bin, yanked it open and puked into it, hurling up her breakfast.

All of us froze, watching her convulse under purging, until she was done. When she looked back at us, she covered her mouth with a paper towel.

"You're sick," I said, "you can't go to work."

"I don't get it," Mary wondered. "I was fine a second ago. Now I'm better."

"Oh," I realized.

"What?"

I looked at Jane and she looked at Mary.

"It's morning sickness," Jane explained to her. "it's beginning for you."

When hearing that, Mary held her stomach, remembering the baby that was growing within.

The lighthearted conversation that we had just been having had quite lost its appeal.

# FOUR
## BREAKING THE BAD

"Your mom and my dad!" Charlotte Lucas, ne Collins, uttered, as she sat next to me. Since the kids were in school, and this was her day off from work, she had the day to herself, so we met and got some lunch from a food truck. We sat down on a bench, eating it as we watched the world move around us. Now that Halloween was over, Christmas decorations were beginning to be put up around the city.

I had just finished telling her the whole astonishing truth.

"Yup," I said, "our parents are dating."

I smiled, amused at Charlotte's reaction.

"You're happy about this," Charlotte noted, reading my expression.

"I am neither happy nor sad about it. I simply had the time to overcome the shock. I'm just amused at your reaction. To be honest, I'm just as scared as you are. At first, I didn't see why this was happening."

"Me too," Charlotte said, rolling her head backwards, annoyed. "Of all the people in the world that they could have met, it was each other?"

"I'm not saying that it's any better than when my dad is dating Anna Gardiner," I acknowledged, "but I just worry that it might all lead to some dramatic moment that no one wants to see."

"That's what I'm afraid of too," Charlotte groaned. "It's not just that, but I'm upset that my dad never talked to me about it. He never told me anything."

"Mom didn't tell us either. I just found out by studying her behavior, and then I put two and two together. I guess they were afraid of this moment. Of letting us know."

"They were being cowards about it."

I gave Charlotte a look and I saw how upset she was.

"Damn it," Charlotte grunted. She stomped the ground with her foot.

"I know why my mom wants to date again," I added, "she's been divorced for a while, and she is at the point where she is learning to live again. With your dad, well, she already knows him, and they both are social creatures. But with Mr. Lucas—can you guess why he wanted to date my mom? They are so different."

"I don't know. He's never been fully himself since Mom died. She was the one who ran everything."

"Then maybe it's because he's lonely. I'm not saying that you shouldn't be upset—trust me, it's right to be. I'm just saying that he was a widower for a bit, and now…"

"No, you're right. As much as this grinds my gears, Dad was alone for a long time, and my siblings and I can't always be there to keep him company a lot. It's not just that, but I should have read the signs. Over the past few weeks, dad has looked more alive and animated. I chalked it all up to him finally getting over mom being gone, but now I see that it's because he was dating someone. Well, at least it's a woman that I know already."

"You're angry," I said, "don't worry, let it out. I'm not going to be offended."

"I just don't understand it all. Yeah, your mom and my dad do love hanging out a lot and are very much people in the mix of things, but still I didn't know that their personalities fit. Then again, when it comes to dating, opposites can attract." She threw her hands in the air. "It's just so strange, knowing that your dad is dating anyone else other than your mom."

"I know. I felt the same way when Dad told me that he was dating Cousin Anna."

We both looked ahead at the park around us.

"We humans are very good at making a mess of our lives, aren't we?" I asked.

"True. And who am I to talk?"

"You'll be okay," I said. "But who am I to talk either?"

———

We were still amidst our conversation when there was a tour guide who stood near us with her tour group. The tour guide was a woman who began with the history of Virginia when it became a British colony.

She gave a brief history of how human bondage began in Virginia, then how Colonial Virginia had become an amalgamation of Algonquin-speaking Native Americas, English and other Europeans, and West Africans. Each culture had brought their language, rituals, and customs.

"During your time as a tour guide," Charlotte whispered to me, "will you get to mention that stuff?"

"Meryton Manor Tours usually focuses on the Scottish immigrants who found Alexandria," I said, "because it's good to begin on a positive note. But I also get to mention the tribes who were here first, and their history. I also get to talk about how Alexandria, during our Civil War, was not actually part of the Confederacy. Soon into the war, the Union army took Alexandria over, and it became a logistical supply center for the Federal army."

"Really?" Charlotte asked. "I didn't know that."

"Yeah, it's true. Alexandria was part of Virginia that still belonged to the North. Especially since Richmond had been the Confederate Capital during that time. Also, I get to talk about the Southern women who were spies for the Union Army. It made sense because we were the best at going unnoticed."

As if on cue, the tour guide began to talk about two Richmond women who were spies. The first woman was Elizabeth Van Lew, who was a wealthy white woman who had created a whole network of spies in Virginia, and then smuggled secrets to the Union armies. Then there was Mary Bowser, a freed slave, who Elizabeth had gotten hired into the Confederate White House, and she was secretly a spy for the Union. Because everyone assumed that Mary was enslaved, they thought she was illiterate, but she had been educated. So, she smuggled all that she learned out of the confederate white house, and got her intel to Elizabeth Van Lew, or another spy in Elizabeth's network.

That was another story that I had been researching and was going to tell on one of my tours. It was a fun bit of history that showed just how hard and complicated the times were. Southern women helped both sides of the war, and I thought to pay close attention to how the tour guide spoke, so that I could take notes on the best way to tell that bit of history.

But then, the inevitable happened. From my time as a tour guide, there was always that person who interrupted your tour, to show how 'smart and progressive, or unprogressive, they were'. What I mean is that, you can be giving a tour about a historically sensitive subject, and someone has to put their 'two cents' in about elaborating on the psychology behind the horrible moment. Especially when it pertains to a particular nation being oppressed, they just *have* to interrupt you about what they have discussed and theorized on the subject matter. Never mind that they are being rude to you by interrupting your lecture with their nonsense. *Never mind* that they have to inject their 'message' into your narrative. You just want to give the history. Attempting to show how 'evolved' they are, when in reality, they are demeaning you. When it comes to tours, this happens more often than you would think.

Like right now.

You see, that's the problem with 'people who mean well'. They can be as annoying as the ones who 'don't mean well'. As the tour guide was telling the story, she was interrupted by a person in the tour five times!

The tour guide was an African American, telling the narrative, and a woman on her tour interrupted her, trying to explain to the others around her, about how women spies were very effective, because of 'lamp-shading'.

I rolled my eyes. I had experienced someone giving that term to me on one of my tours, and it was so annoying, because it was one of those modern terms that clearly was not going to stay in fashion.

"What the hell is lamp-shading?" Charlotte asked, flicking her blonde hair behind her ear, as her face screwed up, in annoyance at the woman who was interrupting the tour guide.

"It's a term about how you view a person as a lampshade," I said, "if I can remember the definition properly, it's something like the person puts the shade on someone else, who is the light. So, the lampshade individual appears to make things darker, when in truth, they are the one who is underestimated. It is political correctness gone mad."

"That sounds stupid."

"It's because it is. When I did tours, I came across idiots like this. It's annoying. And she keeps interrupting the guide."

"Precisely. The woman is trying to tell the history, and she is trying to take the history from her."

Then the woman in the crowd reached a whole new level of annoying. After the woman who could not shut up about lamp-shading, she eclipsed herself on getting on everyone's nerves. She continued to speak of 'lamp-shading', took a step too far, and then said to the tour guide 'not that I'm calling you a lampshade'.

I covered my eyes, mortified, and very embarrassed. But Charlotte, who had a similar look to the lampshade moron, resorted to anger.

"That's it," Charlotte whispered to me, "I've reached my breaking point."

She leaned forward, cleared her throat, spoke from her diaphragm, so that she could interrupt the woman.

"Excuse me," Charlotte interjected, forcefully. Everyone on the tour turned to her. She looked directly at the woman and also at the tour guide, who was now nervously pulling at a couple of her dreadlocks, wondering how much further this tour had gotten away from her. "I know that I am not on the tour, but

I am interested in the subject matter, and I don't have the chance to hear this stuff a lot. Miss, can you let the guide finish her speech, so that I can learn more about it? I'm just really curious, is all."

The tour guide's face switched from anxiety, to ease, and gratitude. She mouthed the words 'thank you'.

"Oh, right," the 'lampshade' woman replied, "continue with the tour."

All the other people on the tour breathed a sigh of relief and gratitude to Charlotte Lucas. The guide continued her tour, and they were able to move onto the next topic, which was the foundations of Alexandria.

———

Once the tour had moved on and Charlotte and I were by ourselves, I smiled at her.

"Well, you're a brave cookie."

"I couldn't take it anymore," Charlotte said. "Call it embarrassment or revelation. That woman was so fast at showing how enlightened she was, that she was disrespecting the very people she was trying boost up. You ever notice how people who are so quick to pride themselves on how progressive they are, they don't see when they are being as prejudiced as the ignorant ones?"

"Oh yeah. It's good to be open to other people's stories about their history, and to help boost their narratives. But you **also** ought to let them *tell their own narratives when they are telling their story*. Talk with them when the time comes to talk with them. But don't talk for them, and suppress their right to talk *for* themselves, while all you're good at doing is talking *at* them. Those sorts of people fit right back into the category of those types 'who don't actually care about people'. They care about ideas, and that's it."

Suddenly, my mind raced to every dream that I had between Darcy and me. Of course, each interaction was an incredible manifestation from my subconsciousness. And yet, on another level, it was still my mind.

All our conversations, all our interactions, were held in my dreamscape, under lock and key.

My dreams controlled our whole relationship.

My subconscious was talking *for* Darcy, and *at* him, rather than letting him talk for himself.

I was telling his story, and he was not even given a moment to tell it himself.

His cousin told me that he had changed. Should I listen to Darcy explain this change?

"See what I mean?" Charlotte asked me. Her question drove me out of my musings, and I returned to the moment at hand.

"Yeah, I get it," I assured her. "That's the thing about progressivism. It's a brilliant concept, but sometimes it is hijacked by the wrong people. And they accidentally give justification to those who don't want to see things progress. They end up validating the villains."

"Precisely. It's tedious. Why do all the good causes get ruined by the worst intentions?"

"It's human nature. We often like a little bit of double standards with our orange juice in the morning."

Charlotte laughed at that, and then my mind turned to Darcy again.

"How long it takes us people to wake up from being blind to spotting the obvious a lot," I said, philosophically.

Then we went back to talking about my mom dating her dad.

# FIVE
# MAKING THE TRANSITION

Later in the evening, I was supposed to go to rehearsal at George Mason, but I couldn't.

I just couldn't.

Since I still had not told Jane or anyone else that Wickham and I were no longer a thing—and how it all ended—I had no good excuse.

But Jane was Jane.

All that I had to do was tell her that I was a little upset about something and was not ready to talk about it. She quietly understood and told me that she would give me the info of what happened when she got back.

Josie and Killian were not as easily satisfied with my reason, but Jane did not allow them to keep urging me to come along.

I was able to go upstairs and practice my lines for the next day.

After eating a Marie Calendar frozen dinner—which surprisingly tasted very good—I raced to the sanctuary that was my room and began to rehearse.

My attempts were futile.

After five minutes of rehearsing, I would burst into tears.

This was the after-effect of everything falling apart so badly. I was still devastated, and I had no choice but to be. Only a cold heart would not crumble, and I was still in the beginning. We all hate this part of the experience.

Of being betrayed.

Of choosing the wrong person to care for.

Of being wrong yourself.

Of thinking that you are an idiot.

Even though there was nothing that you could have done or considered. You had no way of predicting the outcome of the scenario.

But you still kick yourself, and hope that you won't make a scene when you are around people.

Yet, what if I did?

I would feel like that was the worst thing that I could do. But it could easily happen, and I was afraid of it.

I took a shower, cried in there, and kept thinking of Wickham, then I dried my hair. And even that felt like a trial.

Afterwards, I rushed back to my room, and like a glutton for punishment, played the song 'I Can't Make You Love Me', as I lay down in my bed.

To my surprise, Manhattan decided to get in bed with me this time. There is something cathartic about having your pet sit beside you during troubling times. They have a way of making you feel at ease, and not alone. Because you know, deep down, that your pet will always be there. It's a constant comfort.

Manhattan snuggled up next to me, and I cried my way into sleep…

When I opened my eyes again, I was sitting on the park bench, where Charlotte and I had sat earlier that day.

This time, it was cloudier outside, and I knew that I was not alone. A little distance away, Darcy was throwing some food at a couple of squirrels, who were taking those morsels like their lives depended on it.

"Did you give them names yet?" I asked him, about the squirrels.

"Oh yeah," Darcy said, over his shoulder. "That one with the scar on its back paw is Toto, and the other one is Hildegard."

"Hildegard? Fascinating."

"When it came to dishing out labels, it seemed like it was a good idea to break free from my comfort zone."

"We all like to stay in our comfort zone, don't we?"

"Of course, we do. It's cozy."

He finished feeding the squirrels, Toto and Hildegard, and then he sat down next to me on the bench.

"I never got how people can sit in the cold," he began. "I'm not one of those guys who likes freezing."

"I'm not either, but it was warmer earlier," I said, buttoning up. "Do you know, when growing up, I loved the summer. Of course, all kids do—and teachers, for that matter. But it was the heat. I didn't mind the mosquitos, the potential heatstroke, or the sweating... to be able to go out, to run and break free—well, that's all that mattered."

"To break free, that's all that we all want, isn't it?" he asked.

"Yeah, it is. Even popular Mr. Darcy can understand that."

We laughed as we looked ahead.

"I had a revelation today." I narrated all that happened earlier and when I finished, Darcy had many words about it.

"First, I'll start with the smaller stuff," he began, "Charlotte now has to come to terms with the fact that her dad is dating your mom."

"Yeah. I do not regret when she and her dad have that conversation."

"She'll get over it, eventually. But with your mom and Mr. Lucas—maybe it's just a quick sort of thing. Even when people get to a certain age, they can have short relationships. It's not always, 'I met this person after a couple failed marriages, and now I know how to do the whole relationship thing'. Sometimes, they want casual dating."

"If that's the case, I hope the breakup will be mutual. If it's not, then it still can be messy."

"Now that's the one credit I can give to mature people," Darcy administered. "They aren't teenagers or in their twenties anymore. They know how to roll out of a relationship that doesn't know how to work. They know how to recover and move on. But what does your dad think about it?"

I tapped my head, not even thinking about that.

"By the sword of King Arthur!" I groaned. "I never even thought of that. But it shouldn't matter to him, right? After all, he's dating Cousin Anna. Since he's dating someone, it makes sense for him not to be uncomfortable with the idea of Mom finding someone right? In fact, shouldn't this make him happy that Mom is moving on?"

"Not always. Sometimes, people can be strange. They can date someone, but they don't like it when their ex starts dating someone else. It's like they don't want them, but they don't want anyone else to have them."

"My dad is sensible. He'll be the first and not the second."

"For your family's peace of mind, I hope so."

Darcy clapped his hands against his lap.

"Now we get to the uncomfortable part of this all."

"Yeah," I agreed, "let's face the proverbial elephant in the room." I leaned forward, placed my elbows on my knees, and rested my chin on my fists. I looked ahead at the greenery around me. "For too long, I kept you in here." I pointed to my forehead. "Even though I can't control this, I prefer it this way. Here I can keep our conversations regulated, and I could make peace with everything, in my own time."

"I do get it," Darcy assented, with a tone of compassion in his speech, "believe me, I understand. It makes sense."

"Thanks," I said. "I appreciate that, really, I do. But I was doing something else, wasn't I? I was telling your story for you, finding explanations for things, rather than letting you tell it all yourself. Call it being cautious, or being a coward, we'll never know. All that I do know is that it's your story, and I might as well accept that. I can't keep you in my mind forever. You're out there. In reality."

I leaned back on the bench, and willfully did not look at him. It was heavy to admit, but it couldn't be helped.

"I have to meet you now," I acknowledged. "I've gotta get my courage and fire back. And get to it."

At last, I looked at Darcy. I met him smiling at me. Damn the man; his smile was beautiful.

"It's about time," he declared, then he chuckled. "It's about damn time."

I smiled as well.

"But that's the problem," I said, pointing to his smile. "When we meet, I don't think that's going to be there. And I'm going to miss it."

"You don't know that. It might still be there."

"It never was. And if it was a smile, it used to only be there to poke fun at me. But we're not in the classroom anymore. And I do think that I'm getting around to being a match for anything." Then I chuckled. "And I am. By Jove, I am!"

I practically jumped off my seat, turned around and began to pace while speaking to Darcy.

"You know what? I'm heartbroken, sure I am. But I've got my new job. I feel like the rug has been pulled up from under my feet, but I've got my family. I've been betrayed, but I've got people loyal to me. Maybe I'm not in the mood to cry anymore. Maybe running is not the answer. Maybe... maybe I am a match for anything."

Darcy began to clap for me.

"Even for me," he declared, "you might even be a match to face me."

"Yes," I announced. "I think I am." I walked up to him and punched his cheek gently. "I'm Elizabeth Bennet; I'm not afraid of anyone. I once flew planes across the skies and didn't fear a damn thing that I would face in the air. I'm not gonna be afraid of anything on the ground either."

Darcy stood up and offered me his arm to hold.

"Well," I said, "you're getting all Victorian on me."

"Oh, come on. This gesture is much older than the Victorian era."

"I know," I said, placing my arm in his. "Victorian is just the easiest phrase to use."

We walked along through the park and looked at the part of Alexandria that lay before us.

"There's only one problem," I realized.

"What?"

"If I finally meet you, do I still dream of you? When fantasy meets reality, fantasy has a way of fading. Your face won't be here when this is over, will it?"

"There's only one way to find out. I wish I could guarantee this. But I can't. Sorry."

"It's fine. I've had worse goodbyes."

"This isn't goodbye," he assured me, "just see you again, in a different setting." Darcy looked down at me. "Just remember something, and this is very hard."

"What?"

"There is always one thing much better than dreams; reality. Reality is more fascinating. Don't be afraid to live."

I smiled sadly.

"Don't be afraid to live," I repeated his words. "When you're young, you're quick to risk your life for a noble cause. God knows that I did it, a lot. Amazing how life is harder…"

———

I woke up the next morning, and to my surprise, Manhattan had slept with me the whole night.

He rolled over and stretched his paws in the air, opened his eyes and squinted at me.

"Morning," I said to him.

Manhattan meowed and I knew he was responding.

I smiled sleepily.

"This is a day of changes, isn't it?" I asked him. "You're the first proof to it."

Today was the day where I gave my first tour as a historical guide in Alexandria.

I whipped my blankets off my bed, much to Manhattan's dismay who had to jump off in a huff.

Well, best to get to it.

# SIX
# SUDDENLY SEYMOUR!

"Today is your big day!" Josie said as I came downstairs.

"I know it's just a tour," I said, "but you know what? Yeah, it is my big day."

I kissed her on the cheek, squeezed Killian's arm and began to make them breakfast.

"Where's your mom?" I asked them.

"Ironing her dress," Killian said. "I think."

I leaned my head out of the kitchen and called down to the laundry room where the ironing board was.

"Jane! What do you want me to make them for breakfast?"

"We're actually early, for once," Jane exclaimed. "Do you have the time to make them some eggs and bacon and toast?"

"Over and out," I replied, taking the eggs and bacon out of the fridge and began to prepare them. "Which cheese do you want in your eggs today?"

"White cheddar," Killian declared.

"Can you put some onions or garlic in it too?" Josie asked. "My teacher told me that they are both very healthy."

"Garlic is healthier than onions," Killian argued.

"No, you're wrong."

"No, you're wrong."

"No, you're wrong."

"Well, luckily there is no debate," I resolved. "We've got

onions, but no garlic. So, you have to settle for one. Do you know if Mary and Kitty are here? I'll have to make more eggs."

"Aunt Mary had to leave early for work," Killian answered. "And Kitty left with Uncle Richard. He's taking her for a last day on the town since they are going back to the base tomorrow."

"Your grandmom?"

"She's still upstairs."

I called upstairs.

"Mom! Are you hungry?"

"Depends," she called down to me. "What are you making?"

"Eggs and bacon."

"Put some cheese in the eggs and yeah."

"Right."

I began to make breakfast, while Killian and Josie were drawing in their coloring books.

"So," I said to them as I cooked, referring to Richard Fitzwilliam. "You call him Uncle Richard?"

"He likes it," Josie said, breaking one of her crayons. "And it seems like him and Kitty are almost married."

"Yeah," I said demurely, amazed at Kitty's luck. "They kind of are, aren't they?"

"Yeah. I hope they always stay together."

"I hope so too. But even if they break up, I think they will always be in each other's lives. That can happen sometimes. Where two people don't always stay together, but they still stick around. No matter what, Kitty and Richard will always be tied to each other in some way."

"That happens?" Killian asked.

"I've seen people date, break up, and then become best friends. Strange, but true." I made a funny face at them. "We grownups can be so weird."

———

After I made breakfast, Jane and the kids rushed to eat, they got their coats on, Jane kissed my cheek and wished me good luck on my first tour, then they left.

Just as I finished eating and started cleaning up, Mom came downstairs and fixed her plate.

"I heard that you are partaking in the movie nights now," Mom began, biting into her bacon as she sat down.

"Yeah. Tonight, we are watching one of the 'Dragonheart' movies. I didn't hear which one they settled on."

"I overheard Josie and Killian talking. They settled on 'Dragonheart 3'."

"Either one works for me." I chuckled as I put the dishes in the dishwasher. "Jane gave birth to two very interesting characters. I hope they never change."

"I hope so too. They are the best sort of grandchildren to have. They remind me of you five when you were growing up. Five girls and five different voices. I never felt alone. You all always needed me."

"I thought we must have run you ragged."

"I was exhausted all the time, don't get me wrong, and of course, I complained about it. But truth is, I liked it. You all loved me so much."

I turned to her, surprised that she began that way.

"We still do, you know."

"I know. But when children grow up, they need their mama less. Especially with how independent you all got. Don't get me wrong, I appreciate that, but I do miss the childlike need for me."

I didn't know what to say to that, so I continued to put the dishes into the dishwasher.

"Are you coming to the movie night, tonight?" I asked her. "I know that you are having a night with your friends, but just had to ask."

"Now that the cat's out of the bag, I can be honest. Sometimes, I went out with the girls. Other times, I was secretly going out with William Lucas."

I rolled my eyes.

"Ah. And this is one of those nights, isn't it?"

"Yeah. I'm spending the night at his house."

"Now it all makes sense. That's why we don't see you very

much. You're either with your friends or spending a lot of time with him."

"I'm re-discovering myself, Lizzy. You know what that's like, better than anyone."

"Yeah, I do. Don't worry, I'm not judging. Just putting the pieces to the puzzle together."

She turned to me, gently.

"We do like each other, you know."

"I know."

"You told Charlotte, didn't you?"

"I had to. She needed to know."

Mom rolled her lips in between her teeth.

"And did she take the news well?"

"She was surprised, but she took it as well as anyone could take it." Inwardly, I was in a strange state. I didn't know how to break this next bit of information, but I had to ask. "Mom, what exactly is happening between you and Mr. Lucas? What I mean is, is this a casual sort of relationship, and you both know that, or do you both want something more out of it?"

Mom blinked, looked away and yanked a cabinet open.

"Come on," I stressed, "I have the right to know."

"It's not that, Lizzy," Mom said, back, "yes, I'm frustrated, but not at you. I'm frustrated because I don't really have an answer."

She turned back to me, her hands doing their best to add emphasis to what she was trying to explain. "Look. William and I don't know what our relationship is. We haven't really defined it. We never call it anything, and we like it that way. Sometimes, things in life run more smoothly when you don't put a label on it. Don't get me wrong, sometimes, labels are good. And sometimes, labels should be used to define something. But with William and me, we are being loose and free about things. No matter what, I can tell you this. After two months, and we are not together, we'll be okay, and I didn't hurt Charlotte's dad. Nor did he hurt me. And after two months, if we are still together, then clearly, I'm still not hurting Charlotte's dad. You got me?"

I tapped the table as I was leaning against it. I suppose that I had to be happy with that explanation.

"Right. I got it."

"Today is your first tour with Meryton Manor, right?"

"Yeah."

"Nervous?"

I smiled wistfully.

"Petrified. You would think, after doing this so many times before, that I'm used to it. But there's no way of knowing what the group is like, do they want to hear what you have to say, or if they are on the tour because they were *made* to take the tour. Especially when they are in school. You end up being just another boring lecturer to them."

Then I got a faraway look in my eyes—from what I assumed I must have looked like—when I remembered all the tours that I had done before. "But sometimes, you do get through to people. They want to hear the history of how we all came to be. They want to hear the good and the bad. For better or worse. And what's even more amazing is that they care. They care about the history of everything.

And then, you have a tour leading around teenagers. At that age, they are not allowed to care—they don't look cool if they show that they care. But every now and again, there is one of them, that focuses, pays attention to what you say… and you know, that you got through to them. You had an impact, and you made your mark. And even when you were telling hard subject matters, they still believe, they have hope, and they have patriotic pride. That's when you know…and you hope the next tour will be just like the last one. But you never know."

Finally, I was brought back to reality, and I noticed that Mom was staring blankly at me.

"I sound ridiculous, don't I?" I asked.

"No," she answered simply. "I just—I always thought, that once you stopped being a pilot, you were coasting through life, taking jobs here and there to fill up time. I thought you stopped having anything like purpose. But you do like this stuff, don't you?"

"Yeah, I think I do. I'm not saying that I was as satisfied as being in the service, but right now, this is where I need to be. Right now, I need to be home. I need to be around family."

"Why?"

That question seemed so strange.

"Why?" I repeated. "Is it weird to want to be around family?"

"No, not that part. You just turned sad, suddenly. Is something wrong?"

Wickham flashed across my mind.

And so did Darcy when he saw me crying.

The pain must've flashed across my face before I was able to make it disappear.

"Mom," I began, but what could I say? Was I ready to tell anyone that Wickham had betrayed me? No, I don't think that I was. Not even to her, because I didn't know what she would do. Or would she know how to comfort me. We loved each other, but we were never close in that sort of way. Although she was my mother. If there was one person who I could cry to—and yet, I still was unsure. I was not ready at all. "Mom, I just realized something."

"What?"

"That I still don't understand what love is. Or how to go about it. It just still does not make sense to me."

"Oh, is that it?"

I blinked.

"What do you mean, 'is that it'?"

"Lizzy, whether you like it or not, there is no answer to that. There is no way of knowing how to fully go about it, because there is no method to the madness of feeling for someone. Love is just a fundamental thing that we need but is very difficult to come by. Did something else happen?"

I wanted to spill everything, to just let it all out. And yet, the other side, the guarded side, had no desire to say anything at all. I think that maybe I was embarrassed. Maybe I did not like the idea of looking weak. *This* made me look weak.

"I was just speaking generally," I uttered, "that's all. I just like solving problems. And romance, I think, is the only mystery to my life."

"My Lizzy does not know something," Mom said, "that's good."

That was not something that I wanted to hear.

"Good?" My eyebrow arched. "How is that good?"

"You are aware that you don't know something. Believe me, that *will* be a good lesson for you."

I didn't understand what she meant by that, so I didn't respond.

"Never mind," she rushed out. She walked up to me and kissed my cheek. "Good luck today."

I smiled.

"Thanks. I'll be needing it."

———

When the bus pulled up near my stop, I pulled the cord, thanked the driver, and got out.

My tour began at 12:30 p.m., and the requirement was to always show up a half hour before, so I arrived at noon. I was supposed to have Mr. King there with me, to oversee my first tour. When I was on the bus, he texted me, to say that he would be a little late, and to expect him around the time that the group was to get there.

Standing at 301 King Street, I was in front of Alexandria's City Hall and Market Square. That was where I was supposed to meet my group. I was told that it would be one group, from Oregon, and a single ticket was sold, who was independent of the group. I would be able to spot the Oregon group because they all wore blue shirts that said, 'Rockin' in the Free World'.

I put my nametag on, held a clipboard and began to recite my lines. A few people looked at me weirdly, and I gestured to my script, indicating that I was not causing a scene by talking to myself in public, and continued to go about my business.

As I felt the nerves build within me, I looked at City Hall and let the grandeur of the building wash over me.

After my nerves subsided, I went back to memorization, when

I overheard a man nearby, asking someone if he was in the location where a walking/bus tour was going to take place.

The person he asked didn't know, and I deduced that this man was the additional person to my tour.

Wishing to make myself known, I walked up to him.

"I think I'm the one that you're looking for," I said, charmingly. "I'm your leader."

Removing his hat, the man turned around, and the shock hit me too suddenly for me to compose myself.

Losing control of my limbs, I dropped my clipboard on the ground and froze in my place.

"Darcy!"

Standing before me, as one of my guests on the tour, was Fitzwilliam Darcy.

———

It was the best of times.

It was also the worst of times.

And when I say the worst of times, I meant it.

Darcy was the singular one added to the tour, and my surprise could only be bested by the alarm in my eyes. When seeing me, Darcy's expression also shifted.

It had begun as curiosity and calmness, and it morphed into one of disappointment. Yet I was not so much overwhelmed by this circumstance that I was not ignorant of how to read people. The disappointment was not done so because he did not wish to see me. Rather, it was the disappointment that comes from being in the presence of someone who was unhappy to see them.

Darcy was not, and never had been, an idiot.

A jerk, yes.

A bully, yes.

A decider of who was popular in school and who would never make the cut? Yes.

But an idiot—never.

Unobservant—never.

Unaware of other's minds and moods? Never.

He knew that I was frightened at the sight of him being on my tour. And I think—unless I was mistaken—that he was affected by knowing this. He did not like the idea of seeing me so horrified.

"Elizabeth," Darcy began, his traditionally strong voice as weak. "Hey."

I breathed out and in.

"Hey," was all that I could muster in reply. "You're on my tour."

"Yeah. I was meaning to take a few tours around Alexandria and Richard told me that you were a tour guide to old city."

"Richard told you that?" I rushed out, my enunciation flying out of the window as I spoke way too quickly.

"Sorry, I didn't catch that."

I steadied my breathing.

"Sorry," I said slower, "I think I'm letting my nerves get to the better part of my speech and clarity. I said, 'Richard told you that?'"

"Yeah, he did. I thought it would be a good ice-breaker."

"Ice-breaker?" I blinked. "Sorry, I just realized that I keep repeating every word that you are saying."

"Yeah," he said, his eyes half-amused, half-perplexed. If that's possible. "You kind of do."

"I don't mean to be making so little sense, but can you blame me? This whole encounter is helter-skelter. Seriously, talk about a wacky way to begin this. I am just surprised. After all, why would you want me to be your tour guide?"

Darcy rubbed his cheek as he looked down at the cold ground.

"Ah," I said, reading his stance, "you don't know exactly what to say back, and now you need a *moment* to figure out this *awkward moment*."

Now that I was talking again, I think I was getting my courage back.

"Penny for your pain?" I furthered, digging the knife that was 'confrontation' a little deeper.

"You don't like me being here, do you?" he asked me bluntly.

Well-played, Darcy. Bluntness was just his way of being, and it did knock me back. But I was not at the stage where I was going to be afraid any longer. After all, now that we had faced each other, we were in the thick of it, and I've got my nerve. That's how it always was whenever I would be deployed for a mission. I was a little afraid before getting into the pilot's seat, but when I was in the air, I could face anything, without fear. Instead, it was replaced by courage. I think now was one of those moments.

"It's more than that," I replied, "even though you've hurt me, I don't feel like being mean in return. I just—" and here I lowered my voice so that no one would hear, "Darce, didn't it occur to you that taking this tour would be uncomfortable, for the both of us?"

He looked a little apprehensive and he rubbed his lip.

"I do believe that I did not really think this through correctly, huh?"

"I think—that when I met you, this was not how I wanted to go about it. I just think I needed more time to think about what I wanted to say."

"I see your point. Don't worry, I'll leave."

"You would do that?" I asked, surprised at the gesture.

"Why not?" His countenance shifted, and he was preparing to leave. He wrapped his scarf tighter around his neck and put his ivy cap on. "If it makes things easier. I'll see you later, Lizzy."

He turned to leave.

I raised my arm up suddenly, without even thinking.

"Wait!" I exclaimed.

Stopping in his tracks, Darcy turned back to me.

"What?" he asked. "Did you change your mind on me?"

"Welcome to the thoughts of Elizabeth Bennet," I replied, instinctively—yeah, right now I was flying by the seat of my instincts and impulses. When it came to contemplation and thinking things through, I was ignoring that side of my brain. Not consciously, of course. "They shift around sometimes. I'm not a coward, Darcy. I was like that when I was younger, but not anymore. Stay."

Darcy's eyebrow lifted. He was interested, since this was a new shift in what we were like to each other now.

"You really want me to?" he asked.

Did I want him to stay? It would mean me doing my best to remember my lines, and extra facts in my head for whenever a tourist wanted to try to stump me by asking me something that they thought I would not have the answer to—seriously, when people do that to us tour guides, it really does hurt—in front of a man whose presence naturally unnerved me. This could all go horribly wrong. But that was the beauty of it!

"Yes," I stated, "stay. Because if I can survive giving a tour in front of a high school nemesis, I think I can survive anything."

"It's been years since we were in school together."

"We'll talk about this later."

"Later? Does that mean that we will see each other again?"

I didn't want to answer that, but so it was.

"Of course, we'll see each other again. Your cousin is dating my sister, you big dummy."

His eyes turned mischievous.

"Insulting someone on your tour," he asked, "a little misguided, don't you think? I could always give you a bad review."

I looked at him archly.

"You are at liberty to do so, but I would advise against it for three reasons."

"What are those reasons?"

"First, I don't think Richard would like the idea of you giving me a bad review just because I called you a name that I had a right to call you. Second, I could always explain to my supervisor why you left me a bad review. And Richard would back me up, so it would do little good. Either way, I have a way of always bouncing back. And thirdly, I don't think you would go so far to hurt a woman's career for a stupid reason. Or am I wrong?"

Darcy's eyes darkened and he looked seriously at me.

"Well-played," he responded.

"I had a feeling," I declared, staring back blatantly at him. A larger group of twenty people drew near me, and I got the sense that this was my next group. "Now, let's see what will happen."

I walked up to them, asked if they were looking for me, and sure enough, they were.

47

They were a group of adults from Oregon.

"You're all from Salem, right?" I asked them.

"Yes," one of them replied. "It's our state capital."

"Yeah, I learned my state capitals when I was growing up. No one ever made the reference that you have the same name as the iconic town from Massachusetts, do they?"

The whole group collectively groaned.

"Oh yeah," another person on the tour said, "They laugh and would say that, since we are a younger state than the east coast, we are the Salem that never has to worry about being accused of witch hangings."

I laughed.

"Well, that can be compensated for how much we hear about your iconic Shakespeare Festival."

"You know about our Shakespeare Festival?"

"Yes, I worked at the Kentucky Shakespeare Festival, and occasionally I met actors who worked at the Oregon one. They boasted about it, and all the festivals here on the east coast are aware that you've got the most iconic one."

"Good to be known for something," another Oregon-er said. "But you said that you learned all the state capitals. I live in Oregon, but I was born in South Dakota."

"Pierre," I responded, automatically. "South Dakota's capital is Pierre."

He raised an eyebrow.

"How about Michigan?"

"Lansing."

"Kansas."

"Topeka."

"Canada?"

I blinked.

"I said in the USA, but if you want to widen it to North America, then Ottawa."

He was surprised that I knew that, and I wanted to roll my eyes inwardly. Great! I had 'one of those types' on my tour; the know-it-all who will try and stump me somewhere.

Instinctively, I shifted my eyes to Darcy, who was also amused by this interaction. I think that he sensed my inner annoyance because he spoke.

"So," he announced, his voice strong with authority. "What will we learn about on this tour?"

My posture shifted from giving answers to being happy to being put on track. Sadly, I would have to thank him for that later.

"That brings us to the beginning of this tour," I said. "We begin with the town's history and with City Hall of Alexandria. Alexandria was founded in 1749 by Scottish merchants and was named after Scotsman John Alexander who owned the land that became Alexandria. But the original people who belong to these lands were many Native American tribes. By the early 1600s, Virginia Indians lived in three broad cultural groups based on the language families found in the area: Algonquian, Iroquoian, and Siouan. Scholars know most about the Algonquian-speaking Indians of Tsenacomoco, who eventually grouped together into a paramount chiefdom. Of course, colonization occurred and that led to the traditional disruption that it often brought in its wake.

"Today we still celebrate our Scottish origins. And this—" I gestured to City Hall. "This City Hall was built in 1871-74, after America's Civil War, with Market Square and the Colonial-inspired additions that face the plaza built in the 1960s. Market Square is the site of a weekly farmers market, annual holiday tree lighting and festivities throughout the year. This Christmas, it's going to be spectacular."

I began to give them a further history on the Scots who founded Alexandria, then the bus arrived. They got on it, and we began to drive around other parts of Old Town Alexandria, giving facts about the historic sites, and President George Washington's relationship with the city. After all, his home and plantation, Mount Vernon, was not far from Alexandria and being our first president, and the iconic war hero to America's revolution, there would be considerable affiliations to his legacy there.

Near the end of the tour, I concluded with Alexandria's role played in our Civil War.

"When Virginia seceded from the Union, it's important to

remember that not all of Virginia was a part of the Confederacy," I declared. "History today likes to iron things out as simple and 'one side or the other' kind of things. But that's not true. History is complicated and full of contradictions. Same thing goes with our historic heroes, and the same thing goes for our cities."

My attention was seized when Darcy shifted in his place. He did not do it because he was distracted, but only because it was a natural reaction. It was a small action, but it still caught my notice.

"During America's Civil War," I continued, "parts of Virginia were under the control of the North. Just days after Virginia's succession from the Union in 1861, Federal troops arrived in Alexandria to hold the city. It was a Federalist city, in a Confederate state. Troops and supplies were shipped here all throughout the war through the railroads and transported to the fronts. Wounded soldiers were brought here on trains and taken to hospitals."

As I narrated, Darcy found himself moving to the front of the group, listening to me attentively. I confess to being flattered at his interest and was equally amused when he realized that he had to return to standing in the back, once he realized that he was too tall to remain in front of the group. Tall people; they sadly obstruct other people's views.

"From 1863 to 1865, Alexandria was the capital of the Restored Government of Virginia, which represented the seven Virginia counties remaining under federal control during the Civil War. By the end of the war, Alexandria's economy was in shambles, but the city itself had been spared the destruction witnessed by many other places in Virginia such as Richmond and Fredericksburg. That's why there are so many historic sites here and why you can see Alexandria in its glory. It's because it was the Union stronghold, so it was saved."

Darcy raised his hand to ask a question.

"Yes?"

"What of those who were still in bondage?" he asked me. "What about them?"

"Thank you for asking," I replied, "that's the conclusion for our tour. Even though Alexandria was a major slave-trading center prior to the War, it also had a history of a few free black communities. African American life flourished when churches, social and fraternal organizations and businesses were formed. Free Blacks served in the Union army, came here as refugees, and did other things. The Freedmen Cemetery Memorial is dedicated to those who died during the war. That's the moral to the foundations to all humanity: our history is *complicated*."

When hearing that, Darcy blinked, wondering what I meant. In truth, I wonder what I meant as well.

"Well," I said, "that concludes our tour. I want to thank you all for being a great tour group. This is my first time as a guide in Alexandria, and I could not have asked for a better one. Also, thanks for not being teenagers. Remember being that age; it's a social death sentence if you show anything like emotion, or that you are enjoying a tour."

They all laughed, remembering the pains of being that age. They clapped for me, asked for directions on the best place to eat, I recommended Sweet Fire Donna's Barbecue, and they were off.

And then there was Darcy, who decided to stand there, when all was gone and done.

Now time to face the music.

———

When alone, I looked at him.

"Need advice on where to eat as well?" I asked him.

"Actually, yes, I kind of do."

I bit my cheek, trying to think of what he would like.

"Well," I said, "when it comes to taste, each to his own. But when it comes to food, don't get mad at me if the food is not to your liking. All I can do is recommend what *I think* might be up your alley."

"Lay it on me," he said.

"Ted's Montana Grill," I suggested, "great burgers."

"Actually, you're right on the money. I've eaten there twice. It's my favorite place to haunt now."

"What brought you to Alexandria?" I asked. "The base you're stationed at is not even in Virginia."

"Actually yeah, I was originally stationed at Fort Cavazos."

"That's the base in Texas, right?" I asked, trying to remember army bases. "It used to be called Fort Hood, but it was changed to honor Richard Cavazos."

"Yeah," he said, proud of his original base. "He was the first Hispanic American to become a four-star General. It was the best place to start off with because it was not too far from Oklahoma, and it's the third largest base in the country."

I smiled as we walked along together. "From the way you talk, you liked being there."

"It was great. Made a lot of friends there, but I wanted to move around a little. I got myself reassigned to go to Fort Moore in Georgia, but I decided to not go there until January. Years of training, I think I earned a few months' vacation. Richard told me that he was stationed at the Base in Virginia, and I was staying with him."

"You're a soldier who is given time to rest," I said, "from what I remember soldiers told me in the mess hall, when you are on leave, either you enjoy the days off, or you go mad from having nothing to do. Which one of the two were you?"

"The first," he replied, amused. "People who don't know how to rest don't know how to live, in my opinion. I think I've got an old soul to me. I like being in the army, but I'm one of those sorts of dudes who can easily not work and find ways of keeping myself occupied. What about you?"

"I think I'm still finding out the person that I am," I said, "I liked being in the Airforce, but I also like this life. And right now," I said, patting my stomach, "eating is my favorite activity."

"Hungry now? Why don't I take you to Ted's Grill? My treat. It's my way of congratulating you on your first tour here."

I was amazed! Darcy was rolling out the carpet of his gentility, and it was all so very natural, and without pretense. He wasn't being fake, from what I assumed. And yet, there was still one problem.

"You're being kind to me," I determined.

He was a little surprised by this response, but he still replied.

"Well, yes, I guess I am." His eyes shifted as he began to understand what I meant. "You thought that I was going to be different than this, didn't you?"

"Well, yeah, to be honest about it," I acknowledged. "I really didn't see it coming. And I appreciate it, but it does not change the fact that I can't eat with you."

"You can't?"

"No. And it's not that I don't appreciate the offer. I do. It's just that…"

And now it came down to the moment. All that had been building up inside of me, and I knew that I would not be happy until I told him the truth.

"Darcy, I learned to hate you for many years. Seeing you now, after so long, hasn't changed that. And if we eat together, I know what's going to happen. I'm going to remember how angry that I am, and I'm not ready to put us both through that. It's my first guide day, it went well, and I don't want to ruin that. Thanks for the offer, but I need more time. Judge me for that if you dare."

"I don't dare," he replied. "I just…it's been years. You can get passed it, right?"

When hearing that, I was angry, suddenly. After all, it was very easy for him to say that. But the years of bullying, of destroying my confidence, or ruining my life were not something that could be erased so quickly. And he expected me just to forget it.

"It's been years, yes," I said, "it's been years *for you*. But when you get bullied, when your life is destroyed every single day, it leads to demons in here," I said, pointing to my head. "It leads to so much pain, and it cannot be forgotten. So yes, it has been years —for you. But for me, I live it every day. Please, don't ask me to forget it. We people cannot forget our memories, nor can we escape them."

"I didn't mean it that way," he explained, "that's not what I had implied."

"I know. That's why I don't want us to eat together. I know what's going to happen. It's *this*. *This* is what's going to happen.

So no, I'm not going to put us through this. We both deserve better than that, don't we?"

Darcy didn't respond, and it wasn't his fault. I think I had rendered him speechless, and I kind of liked it. Leaving him speechless was a unique form of revenge for the man that he once had been.

"Thanks for not leaving the tour," I said, tightening my scarf around my neck more. "You were great. And you also reminded me that I have it in me to stand up to anything. Even a person from my past."

I smiled.

"Thanks for that."

Turning my heel, I walked away from him, and to the nearest bus stop that would take me in the direction of home.

# SEVEN
## MADNESS

A s I walked to the bus stop, I could not help but think of everything that happened in the last few hours.

I had done my tour.

Check!

It had gone well.

Check!

I had faced Darcy again, and I managed to pull through.

Check!

So much I had overcome in this one morning. They were small accomplishments, but they meant something anyway.

Eventually, I reached my bus stop, but I found that I wanted to walk a little further. There was something about the morning that brought out the wanderer in me.

So, my feet began to take me where they would, as I looked around, at the architecture and layout of the city that surrounded me.

Alexandria was a place like any other: I was walking around in the present and had hopes of what things would look like in the future. But I also was walking around in the past, in a place that clung to many a yesteryear, of the charm of where humanity had been, to justify what it had the potential to be.

My past had returned to me often when in Alexandria, to a place where I did not want to go but had no choice but to.

Yet I saw the present before me, and a sense of a bright future ahead.

Suddenly, I passed a bookstore on the other side of the road. It was interesting, because since so much of the world has gone electronic, hardcopy books are not as popular as they once had been. How could a bookstore be maintained in such a time of history?

But there it was.

Stricken with an impulse, I walked in and asked if they had a book in stock.

The worker looked it up and helped me to the correct place that I would find it. We looked through the shelves, and eventually came on the title. Taking the book from the shelf, she handed it to me.

"Is this what you were looking for?" she asked.

Taking the book, I turned it over and saw the title:

It Takes a Witch
By
Heather Blake

The cover was cool to say the least.

"Yup," I answered, "that's it."

"Fan of the magical genre, eh?" she asked.

"Actually, I never read this series before. I just saw it online, liked the cover, and it seemed to rest in my subconscious for a while," I said, remembering when Darcy handed the book to me in my dreams. "Sometimes, a book gets under your skin, and you're not happy until you give it a try. I think I will risk it."

Without even reading a word—despite how illogical that is—I bought the book. I walked to a bus stop and thought to read the back cover while waiting for my ride.

Turning the book over, I read the description and soon found out the name of the lead character, who was a young woman who moved to Massachusetts and discovered that she came from a long line of witches and had been a witch herself.

"Darcy!"

I shouted the name so loud that I scared passersby. Apologizing to them for my sudden bit of madness, I quieted down and kept my astonishment internalized.

When reading the book description, I found out that the lead character's name was Darcy Merriweather, a woman who had moved to Massachusetts after suffering a major disappointment. She had gone back to stay with her family, and got work there, discovering how much she was needed amongst them.

Coincidence is a real thing, I grant you.

But this was just too uncanny.

Opening the book, I quickly began to delve into the world of a heroine who found herself thrown into a situation that was so fast, and again…her name was Darcy.

My subconscious really felt like pulling a number on me that was too intense.

The bus came, and as I continued to read the book, I got a text message from Delores. She asked when I was going to drop by for Thanksgiving dinner. They were a smart family and realized that they had to celebrate their dinner on the day before actual Thanksgiving, because on the actual day, they were always invited to another family's dinner, and so I could swing eating with them the day before, and then eating our family's dinner the night after.

It was strange, because that was when I felt that I could release all my inner frustrations about Wickham to her. I was still not ready to talk about it with my family. And yet Delores, who had warned me about him from the beginning, had always believed that I was too good for him. Also, Delores was good at not being judgy. She was an affectionate mother, to more than just her own kids.

I replied in the affirmative, and then added:

> You were right about Wickham. We're no longer
> a thing.

After a couple of minutes, I got a response from her. What the hell did that womanizing idiot do?

Usually, I was not the biggest fan of the word 'womanizer'. I never begrudged men for wanting to date lots of girls, provided that the men were always honest about their intentions. It's the same way that I never disparaged women who dated lots of guys and I despised the word 'slut'. I never believed there was anything wrong about wanting to be around the opposite sex, or the same sex, if that was your pleasure. We are meant to adore each other, and perhaps that was a good thing.

However, in some circumstances, the words 'womanizer' and 'slut' are properly distributed to the right directions, because the person did something despicable enough to be worthy of that title. And in this case, Wickham was precisely what Delores labeled him as.

Feeling the familiar sense of empathy that she exuded, I wrote back:

> He never cared about me at all. He…cared about someone else.

She wrote back.

> And by that, you mean that he liked this other girl while he was dating you.

Suddenly, tears formed and began to roll down my cheeks. The shame, the humiliation, came on me. Texting her back about it, opened the wound again, and made it bleed afresh.

Wishing for no one to notice, I wiped my face with my sleeve and turned to the window.

Sometimes, the best thing to do is to get away. To go somewhere and find a change of scenery.

For some, it's getting a makeover.

For others, it's writing down your frustrations.

For me, it was observing others, and a scene around me.

Staring out of the window, I was able to see people on the street, or in their car, and that helped distract me.

From the person who is walking down the road, on their cellphone, to the person who is sitting on a bench, reading. To the person who is crossing the street on a red light and hoping not to get hit. Or the homeless person who is begging for money.

All of them have been heartbroken. All of them, if they lived life correctly, have shed a few tears. My pain was no more or less special than theirs had been. I was nothing new, or nothing unique. I was just another heart in the crowd. There is something to be said for fading into the many heartbeats that burn brightly on the road to romance and love being lost. You can get lost along the masses, but then you can drift a little above them for a time, floating above their heads, and the world shows you that your pain is more pronounced at the moment. It has the right to be above the rest for a little while, before it sinks back below, and mixes with everyone else's grief. But then you get over it. At first, you rush to do that, but looking at everyone that I observed, I knew that they were like me: being betrayed was never easy to get over. It takes time to recover, and right now, I suppose I had no choice but for things to suck for a little bit longer.

I knew that I was going to overcome this.

If we develop correctly, we all can rise above heartbreak.

But again, I was no different on my road to recovery than many others. This path would unwind for a little longer. But at least, I was not alone.

So, I was able to text back:

You hit the nail right on the cheating head.

A minute later, I got her reply:

When are you available to come around? I'll fix you some pastelillos acapulgueas relleno de papa arroz con gandules ajo con chuleta. It's better than ice cream. There's nothing wrong with eating your pain sometimes. Btw, it's best to come in less than a week. If you don't, you'll get to that point where you will start crying in public.

I froze. How, in the name of Coincidence, that she was worried that I would do what I literally had just been doing.

It's amazing how quickly my crying came to an end.

Her invitation—and coincidence—made me feel better immediately.

I told her that I was open to swinging by on Friday, because a tour I had was early in the morning and would be over by eleven AM. I told Delores that I would get to her home by around two, and she confirmed the date.

Knowing that I would be met with nothing but a good meal, lots of warm hugs and a welcome environment, I had something to look forward to.

With the tears dried up, and aware that I had escaped making a spectacle of myself, I picked up the book, 'It Takes a Witch', again and continued to read.

At first, I feared that I was reading *without* reading. You have been there, I am sure, where you are reading something, but not remembering any of it, because your mind is elsewhere.

But the fact is that the lead heroine was named Darcy Merriweather, and Coincidence reigned supreme at helping me focus. Soon, I found myself reading a leading lady with an old acquaintance's name, and like me, was recovering from being pushed aside by a man that you adored. Like me, Darcy Merriweather had moved to a new place, looking for a new life.

That is the great thing about books: you open them, and they look to connect to you.

I read on.

———

Eventually, I got home, and to my surprise, Kitty and Mary were there.

"How did your first tour go?" Mary asked, but then she looked at my face.

Clearly, I looked flustered, and it showed all over my face.

"Uh oh," she continued, "what happened?"

"Darcy is what happened," I answered. "But it's more than that."

"More than what?" Kitty asked, holding some laundry in her arms.

"First, I have dreams about Darcy for weeks, then he shows up in Alexandria, then he put himself on my first tour, and then I get confused about how to talk to him, and then I buy a book where his name is the heroine of the book that my dreams told me to read. I'm going mad, I think! It's pure madness. Life is so weird, and I don't get it. I don't get it at all."

I raced up the stairs, with Mary calling after me.

"Just remember, I'm the one who is pregnant and my whole life has been turned upside down. So, keep it all in perspective!"

At first, I was humbled as I stood in my bedroom doorway, but then I heard Kitty snipe at her.

"Mary," Kitty hissed. "It is our God-given right to complain about our lives, every now and again. Don't take that from people by pouring your life down on their parade. Without complaining, we humans don't have much to talk about."

"Oh, right, good point." Mary called back up to me. "Go ahead, Lizzy, complain all you want. You do you!"

"Thanks, Kitty, and precisely, Mary," I replied, then I closed the door behind myself.

Without the right to complain every now and again, even on frivolous matters, what do we humans have to talk much about?

Sad to say, but that is a good point.

# EIGHT
## A LANDMARK MOVIE NIGHT

Before movie night, I used my room as a sanctuary. Cop and Police comedies always put me in a calm state of mind, for reasons that I cannot explain, so I turned on the show 'Brooklyn Nine-Nine' and let the genius of the show help me find my way back to a lighter shade of thought. At first, I sat down, surfing the internet, which never fails to be a little cathartic. Until you read—shudder—the News.

Once you get past the occasional political parties who are so busy fighting each other rather than working together to improve the nation and attend to its safety, to another crime being committed, then you have the occasional pet videos that help give you hope for mankind, you need another outlet. As such, you cannot help but give into your selfishness and go to online stores and shop for something to make you feel better. I call it sympathy shopping: buying something that helps you rise above the funk.

I saw a nice winter dress that would fit my curves but flared out at the hip. As I thought about it, I remembered Darcy at my tour.

Now that I had time to reflect on it all, I was able to analyze the man from my past.

When telling history tours, it's natural for someone to occasionally daydream and not focus on your lectures, but I did the best I could to always be animated and inflect my tones, to keep the viewer tuned in.

Unless I was mistaken, Darcy was the most attentive in the group. He focused on me and seemed to be very good at listening to all that I said. And by the look on his face, I do believe that he remembered it. I was not surprised, because from what I remember of school, he always had good grades, on top of being a football player. Yeah, despite my hatred of him, he really didn't fit the other stereotype of athletes skimming past classes and their skill on the field made up for their bad grades. No, Darcy did care about how he performed in classes and often boasted about how he never got a 'C' on a test.

He was the type who knew how to learn from listening.

Was he listening now?

He clearly had changed. That cannot be denied. And yet, I still clung to my anger from the man he once was. I was aware that a metamorphosis had occurred, but I was not ready to accept him just yet.

However, he was kinder. Unless he was presenting another image.

After all, I had been wrong about people before.

Wickham was the prime example. That was the ultimate deception, and now I was going to be more on my guard than ever. I thought I had everything figured out, that I knew the world and what made it turn. But Wickham's behavior had proven that I still had a few lessons, or two, to learn.

Richard Fitzwilliam said that Darcy had mellowed out and had grown a conscience.

Kitty also said this.

But I was not going to be sent on a fool's errand again. With Darcy, I still did not know if we would see much of each other, but if I did ever see him, I would be astute, scrutinize him, and see how he really was.

However, the first thing was first: I would not see what I wanted to see, or what I did not want to see. I would see what was *actually there.*

I realized that I did like the dress and so I bought it.

Soon I felt my eyelids grow heavy.

'Brooklyn Nine-Nine' always had a way of getting me out of my head and into a Zen state. Closing my laptop, I got into my pjs, got under the covers, and let myself fall asleep to the last episode of the second season.

My eyes were closing just as the lead cops, Jake and Amy, had finally kissed each other, after two seasons of them picking on each other and constantly bickering. That scene had always put me in a tranquil state... because, for me, it was the most much-anticipated kiss on TV, only bested by when Jane and Raphael kissed each other on the show 'Jane the Virgin'.

My eyes closed to the happy scene, and I fell asleep.

———

"Lizzy!" I heard Mary knocking on the door. "Movie night is in an hour."

I woke up, to see that my tv was on 'Brooklyn Nine-Nine' DVD menu, since I had finished watching the whole disc.

"Did you take a shower yet?" she asked, from the other side of the door.

"Nope," I said, rubbing my eyes, and sounding groggy, "thanks for waking me up. Did Josie and Killian bathe yet?"

"Yeah. All bathrooms are free."

"Great. Tell Kitty that I'll be quick and then be down to help with the movie night dinner."

"Don't worry. I'm staying this time, and I'll be helping her. It's your first day on the job. Relax."

"Great, because I think I want to do the whole bubble bath thing," I said. "And how are you feeling?"

There was a pause. Then Mary finally talked.

"The food cravings are getting worse," Mary responded, "and I've started to want to eat a lot."

"That's the great thing about being pregnant," I said, "you've got all the excuses in the world to pig out."

"Yeah, yay me."

I heard her leave and walk downstairs. I was very worried

about her. Mary was still in limbo between being open to having the child and being angry about keeping it. When the baby did come, how would she look at it? Either she would look at the baby and fall in love with it, or she might very well see it as the source that destroyed her life.

All we could do was believe in her and know that she would find her way.

Going to the bathroom, I cleaned out the tub, filled it with bubble bath liquid, ran the water, and washed my face as the tub filled up.

Once it was at the right height, I disrobed and stepped into the water.

The soap, bubbles, and suds were brilliant. I do not believe that I had a bubble bath since I was a kid. The things we give up when we grow up!

Dunking my head under the surface, I was submerged completely. Holding my breath, I rested my head at the bottom of the tub and thought of romantic love.

Love!

The one thing that every human needed, and also the hardest thing to get ahold of.

'Wickham, what did you do to me? What have you done to many women before me?'

You were fiction, not fact.

And Darcy…what are you? For better or worse, you are fact and not fiction.

And fact is not nearly as fun or a fantasy. Fact is real, but also hard.

But fact is still truth.

Both men circled around in my brain, and continued to revolve until my head began to spin.

Then there was a slight banging on the bathroom door.

I raised my head back up to the surface.

"Who is it?" I asked. "And what do you need?"

"Um… Elizabeth?"

If I was standing, I would have fallen back in the water.

"Darcy!"

———

When hearing his voice, I ducked my face under the water, just below my nose. Literally, I was using the water like it was a shield.

I don't know why I was afraid. After all, it's not like I was not trained in combat, but still—this was different. I was naked, in a bubble bath, and a shadow was on the other side of the door.

"Darcy?" I rushed out, from over the water. "What are you doing here?"

"Sorry," he responded, "I didn't catch that."

Closing my eyes, I slowed down my speech.

"What are you doing here?"

"Oh, well, you know that it's Richard's last night before he heads back to Fort Barfoot for the next few weeks and Kitty heads back to Anacostia Base. They invited me to their last movie night."

"And you thought it was the best thing to tell me when I was in the tub, in the bathroom."

"Well, I had to go to the bathroom, and this was on the way. So, I figured that I'd better make myself known, rather than you come out of the bathroom and saw me suddenly walking down the hallway."

"Oh," I said, "sorry, I was being rude. Forgive the shock."

"I get it. You really didn't expect me, so it's better that we spoke without having to look at each other."

"Your heart is true," I said lightly, showing him that I understood why he thought this was the best way of explaining why he was there. "I just have to brace myself. I'm going to be in the bathroom for ten more minutes. That gives you time to do your business, and then go back downstairs before I emerge."

"Good to know that my instincts worked."

Pause.

"Does that mean that you are heading to the bathroom now?" I asked.

"Oh, yeah, sorry. I was waiting to be dismissed."

I chuckled, despite myself.

"You are dismissed, officer. Go and relieve yourself."

"Aye, aye, sir."

He left and went to the other bathroom that was down the hall.

When hearing the door close, I sighed, and my heart was able to stop beating in my chest like it was charged by the Energizer bunny.

Darcy had come to our movie night.

The one safe place that I had, that kept the outside world at bay, and now it had been compromised. Now the stress of the outside world had come in.

But *perhaps* it was better this way. *Perhaps* this was something that had to happen, and it ought *to happen*. Richard Fitzwilliam was a part of Kitty's life. In a pretty permanent way. As such, he was a part of our lives. Darcy was a close cousin to him. Therefore, this really was only a matter of time, as I had already been told.

Well, now was the hour of our discontent!

Oh, crap! Now I'm quoting Shakespeare. I only did that when I was flying my jet into enemy territory. I was getting serious again, and I really had to calm down.

I needed to learn to move on from the past. This was the only way that I could move forward. After all, this had long been a habit of mine, and would continue to be so, I wondered. The past was important; it helped you make sense of things, and what ought not to be forgotten. It keeps you from allowing yourself to be made into a victim again. Knowing the past is education. Education is knowledge. And knowledge is power. It's good to have power over your past. Yet, at the same time, holding onto the past can hold you back. So, what should I do? Remember the past or let it go? Remember it in a way that gives me knowledge, but forget it in a way so that it does not hold me down?

It's easy to do one or the other, rather than do the right thing: which is to do both.

I could do things the easy way.

Or the harder one.

But then again, at some point, I stopped being afraid of life. Now it's time to stop being afraid again.

I heard Darcy come out of the other bathroom, walk past the door and then back downstairs.

Knowing that the coast was clear, I got out of the sanctuary that was my bubble bath, wiped myself down with a towel, put on my bathrobe and went back to my bedroom.

To keep my nerves calm, I watched another episode of 'Brooklyn Nine-Nine' while I was getting dressed and blow drying my hair. When it dried, it was fuzzier than ever, but there was no one to impress. I pulled on my 'School House Rock' fitted t-shirt, some comfortable sweatpants, and then I walked downstairs.

With each step I took, I told myself to be casual and cool. When I came into the kitchen, it was to see Kitty, Richard and Mary preparing the food.

They looked at me, their expressions changing from ease to apprehension.

"You've been thinking about me," I stated, determined to get to the heart of the matter. "Admit it?"

"We were never going to deny it," Kitty responded.

"Why do you think I offered to help prepare the dinner?" Mary asked.

"Thanks," I said, "at least I can prepare the drinks."

I went to the fridge, took out some Pepsi and grapefruit juice. Two different types of taste appeal to as many as possible.

As I got the cups, Richard came near.

"Liz? Are you angry at me? For inviting Darcy, I mean."

I smiled.

"I was for, like, three seconds. And then I realized something." He looked quizzically at me. "That maybe it was better this way."

"He told me that he was on your tour. Since that happened, I thought this would be okay."

"That makes sense," I administered, "but in the future, give a girl some more notice! Richard, really?"

"Oh," he said, chuckling, "yeah, I was a little scared to say anything."

"What is with us soldiers and being unafraid of battle, but afraid of conversation?" I laughed, until I noticed Mary looking curiously at me. "What?"

"Soldiers. You just referred to yourself as a soldier."

I blinked. When thinking back on what I had just said, I saw what she meant. Kitty and Richard also looked at me, knowing why Mary had noticed that.

"I guess that I did," I admitted, equally surprised with myself. "I didn't even know I said that. Old habit, I guess."

Ignoring their expressions, I went back to my business and carried the cups into the living room.

When I walked in, it was to Josie drawing in her coloring book, and Killian playing his video games. To my surprise, Darcy was also playing the video game with Killian.

My entrance distracted him, he turned to face me and that led to Killian defeating him.

"Ha!" Killian cried.

"Not fair," Darcy replied to him. "Your aunt just came in."

"Oh, it's fair alright," Killian replied, "right, Aunt Lizzy?"

Putting down the cups, I refused to get in the middle of it.

"I will not take sides," I said, "that is what I call making it easy for myself. So, what level are you both on?"

"Nine," Killian replied, as Darcy looked down at his lap. "Want to play again, Mr. Darcy?"

Darcy looked at me, as if he wanted my approval.

"Go ahead," I said, "you've got fifteen minutes. Make the most of it, boys."

Killian socked the air, triumphant. Darcy smiled gently and they both went back to playing.

After we brought the food out, we all took our places in the living room, and Jane put the DVD in.

Jane, Killian, and Josie sat on the middle sofa.

Mary sat on the armchair, Darcy sat in the rocking chair on the other side of the room, and Mary and I sat on cushions on the floor, in blankets with our backs propped up against the sofa's arms.

Richard, and Kitty, naturally, rested their heads against each other's.

As the movie began, we ate and watched the iconic familiar music of 'Dragonheart' begin with the opening title sequence.

Instantly, I was hurled back to my past. The movie was released when I was a teenager and had been a refuge before the dark days came. The depressing times of being a teen. Often it was movies, music, and books that saved us from that era of our lives when we didn't know how to keep going. Especially tales of magic.

As we ate, we were all so wrapped up in the movie, that we barely spoke.

But you know how when you have a papercut, or a half-grown pimple, you can't help but pick at it?

Such was the way with Darcy and me.

It wasn't just a tour where I spoke, and he listened in a group.

No, this was different. We were in the same room, now connected through family. Our lives would possibly be inter-twined from now on. We had entered another chapter. A turning of the page if you will.

As a result, I couldn't help but, a couple of times, glance at Darcy.

Fortunately, I was able to do so when he was not looking. This was good, because sometimes, you don't have to look at some-thing to see it. As I watched the movie, out of the corner of my eye, I saw his eyes rest on me.

Life had brought us together in the oddest of ways. I wonder if it was as hard on him as it had been on me? There was only one way to find out.

I had to ask him.

———

After the movie was over, it was time for cleanup.

"Don't worry," I said to Kitty, Richard, and Mary, "you cooked. The rest of us can do cleanup."

Killian and Josie groaned.

"Listen to your aunt," Jane ordered as we got the plates, cups, and other stuff.

"Can I help at all?" Darcy asked. At first, it threw me for a loop, but luckily, Jane swooped in.

"You're a guest," Jane said, "but if you really don't mind, it will make the night go faster."

Without responding, Darcy began to help us as we did the cleanup. Mary, Richard, and Kitty sat there and discussed what their favorite part of the movie was. Then the conversation shifted to what was their favorite actor to voice the dragons, because in each movie, the actor who voiced the dragon changed each time. Chances are everyone's favorite voice actor would be Sean Connery, but it was a close call, because they all were pretty amazing.

As the rest of us were cleaning up, it was left to me to fill up the dishwasher and clean any other dishes that could not fit.

It led to Darcy lingering with me, handing the dishes to me, and drying any other ones that I handed to him.

"Liked the movie?" I asked him.

"A tale of magic, dragons, and surprisingly good writing for a sequel," he replied. "Works for me."

"You know," I said, "when growing up, I so much wanted magic to be real."

"Every kid does."

"Yeah, but it continued in my teenage years. It was because I needed to know, so much, that there was more to life than the mundane. Or to help explain things better."

"Explain what kind of things?" He asked, handing me a dish as I put it into the washer.

"Why life was so hard," I said simply.

"Oh."

"Sorry," I replied, "I didn't mean to get so serious after a fun night."

"It's okay. You have a point there."

"Good, because now I have to be serious," I said, organizing the dirty dishes on the shelves. Avoiding Darcy's gaze, I decided to address the issue directly. "How are you feeling?"

"Feeling?" he repeated.

"What I mean is this: being here, at movie night with this family… and seeing me again. I know that you came to my tour, and I appreciate that. Really, thank you for that. But let's be honest here, it's not *just* my feelings that matter. But yours too. It's been years, and now here we are. What's it like being here and seeing me again, like this? Is it awkward, is what I mean."

Darcy did not respond, but only handed me a glass that I began to stack.

"Darcy," I said even lower, "come on, that was not an easy question for me. It deserves an answer, don't you think?"

Darcy sighed and handed me another dish.

"It is awkward," he acknowledged, "there's no point in denying it. This is weird. Yeah, it's very much that. And how about you? I thought the tour would help things, but I guess that there are some things that a person can't breeze passed. It's strange, seeing someone when our past was so turbulent. Guilt's not the most enjoyable thing to feel, especially when you have to face the person, but I assume that it's necessary."

"You feel guilty?" I asked, hopeful.

"Yes, I do. I thought that going to the tour would show that, but sometimes, things have to be said, don't they?" he asked, a little low in his speech. It was probably not because he didn't mean it, but rather, I think he was just trying to find the right words to say, and there's no real 'right words' in these circumstances.

"That's good," I asserted, "and I'm not going to apologize about calling it good."

Since we ran out of room in the washer, I cleaned a plate, handed it to him and he began to dry it. After washing the last dish, I turned to him.

"You mentioned before that things have to be said."

"Yes," Darcy responded simply, "I did."

"Well, you're right."

After he dried the last dish, I put it away and put a detergent pod into the dishwasher.

"And I don't think that I'm going to be able to be comfortable around you until I clear the air. And when I say 'clear the air', I mean that I won't be happy until I have told you everything that I've been feeling."

Darcy uttered a sigh, and then placed his hands in his pockets. It was obvious that he was bracing himself.

"About the way that I treated you before?" he questioned.

"Yes. You see the problem was not just how you treated me... it was that I never stood up for myself in a way that made you stop."

When hearing that, his eyebrows raised, but that was the only change in his expression. Darcy was a strong man, and men like that were trained to be stoic about things. Especially if you also had been in the military.

"I did," I continued, "and I hated myself for not having enough fight in me. Well, it took the army, the Airforce, and many more life experiences, and now I know what to say. And please... don't run away. Don't interrupt, and don't groan or shrug when I'm talking. I'm asking you to do me a favor and let me tell you what I should have told you many years ago. Please?"

Darcy did not respond to that, and I took it as encouragement. Gathering my nerve, I began my rant.

"Fitzwilliam Darcy," I began, "the wonder years can some-times accidentally be some of the hardest times on a person's life. But you made it a certainty. You made my life hell, you made me a laughingstock, you turned everyone against me. Every day that I walked into school, I did my best to look and act invisible, hoping no one would see me. I always sat in the back of the class, which was harder to see the board, so that everyone would ignore me. I hardly ever raised my hand in class because I knew that, if I did, you would start passing notes to your friends about me. I didn't go to my proms because of you. I ran home crying so much, *because of you.*"

At this point, I was fighting back tears. "I missed out on what could have been some of the best times of my life, on many expe-riences, *because of you.* But I grew up, I did something with my life, and I realized that you weren't worth giving a damn about. You weren't worth another moment's notice. I should have walked past you every day, and not cared about what you said, and who you turned against me. I should have lived to the very fullest. No matter how bent you were on destroying my life. And I should have kicked your ass like the worthless spec that you were. And from this day forth, there will not be a day that I do not stand up to you and face the worst."

I expelled a long breath, holding my hands on my hips to steady my nerves.

"There," I uttered, relieved. "I did it. It's done."

Opening my eyes, I saw that Darcy was standing there, not knowing what to do.

"I get that you don't want to see me after this," I realized, "And it's okay. I get it."

I walked to the doorway and was about to walk up the steps, then I turned back to him.

"I'm sorry," I said, but I was not really sorry, "but that felt great! Good night."

I dashed up the steps, perfectly fine with him thinking that I was insane.

When I went into my bedroom, I saw Vatalie and Manhattan lying on my bed. When I closed the door, they looked at me but stayed where they were.

"I'm about to jump on the bed, happy as could be," I said, "sorry for what comes next."

I jumped on the bed, which led to them jumping off, frantic.

"I stood up to him," I exclaimed, into the pillow. "I stood up to him." I began to sing the song 'Oh Happy Day', until I forgot the rest of the lyrics.

I got into my pjs, opened the door to let the cats come and go as they wanted, I turned off the lights, turned on 'Brooklyn Nine-Nine' again, and then watched it until I fell asleep.

# NINE
# LET'S FACE THE MUSIC & DANCE

M y alarm clock pushed through my dreams, and I opened my eyes, groggy. Rubbing my face, and yawning, I looked down to see Vatalie lying at the bottom of the bed.

She squinted when looking at me, and I repeated the gesture. With cats, if you squint at them, that was a way of letting them know that you are looking at them affectionately.

I woke up happy and had more reasons for that than one.

Yeah, I talk to myself occasionally, but this time, I had Vatalie for an audience.

"I dreamt about waking up in the Renaissance, in modern clothes." I laughed. "Like literally, I showed up, in jeans and a thermal shirt, while everyone else was in long gowns and men were still wearing tights. I didn't dream about Darcy. It's over. And I stood up to him. I stood up to him, and my dreams about him are fully over. Finally, it's over!"

Laughing, I dug my face in the pillow, giddy.

When I went downstairs, I began to make breakfast for everyone, as Jane was busy getting Josie and Killian dressed for school.

Just as Kitty walked in to help pull out the bacon the laptop downstairs clicked on and there was an incoming message.

"It's probably Bingley," Kitty said, clicking it on, and sure enough, Bingley's face appeared.

"Kitty and Lizzy?" Bingley said. "Morning!"

"Calling early, huh?" Kitty asked. "You're eager about something."

"You would think that I would have something important to say."

"Because you do," I said, "whenever I called back from base at an early hour, it was to give good news."

"You guessed right."

"Jane's going to be down in a few minutes," Kitty said, "she's wrangling the babies."

"Nothing harder than getting kids up in the morning," Bingley said. "I'd rather go into a raid. So, how is everything going?"

"Last night, we had our movie night," I said.

"Ah, what movie?"

"*Dragonheart 3.*"

"Curse of the Sorcerer? I love that one!"

"Yeah," Kitty said, "it's so good. It was Richard's last night. He had to leave this morning to go back to Barfoot."

"And you're stationed at Join Base Anacostia-Bolling."

"Yeah, but after Thanksgiving, we go overseas together."

"At least you both will get to be together. You're at the stage where you need to be connected. I remember when Jane and I were dating. We made sure to be at bases in the same state and we always made sure to be stationed at the same forts when we went overseas. It was a special time."

"That's what amazes me," Kitty said, putting the bacon in the air fryer and turning it on. "I never thought that I would fall in love. I've had tons of crushes, but what I mean is that I didn't think I would fall in love with someone who would fall in love with me back. I love Richard a lot. I still can't believe it."

"Believe it. Sometimes things do work out."

Bingley looked at me.

"Oh, we sappy romantics are probably boring you."

"We're not," Kitty assured him. "Lizzy has her own romance going on."

"Oh! Who is the lucky guy?"

I closed my eyes, my insides in knots.

"Was," I stressed, "I had a romance and it's over, so his name means nothing to me anymore."

Kitty looked at me, surprised.

"You and Wickham aren't dating anymore?"

"Nope," I said, "it's over."

Kitty was astonished.

"Well, this was sudden. You two were hot and heavy for a bit."

"And it burned itself out," I said, putting the bread in the oven so that I could toast many pieces at one time. "I learned my lesson, believe me."

"What happened?" Kitty asked.

"Not much to talk about," I smoothed over, still not ready to tell the truth. "Kitty, I wish that I could give a better answer, but I need more time to make sense of it. I need time to get my head around it, but now I don't care about him at all. I don't mean to sound cold, but believe me, Wickham didn't care either. And I—"

Luckily, I was spared having to go into more detail, because Jane came downstairs with the kids, who all rushed to speak to their father.

"You're early," Jane said as I put cheddar cheese on the bread so that it could melt. "That means only one thing. You have good news."

"I totally do," Bingley said, smiling, "I've gotten leave from the fort for the holidays."

When hearing that, Jane's eyes brightened.

"Then that means…"

"Yup. Children, your dad is coming home for Christmas."

Everyone cheered! Bingley was coming back home.

———

Since Bingley had some more time on his hands, he was able to stay on facetime while we ate.

Josie and Killian went into epic detail about movie night, and then Killian talked about how he played video games with Darcy.

When hearing the name, Bingley perked up.

"Darcy came to dinner?"

"Yeah, and I beat him!" Killian boasted.

"You know Darcy?" I asked, surprised.

"Oh, yeah. We went through training together and entered the army on the same year. Yeah, we were stationed at Fort Cavazos, in Texas, back when it was called Fort Hood. When it came to Darcy, talk about a transformation."

"Transformation?" I asked, very curious. "What do you mean?"

"Well, when he began, he was a little...stiff and standoff-ish. Do you follow?"

"He was mean," I summed up.

"Oh yeah."

"I heard that the drill sergeant who trained him was intense."

"Masters. The drill sergeant was Masters, and he took a natural dislike to Darcy, for obvious reasons. Darcy was proud, and very high on himself. He kind of didn't understand humility and all that. Well, between that and how the other trainees treated Darcy, he learned humility fast. He made enemies, they ganged up on him, and he got his butt kicked so many times that it pushed him off his high horse. Sometimes the only way to defeat a bully is to bully them back. Darcy realized that he was not the 'end all be all', and he just got better over time. Once I saw that he was more open and willing to be nicer to people, I thought that he might be open to talking to me. We started getting along after that. I think we became friends eventually. Or at least, I thought that we were. You got to ask him if he grew to like me enough."

"Well," I said, "he's here till Christmas, so you have time."

"He is?"

"Yeah," Kitty said, "he's staying in Richard's apartment until the lease ends."

"I'll see Darcy again? Well, that will be interesting."

We were interrupted when Mary came down the steps, holding her cellphone in her hand.

"Mary, we have more breakfast for you," Jane said.

"Cool. Did you all check your phones? We got a text."

"A text? From whom?"

"From Dad. His plane lands tomorrow and he wants us to pick him up."

Quicker than you could say hocus pocus, I went to the desk and opened my phone. Dad had sent a text message:

> Hey girls. My plane arrives at DCA tomorrow at 11:00 a.m. Can one of you pick me up, because you know that I've never been good at ordering an Uber. And tell your mom, too.

"Yes," I said, "Dad's coming home tomorrow."

———

After school was over, Jane and I met at the kids' afterschool for our next rehearsal.

We learned the very last song that was written for the show, and Mr. King had some very good news for us.

"The dates for our performances have been confirmed. We will perform for three nights: December 10, 11, and 12. And tonight, I promise you all that this is the last song for you all to memorize."

We all breathed a sigh of relief. To be the crew for a children's musical was one thing. However, none of us adults were professional singers, except for the music teacher. A few of the children also had songs, but only as goblins, and if they were leads. We were there just to cover up scene changes, and for the complicated stuff.

Pages of the lyrics were handed out, with sheet music above the words.

Time had taught us to harmonize, and we first began the song without musical accompaniment, to learn the tune:

> *A man undone.*
> *A man who learns.*
> *A man now humbled.*
> *A journey earned.*

*He rises high.*
*He rises tall.*
*And returns to our world.*
*Despite it all.*

*A heart no longer cold.*
*Fallen from harshness.*
*A soul now filled with gold.*
*And saved from darkness.*

*He rises high.*
*He rises tall.*
*And returns to our world.*
*Despite it all.*

*He rises high.*
*He rises tall.*
*And returns to our world.*
*Despite it all.*

*Now that he moved passed this fight.*
*He hopes there's still time to set things right.*

Once we succeeded at harmonization, the pianist began to play, and we had to adjust to singing to music again.

Amidst the rehearsal, a woman entered the auditorium and walked up to Mr. King.

I was so busy trying to get the melody right, that I was standing off and rehearsing on my own.

"And there is the best teacher in George-Mason!" he said to her.

She kissed Mr. King on the cheek and spoke to him with affection. At first, I didn't care, but then I was called over.

"Elizabeth? Have you met my daughter yet?"

"Coming," I said, still looking at the music. I walked over, preoccupied with the lyrics. When I reached Mr. King, I finally closed the music and was prepared to meet his daughter respectfully.

When I looked in her face, I froze, and so did she.

"Mary," Mr. King said, "this is Elizabeth Bennet. Lizzy, this is my daughter, Mary King."

Mary King!

I was looking into the face of the woman who I caught with Wickham on Halloween.

In her face was embarrassment.

Mine was agony.

Mr. King was not an idiot. He could tell that there was a problem.

"Is everything okay?" he asked, a little anxious.

If my emotions betrayed me before, I would not let it continue now. Willing to compose myself, I wiped the sadness off my face and switched to casualness.

"Oh, sorry," I said, "it's just that your daughter reminded me of someone else when I was living in Kentucky. It shocked the heck out of me." I looked at Mary King, who knew that I was lying. "It's nice to meet you, Miss King."

"It's nice to meet you too," she responded, breathy.

Determined to make sure that her dad did not suspect anything, I decided to stick to the usual chitchat that you say when you meet someone.

"I like your dress," I said, a little forced, but I had to start somewhere.

"Thank you," Mary King replied. "I like your singing voice."

"Oh, you're being nice. Truth is that I can't sing for my life. But I'm trying."

"It's obvious that you are."

The piano teacher called Mr. King over, and he excused himself.

When we were alone, I breathed a sigh of relief. And so did Mary King.

"Well," I began, "this is awkward, isn't it?"

"Yeah, it is," Mary King said, chuckling nervously. "Thanks for not saying anything to my dad. I still am working up to tell him that I have a boyfriend. He's a little overprotective, which I get. Dads' ought to be. But for him to find out that I was with my boyfriend at the school I teach at. Well, I would never hear the end of it, you know? Parents and their lectures."

My eyes glazed over in wonder as she talked. I just realized that she did not know about George Wickham and me at all.

It all made sense. After all, why would she? All that she saw was that she was kissing her 'boyfriend' on school property, and I was the one who walked in on them. That's all that she knew and naturally, Wickham would never have told her about me. But wait! Didn't I call him out on being unfaithful before I ran off? Wouldn't she have wondered about that?

"That man you were with was your boyfriend?" I asked.

"Yes. His name is George. I'm sort of crazy about him. You probably didn't get a good look at him, but he's the most perfect man I've ever met. I know that I shouldn't have let things get that far, but come on, you know how it is, right? You meet that person who sweeps you off your feet, and the rules fly out of the window."

She saw that I looked perplexed, and naturally mistook what it meant.

"Or maybe you don't know what I mean," she said.

"No, no, I get it," I rushed out. "When things get hot and heavy, it's easy to get excited. I've been there, and the whole 'getting swept off your feet' thing does feel great."

"It does."

"How long have you both been together?" I asked. "It seemed like it was intense. I never was great at long-term relationships, so I wonder how it works."

"Oh, we've been dating for five months."

Five months!

When Wickham asked me out, he was already dating Mary King.

Truth is a double-edged sword; it can be a weapon that sets you free, or it can slice even harder into you. This was that circumstance. Days later, I would appreciate the truth, because it did set me free. However, right then, it sliced into me, and the slice was painful.

Mary King was never the 'other woman'.

I was the 'other woman'. Plain and simple.

To know that you cared for someone who never cared for you.

I suppose this was what growing up was like, even when you were already an adult.

Sadly, there are just some experiences that you cannot sidestep.

"By the way," I had no choice but to bring it up, "when I shouted at him…"

"Oh, yeah, Wickham had a theory about that. He was confused since you and he had never really met. He figures that you mistook him for someone else. That must have been strange for you, huh? Was he right?"

Ah! It was all willful ignorance.

Now there was another problem. Here a woman was wholly in love with George Wickham, and she didn't know the type of man that he was. He was, in fact, the worst, covered in perfect wrapping. Oh, why did those two combinations coincide more often than one wishes?

I was now caught in a bind.

I had two choices here:

I could tell her nothing and leave her in the happy ignorance that she was in. Truly, she looked happy, like I must've looked when I was dating him.

Or I could tell the truth. I could tell her about how Wickham had dated me while he was dating her.

But then would she believe me? She would easily get angry, and we were in public, telling her would be the worst thing to do. It could lead to us causing a scene.

Or maybe she would take her anger out on me. She could easily blame me. It was customary, despite being illogical, to blame the other person in the relationship rather than to blame the actual cheater.

Everything could go wrong.

As a result, I did what I did not expect.

I froze. I couldn't tell her just then. It was the worst timing imaginable.

But I didn't want to leave her in darkness.

All that was left for me to do was to smile and nod.

"That's great. Nothing better than when you find that one person that you care about."

"I know, right? And to think, I never thought it would happen. What about you? Do you have a special person in your life?"

I chuckled.

"Still celebrate Valentine's Day by sitting at home, watching 'Living Single' and the 'Unbreakable Kimmy Schmidt'."

She looked at me in confusion, and I realized that she had no idea what I was talking about.

"Those are two tv shows," I explained. "One's from the 1990s. Good time for television. Diversity was very organic on tv and movies back then. You didn't have to worry about filling up obligatory quotas. It was just a given."

She looked at me confused, again. It was obvious that she didn't know that I was just making fun chitchat.

"Yeah," I said, rubbing my lip, "this is one of those moments where I realize that my humor is not for everyone. What I mean is that, since I'm watching shows about women who are mostly single throughout the show, it means that I'm still single."

"Oh," she said, tapping my shoulder in a 'sympathetic' fashion. "Sad heart."

I tried to hold down my lunch, because I was afraid that I was going to barf.

Her lips moved downward, in a 'sad face' kind of look, and continued to coax me.

"Don't worry, I firmly believe that there is a special someone out there, for everyone. You just haven't met him yet."

"Thank you," I said, saying my words carefully and slowly, to concentrate on keeping a lid on what I really felt. "Maybe he is there. Or maybe he's not, and I can adjust. 'Living Single' and 'Unbreakable Kimmy Schmidt' are great shows. I love watching them on repeat."

She looked at me quizzically.

"By any chance, do you watch any *current* tv shows?" she asked me.

"What can I say? I just like having knowledge about the *past*."

Uh oh. I was slipping into cynical, but there was no way that she could suspect anything.

Luckily, Mr. King had come back to tell me that rehearsal had resumed.

I said goodbye to Mary King, walked away gracefully, but truth is, I wanted to run.

The second I got home I went to my room and texted Delores about how I saw the woman that was dating Wickham.

She wrote back.

> Make sure to come on Friday. You need some therapy.

I wrote back an agreement. I did need therapy.

# TEN

# SHIFTING FROM ONE BIT OF DRAMA TO THE OTHER

After Jane had taken the kids to school, I borrowed her minivan and drove to DCA Airport. She had to remain home to get food and make sure that the spare room was available for dad, and that it was all prepared.

As I rode into Washington D.C. I was looking at it from a different light.

You see that's the problem, and simultaneously, the blessing of when your life is telling people about their history. Since I lived so close to our nation's capital, and to George Washington's home, I had been doing constant research about our country's past.

First, I found out that, no matter what I did, I could easily say something historically inaccurate, because sometimes history is not written by the factual, but by the opinionated. Human error will always exist, naturally. As a result, I could give facts that will be countered a few years later. However, when you research history, it helps put everything into perspective. Ironically, despite the human constant need to complain, as we all have the right to, you learn that we are still living in the better times.

For example, when D.C. was chosen to be our capital, soon British ships were sailing up to burn it to the ground during the War of 1812—the war that both countries probably want to forget, because that was the war where both countries were not in the right at all. Using my imagination, I swiped away all modernization and replaced it with images of D.C. citizens running to and fro, trying to escape the oncoming invasion as the British ships sailed up the river, landed and stormed the city.

I even had sudden images of when the White House was burning, when the First Lady, Dolly Madison saved George Washington's portrait, and when a clerk named Stephen Pleasanton had rescued our Constitution, Declaration of Independence, and Bill of Rights, from the burning province…

…Only for over two centuries later, a mob of idiots would attack the capital for a stupid reason, cause an insurrection, and had the audacity to call themselves our own people. And one day, that would be our distant history. How embarrassing. At the same time, the right to fight… but also, the right to be loyal to tradition… We all have the right to think and believe as we do. But that's just it… think before you decide to fight. And then ask yourself, is the fight the right fight?

I blinked; was I still thinking like a soldier? As well as a citizen? Loyalty and freedom.

Since I had arrived in D.C. earlier than expected, I rode past address 1600, and glimpsed the White House, but my thoughts swept over all the government; a house divided is no house at all. How can you unify a people when you refuse to be unified?

Eventually I fell back into the present, eventually arrived at Ronald Reagan Airport, parked, and went to the terminal to wait for dad.

Looking out on the airstrip you see planes roll in and you wonder how much we humans do need to escape. The desire to get away, to discover yourself by going somewhere else.

Eventually, a plane landed, rolled into the terminal and it was evident that it was Dad's plane.

It connected to the walkway, and soon passengers were disembarking, meeting with their loved ones, or being met by no one at all. Usually, the latter was me. Whenever I traveled anywhere, I got off the plane and took a cab to wherever or to my home. Often there was no one to meet me. You would think that solitary existence meant that we types are lonely, but not really. We know how to be by ourselves and not ask what's missing.

As more passengers passed me, I was wondering where my dad was, when suddenly, his head appeared from behind a freakishly tall guy.

"Dad!" I exclaimed, a smile spreading across my face.

When seeing me, his eyes lit up. He didn't smile, but he didn't need to. I knew that he was happy to see me.

Racing up to him, laughing, I jumped into his arms as he embraced me.

"Well, well, well," he began, kissing my forehead.

"You said 'well' three times. That must mean that you're happy to see me."

He released me, to take in how I looked. "You look good, Liz."

"Thanks. I'm actually doing well, if you can believe that."

"I can. You always had a way of redefining yourself."

"It's my nature to be a wandering hobo right now," I said. "Thanks for not giving me the 'what have you done with your life' speech?"

"If I did that, what would be the point?"

We walked to the luggage claim and waited for his suitcases to come out.

"You would think after years of being in the army," he said, watching the luggage rotate around, "that I would learn to travel light."

"But that was a lesson you never acquired," I finished for him. "Dad, you always say this whenever you have to get luggage from off a plane."

"Do I?" he asked.

"Yeah, you do."

"Oh great. I've gotten to that point where I've grown to be boring and now repeat myself."

"You have no choice. That's what it means to be getting old," I teased.

"Can it!"

I laughed.

"So," he continued, "where are my other girls?"

"Don't blame them for not being here. Jane is preparing your room for you and dinner. Mary is working. She needs all the money she can get now, because, well, you know why. And Kitty has gone to get Lydia. Then her leave is over, and she heads back to base."

"And your mom? Is she prepared to see me, or will she poison my food when I'm there?"

Pause.

"I hope that you packed a food taster in your suitcase," I jested.

"Nope. That was an oversight on my part."

"Yeah, it sure was." Dad and I smiled at each other. "Truth is, you don't have to worry. And if you wanted to bring Anna along, then it turned out that it would have been okay."

"Really? Your mom would not have wanted to kill me, then kill her, and then kill me again?"

"Your dating Anna probably would not have been hard for her, because Mom is dating someone right now. You both moved on at the right time."

"Your mom is dating?" he asked, with a raised eyebrow.

"Yeah."

"Who is the sad soul who fell for her charms? Or lack of charms."

I didn't respond immediately, because I was wondering if telling dad who it was would be a good idea. But like peeling off a band aid, it had to be done.

"Mr. Lucas. Charlotte's dad."

When hearing this, Dad didn't respond. At first.

"Uh oh," I said, reading the vacant expression.

"Him?" Dad said at last. "He's dating Ariella?"

"Yeah. He is."

"That makes no sense. They are too different. What could possess him to like your mom?"

"Dad!" I stated. "I know that Mom is not perfect, but what's that about? Come on, you married her."

"She was younger back then and was gorgeous. And still sane."

"Dad, I've got news for you," I whispered. "Mom's always been a little insane. She was a fighter pilot. To do that job, you've got to have a little bit of crazy in your bag, because you never know when you might need it."

"True." He smirked. "Are all five of my girls crazy then, by rule? I mean, I know that Kitty and Lydia are, but what about you, Jane, and Mary?"

"I know that I am," I confessed, remembering my dreams of Darcy, and how they died once we met again. "I admit it freely. I just don't walk around advertising it."

Dad's luggage came, we retrieved it and began to lug it through the airport.

"Well, now it's time to address the elephant in the room," Dad said, "Or the elephant in the airport, in this case? How is Mary? And don't sugarcoat it for me. How is she really doing?"

"Scared," I admitted, "she puts on a brave face, and that's good. Putting on a brave face helps you become brave. But I know her. We all do. Dad, she's terrified. And it's not just about money, but it's also about the fact that this kid is going to change her life completely. And being a parent is pretty much the hardest thing ever."

"Tell me about it," he said. "I did it five times."

"Yeah, but you had Mom, and you planned for us. Mary didn't plan for this. And I think she's scared that she will be a bad mother."

"If that's the case, then that's good."

"It is?" I asked as we left the airport and began to go to the parking lot.

"Oh yeah. That's one thing that everyone should ask themselves before they have a child. You have to always ask yourself if you will be a bad parent. Because only by asking that will you know how to be a good one. More often than not, it's good to question yourself occasionally. Parenthood is the perfect time to do that. Either way, we don't have to worry. Mary will be a great mother."

"I know."

"I know that you know, but here's the main reason why."

Dad looked pointedly at me.

"She cannot be a bad parent," he declared, "because if she is, then she would never forgive herself."

We reached the car, and I drove him to Alexandria.

———

"So," Dad inquired, as we got near Longbourn Road. "Do you have anyone special in your life? Some man that I have no choice but to meet."

"You're safe," I assured him. "All quiet on the western front, regarding my love life. There's no guy, and there's no chance of me finding myself waking up with a baby on the way."

"Good," he said, "keep it that way. Especially since…"

He trailed off. As we stopped at a red light, I decided to translate that incomplete sentence.

"Especially since what?" I questioned. "You had a thought and then you chickened out. Spill the beans."

"I never have spilled beans my entire life. I'm not about to start now."

"Nice attempt at deflecting me from what you meant, but I got my deduction skills from you, so there's no point in trying to distract me. Especially since what?"

He sighed, trying to find the best way to phrase his answer.

Yet, I had a guess about what he meant, so I took a shot.

"Especially since I might go back into the Airforce," I finished his sentence for him.

He didn't respond, but only looked away from me and nodded. That was confirmation enough.

"Dad," I extoled, sighing, "you have to consider that I might never go back."

"Never say never in this case," he responded. "Lizzy, look me in the eye and tell me that you still don't have the instinct to be willing to lay down your life to protect the free world. No really, you're telling me that you don't have that voice in you, deep down somewhere."

The light turned green, and I drove as I thought about it. Darn it, dad. Sadly, he was right.

"Yes," I confirmed, "it's true. I still believe that."

"I know you do. That's why I'm saying that you shouldn't have kids just yet. You still might go back into the service. Only settle down when you fully know when that life is behind you. And I don't think that life is done with you just yet."

Not done with me just yet.

When we arrived home, Jane was excited. She rushed to the car, hugged Dad, and he was willing to get gushy over her.

Eventually Kitty returned home, with Lydia.

"Well, this is going to be fun," Lydia said, as Dad hugged them both. "You and Mom in the same room again, while dating other people. I have made some predictions."

"Of course, you have," he said, rolling his eyes. "Go on, lay it on me."

"You and Mom will be nice to each other for an hour, then an argument will ensue, and by the end of the week, there will be a thunderous fight. After the fight, you will make up, and wish you had never come, but then you will still stay, because you will not be happy until you have fully convinced Mary to meet this Atkins guy. And you also will want to meet him yourself."

"Right on all counts, probably," Dad said.

"Probably?" Lydia asked, skeptical. "You know that I will be right."

"But that's why you will be wrong," he countered. "You told me what would happen, and it probably would have happened. But since you told me, now I know how to avoid my fate. Thanks for telling me the direction that I'm in. Now I know to go in the opposite direction to what you said."

"No," Lydia refuted, "it doesn't matter what I say. It's going to happen. Sorry, but my logic is undeniable."

"Well," Dad said, using his tone to cut to the chase. "Before she gets here, I gotta ask. How is Mary really doing? How does she look?"

"She's beginning to show," Kitty explained. "Morning sickness has kicked in."

"And I'm correct to guess that none of you have met this Atkins jerk."

"We don't know if he's a jerk yet," I said.

"He got my daughter pregnant; I hate him. It's the way of us dads." He looked at Kitty. "And in a couple months, you and that Richard guy are deployed overseas."

"Yeah. Right now, he's at Barfoot. And Bingley is coming back for Christmas."

"That's great," Dad said, clapping his hands together. "Thank God Jane married a guy that I don't entirely hate. She was very good at doing that."

"Dad, if you met Richard," Kitty argued, "you would know that he's actually pretty great."

"I'm tired of meeting men that my daughters' date. When most of you went to prom, I was in hell. Each and every time."

"We all went with a guy who was a friend," Jane said.

"Please!" Dad said, swiping the air. "There's no such thing as a guy who just wants to be friends."

"Come on," I said, kissing his cheek. "Some men out there befriend us with entirely innocent intentions."

Dad gave us a sly look.

"Fine then," he said, turning to Kitty, "when this Raymond—"

"Richard," Kitty corrected.

"Fine, *Richard,* then. When you met this Richard guy, did you both start out as friends?"

Kitty's face screwed up for a minute.

"How did you know that?" she asked.

"Being a man, I understand them."

"It's no different than with Lizzy," Lydia said, "after all, she and George Wickham started out as friends from school, and now look at them."

Everyone looked at me.

I wanted to die.

———

Over the last few days, I had not really talked about Wickham, and I never spoke about him to our dad. As a result, it was perfectly natural to assume that I would bring him around soon.

But I had no intention of doing that.

"George Wickham?" Dad repeated. "That name sounds familiar."

"We went to Santa Fe High School together," I said. "We were friends at the time."

"And he's your boyfriend now? I thought you would have mentioned it at least once on the car ride here."

Inwardly, I rolled my thoughts like someone rolls their eyes. Between the fact that our father was naturally overprotective, that Kitty was dating someone that Dad hadn't met yet, compiled with the fact that Mary got impregnated by a guy who Dad was quick to belittle, and hearing that I was dating someone naturally would spark another nerve in Dad's 'daughter-date-o-meter', was not the best situation to be in. Especially since he always had a deep love for me.

"If you're about to give me a lecture," I noted, "Dad, I am perfectly happy to spare you from any annoying news. I'm as single as ever."

"Single?" Lydia questioned. "When did that happen? You and George are no longer a thing?"

"Yeah," I said, "sorry if I spent a lot of time talking about him. I think I was so quick to like him, that I made something out of nothing. It was one of those things that was a quick sort of romance that burned itself out even before we got serious. We're completely over—in fact, I wonder if we ever began anything."

"Well," Dad said, relieved, "that solves that chapter. When it comes to Mary's life going through this, it's nice to know that it's all Quiet on the Romantic front with one of you." Then he looked at Lydia. "I know that, with you, I know better than to ask questions. What I don't know won't hurt me."

"I'm in college," Lydia remarked, "you're right not to ask me. Ignorance is bliss."

"She's single again," Kitty said for Lydia.

"Kitty!" Lydia groaned.

Kitty grinned.

"In this moment," Kitty said, "I'm the wildcard that you didn't predict or see coming, eh? Don't worry, it will make dad happy to know that, under all that cynical cleverness, you are pretty independent." She turned to Dad. "Lydia likes to make herself look worse than she really is. She hasn't even kissed a guy in almost two months."

"Or girl," Lydia added, "I'm pretty open to other experiences, FYI."

"Is this true?" Dad asked Lydia, smiling, "you're still doing that thing where you try to make yourself look hedonistic when you prefer just to go to class, do homework, and read books?"

Lydia rolled her eyes and looked at him.

"What's the fun of doing the whole virtuous thing when it doesn't make you interesting? Sorry, but good people are always so boring. No one ever wants to hear about them. It's wrong, but it's true, sadly. Just watch the news and you'll see that. If I like to embellish my flaws, then it's better for everyone around me. I bring more to the conversation by looking perverse. Believe me, it's for the best."

Dad sighed.

"Why must you be too smart?"

"I regret nothing," Lydia replied, smug.

Dad and the rest began to talk about other things while I told Jane that she could keep up with dinner and I would pick up the kids.

She agreed to this, and I was about to leave the kitchen when Lydia approached me.

"So," Lydia began, her voice low, "you and this Wickham guy was a passing thing?"

"Yeah, it was. If you're worried that I'm leaving out any juicy details, don't worry. There was nothing really interesting about anything that happened between us. It was a few kisses and then he went."

"And by that, it means that he cheated on you."

Astonishment was put mildly.

The color drained from my face as I looked at her, alarmed as God knows what.

I didn't have to say anything for her to read my expression.

"Yes," Lydia said, "I had a feeling that was it."

Losing not a moment, I turned to everyone else.

"Lydia is coming with me to pick up the kids," I said, not even waiting to ask her.

"She is?" Jane asked, cutting some carrots.

"Yeah," Lydia said, reading my thoughts, "I guess that I am."

We got on our hats, coats, and walked to the car.

I was in a state of surprise, but why was I? Lydia was born with deductive skills that were worthy of Sherlock Holmes.

"Well," Lydia said as she opened the car door, "you could have *asked* me to come along. I would have said yes, you know."

"I didn't want to leave anything up to chance," I retorted, getting into the driver seat, and shutting the door.

As we buckled ourselves in, I turned on the ignition.

Now that we were inside a car, and no one could overhear us, I unleashed my frustrations.

"Really?" I groaned. "Lydia, how could you possibly have known that?"

"I just reasoned it out," Lydia explained. "Some people lay all their cards on the table by talking. Others show what's really going on with them by not talking about much. You went from talking about Wickham, to not talking about him. Now if the breakup had been mutual, or he broke it off respectfully, then you would have told us the details. In fact, you would have told us about it all."

She gave me a side glance as we stopped at a red light.

"But you didn't," she continued, "rather you have been very secretive about it. That means that there was something humiliating about the whole experience. And you adored this guy. Which means that he had to have done something that caused irrevocable damage. And I know that you wouldn't have done anything because you were excited about this. When it comes to lovers, nothing is worse than cheating, so it had to have been him who made the mistake. And I was clearly right."

The light turned green, and we drove to the school.

"Lydia?"

"Hm?"

"For once, can you just not be right?"

"No," she replied simply, "because if it weren't for people like me, what would happen to the world? So, when are you going to tell the family?"

I rubbed my lips as I turned the car with my left hand.

"You're going to have to eventually, you know?" Lydia said.

"Why?" I asked. "Why do I have to? Why did you have to discover it? There was nothing wrong with me just saying that we were broken up."

"Because it hurts your pride to admit that you were wrong there."

"Yes, it is," I admitted. "It wasn't till after that moment that I never actually knew myself."

"It happens to many people. Even sexy people get cheated on."

Since Lydia knew everything, I suppose that I could talk to her about it. It was strange, because she was the least likely person that I wanted to have this discussion with.

"I thought I knew him," I acknowledged. "I honestly thought he was the right one."

"That's what many people think when they are in this predicament."

"Have you ever been in this situation?" I asked.

"No," Lydia answered, "but that's because I've never been in a relationship long enough for someone to cheat on me. I may have many friends, but people don't like to date girls who have a brain like mine. Since I'm very good at knowing the outcome to any situation, I'm a little intimidating."

I could well believe that.

"But I also don't seek romance out very much," Lydia pursued. "When you've got a brain like mine, falling in love for too long makes things fuzzy. Besides, I want to be in the Airforce, and that dream takes up much of my imagination. You and I both know that life as a warrior is romantic, in its own way."

Hearing her say that astonished me.

"You know that?" I asked.

"Oh yeah. Grandmom did it, and so did Granddad, because there clearly had to be some sort of charm to it all. After all, why else would someone willingly risk their lives, unless there was some beauty to it all?"

"True," I acknowledged, unable to deny it. "A fighter jet is beautiful. Like the ultimate bird flying among the clouds." I chuckled. "When I was a kid, mom showed me a picture someone took of her jet when she had her first liftoff. I thought it was like a dragon, but in the best sense. A dragon to protect the land. I thought our mother was magical when seeing her in her uniform. And Grandmom."

"So did I," Lydia acknowledged, "so did we all."

Lydia gave me a look.

"What?" I asked her.

"Nothing much. I just know something."

"What would that be?" I asked.

"I'm not going to tell you. You'll figure it out on your own."

"You're getting elliptical." I raised my eyebrow. "You only do that when you start to predict the future."

She smirked.

"You're learning to read my expressions. Well, it's about darn time."

"Fine," I accepted, "keep your secrets."

"I will, thank you very much."

We pulled up in front of the school. Since Josie and Killian were aware that they would be picked up at this time, they were waiting at the front door. When seeing their mother's car, we saw them putting on their backpacks.

"But one thing is certain," Lydia said, waving at them through the car window. "If you're going to start entering the dating world, this was inevitable."

"Me getting betrayed?" I questioned.

"Yes. Love is like everything else in this world; you get better at it through practice. And practice makes perfect. Since you don't date very often, you weren't blind, Lizzy. You just didn't know because you lack experience. The more you date, the more you understand what you want, and what you don't want. What's real, and what's not. There are some life lessons that you can't jump passed or skip around. You just gotta live through it, and then come out of it on the other side."

"I thought I was past this," I admitted.

"You can't be. Life is a test. Or a series of tests. You hadn't taken it yet. And now you have. I won't tell everyone what went down between you and Wickham. But you might as well get around to telling the rest of the family eventually. Think of it as just another test."

Killian and Josie came up to the car, Lydia opened the door, jumped out to greet them and they rushed into her arms.

As she twirled them around, I looked at Lydia. Was she right? In my eagerness to not get hurt anymore by things, did I open myself up to inexperience?

What's the point of running away from something if you only run back to it?

For the love of Captain Kirk! Lydia was right. Of course, she always is. But now more than ever, Lydia *was right*.

───

Once we drove Killian and Josie home, they were both excited and nervous to see their granddad again. Kids are neither ignorant nor unaware of vibes that we adults give off. They knew that he and their grandmom were divorced. They were aware that there was tension between them. And they were never as close to our father as they were to our mother, since he didn't live with them.

They loved each other, but he was an outside force to them.

As such, when our father wrapped his arms around them, they were happy, but didn't know what to say. He sat down and asked them about school, letting them talk about what they learned in class, but there was a stiffness to it all.

As I helped with dinner, I watched him talk to them and wondered about Mom.

"Is Mom coming tonight?" I asked.

"She knows that he's coming," Jane said, "so probably not. Do you think she might be…"

"With Mr. Lucas?" Kitty finished that sentence. "Most likely. Personally, I think it might be better this way. If there is going to be drama, let's get into it gradually."

"True," I said, "Dad's home. Let's plunge into the abyss slowly."

The front door opened, and we all quieted down as we heard Mary's voice.

"I'm home," Mary called, locking the door behind her. "It's colder than I thought." She came into the living room, removing her coat. "And I spent the whole day wanting to eat nothing but burgers and fries. The cravings are getting bad and—"

She stopped talking when she saw dad, sitting near Killian and Josie.

His eyes fell on her.

And she gazed at him.

Dad's eyes lowered to Mary's belly, which was beginning to show.

Slowly, he began to stand up.

"Mary…"

"Hey Dad," she said, slowly. "You came home."

"Yes, Mary, I'm back."

Then her face transformed from complacency to sadness, horror, and embarrassment.

"Dad…"

Dad rushed to her and hugged her. Like a little girl, she fell into his arms and let him hold her.

"Dad, I am so sorry," she wailed, weeping into his neck. He rocked her where she stood, becoming the child that she once had been.

"It's alright," he assured her, "I don't hate you. Mary, I don't hate you at all. So please, don't hate yourself."

"All my dreams!" she cried. "Everything that I had planned to do…"

"I know. We'll find a way. I promise that you will find a way."

Killian and Josie sat where they were, motionless.

Jane, Kitty, and I stopped cooking and watched the scene.

Only Lydia sat there casually, eating some beef jerky.

I looked at her and mouthed the word: 'Really?'

She mouthed the words back: 'I knew this was going to happen'.

Of course, she did.

Life is about being surprised every now and again. How can Lydia always be so cheery when that kind of excitement will never be something she will experience?

———

We all sat down to dinner, and Dad told us about his vacation in Vienna. He left out any talk of going with Anna Gardiner, and we preferred it that way.

After we finished eating, I was putting the dishes in the dishwasher, Jane was putting away the food, Kitty was wiping down the dinner table, Lydia was sitting in the corner, doing her homework, and Killian and Josie had already been sent upstairs to take a shower.

Now that it was just us downstairs, Dad could approach the subject.

"So," Dad said, "be honest with me. Have you talked to this Atkins guy about him being the father?"

Mary sighed. After all, we hadn't approached the subject for a little while, if Mary had talked to the man. Mary opened her mouth, putting on a brave face.

"No," Mary replied, "I still haven't talked to him about it."

We all turned to her, except for Lydia, who was still doing her homework. And we all knew why, because it went without saying: she probably knew that Mary had never called the baby's father.

"Why not?" Dad inquired. "Mary, your sisters talked about this. You have to tell this man about what he did to you."

"It was complicated," Mary responded.

"I'm a man with five daughters; I don't see what's complicated about this. He got a woman pregnant. He ought to know what is going on."

"At first, I had my reasons," Mary said. "Remember I was still thinking, for a while, that I might not keep it. I was very much exploring that option. Then I thought I might have a miscarriage. After all, I'm still very active. So, there was no point in me informing him about something that might never happen, or I would not follow through with. Or at least, that's what I told myself in the beginning. And I was right to. But it's more complicated than that and I just didn't want to tell him. I know that I should explain. I just don't know how to tell you or put it into words."

Mary took a drink from her cup, trying to sort out how to go about the discussion. However, Lydia is Lydia, and she was never very patient when it came to personal revelations.

"It's the fear of not knowing what will happen next," Lydia translated. "If she tells this Atkins guy, then two things are going to happen. Either A) he will be upset at the idea, want nothing to do with her or the baby, and even accuse her of trying to trap him in some way. Hearing him say that would hurt. Or B) he will be open to the idea of being in this child's life, but in what way? Will he be a good father, or a bad father? Or a dad who's there and then who's not. And how will he treat Mary? After all, he and Mary don't know each other very well. By having him in her life, things could get worse. She'll need money to help raise the kid, but what if the cost of having him in her life is not worth the money that he can bring by supporting his kid? There's just too much at stake."

Dad processed this all for no more than four seconds before he turned to Mary.

"Mary, is that what you're feeling and thinking?" Dad asked.

Mary didn't speak, but she looked at her lap, nodding. Turning to Lydia, dad was a little annoyed.

"Lydia, you couldn't wait for her to tell me. You had to determine things for her."

"Come on, Dad," Kitty defended Lydia. "You know that it helped."

"It did," Mary accepted. "Dad, truth is that I didn't know how to phrase it well. In fact, I kind of was scared to. Lydia said it so that I didn't have to."

"Precisely," Lydia said, still doing her homework. She could do work and converse all at the same time. "Sometimes it helps for someone else to speak, so that you don't have to think of the words. This *is one* of those moments."

"Fine," Dad determined, "just this once, Lydia, I'm happy that you were unafraid to know it all."

"Ah, a compliment," Lydia extoled. "Heavens rejoice! He actually complimented me on something."

"If I complimented you on knowing everything, I'd make you high on yourself," he explained. "And we can't have that."

"Luckily, my self-confidence does not live or die by your compliments," Lydia announced.

Dad and she gave each other a look.

"Please," Mary said, "don't start right now, you both. I don't want you fighting because of me."

"Fine," Dad said, putting his hand on hers. "But I need you to call this man. At least give him the chance to know that he will be a father. Whatever happens, things will work out on their own. Promise?"

"You're right. I've just been a coward about it."

"Do you need me to write the text message for you and send it on your phone?" Lydia asked, still doing her homework.

"Lydia!" Jane and I declared.

"What? It was an offer, to help."

We all did the face palm.

"The offer is still on the table," Lydia continued to offer, still doing her homework.

We face palmed again.

"Maybe Lydia would know how to phrase it," I suggested.

Everyone looked at me, surprised. Even Lydia looked away from her homework, which she clearly would get an A+ on.

"Yeah," I acknowledged, "that has got to be a first for me."

"And speaking of dysfunctional situations," Dad brought up, "where is your mom?"

We all were silent.

"Why did I even ask that?" Dad said, reading our silence. "In fact, why do I even care?"

———

With Josie and Killian still upstairs, Jane was getting them into bed. Since she was spending the night, Lydia was pulling out the cot in the basement, since dad had the guest room. As such, Kitty, Mary, and I were sitting in the kitchen, with dad sitting on the opposite side of the table.

Mary's cellphone was on the table, and we were all staring at it.

"Go on," Dad encouraged Mary, "if he starts getting fresh, I am perfectly willing to butt in on the conversation."

"Dad, please don't," Mary said.

"Keep staring at the phone, and I will make no promises."

Breathing out and in heavily, Mary opened her phone, searched through her contacts, and clicked on Henry Atkins's number.

"Put it on speaker," Dad ordered.

"Dad?" Mary groaned.

"Hey! I'm half the reason that you are alive. Indulge your dad."

Mary clicked it on speaker.

"He's probably not even going to pick up," Mary pointed out, "many people rarely answer their phones, because they're too busy—"

The phone clicked on, on the other end.

"Hello?" a man's voice said.

"Henry?" Mary said, her voice shaky.

"Mary?" Henry Atkins replied.

"Yeah, it's me. Hey."

"Hey. It's been a while."

"Yeah, it has. Thanks for keeping my number in your contacts."

"Yeah, I've gotta get better at emptying out my contact list, for data storage."

We all raised our eyebrows, and Dad looked like he wanted to murder that guy.

"It was a joke," Henry replied, reading the pause that he wasn't there to witness. "Sorry if that sounded awful."

Mary breathed a sigh of relief.

"Sorry, I should have laughed. That's the problem with phones; you can't always read people's expressions by the tone of their voice."

"I know, right? That's why I reduce my phone conversations to no more than three minutes. Less likely for things to get lost in translation."

"You're preaching to the choir."

Mary laughed awkwardly, then stopped when she realized how stiff that was.

"Don't worry, I called with a purpose."

"Sure, what's up? You want to hang?"

Dad whispered the word 'pig' under his breath.

"That's up to you."

"Well, I'm still open, but right now I'm at the base. But I go on leave in two weeks. Is that soon enough for me to drop by Alexandria for a while? I can only stay for a week, though. I promised my parents I would come home."

"Again, that would depend on you."

Henry paused.

"What is that supposed to mean?" he asked. "I kind of put myself out there already. It's kind of up to you now."

Mary ground her teeth, looked at our dad, and clearly was uncomfortable.

"You know what, I realized that what I have to say shouldn't be said over the phone. I should say it face to face because it's kind of important. Maybe we should zoom each other."

"You hate zoom and face chatrooms," he pointed out, "And so do I."

"You remembered that I only believe in zooming if you won't

see someone for months at a time, and if not, just wait till you see them again?"

"Of course. It makes all the sense in the world."

"That's really sweet," Mary cooed.

"Yeah," he said, chuckling, "I'm sweet."

Our father looked like he wanted to puke. When you're a dad, all men are a waste.

"Mary," Henry said, "what is it?"

Mary looked at us, and we all gave her the thumbs up, encouraging her.

"Alright," Mary said, "what I have to say is something a little big. Oh, that's a terrible way of putting it. It's big, and before I tell you what it is, I want you to understand that I wouldn't tell you this unless I was completely certain. And the reason that I'm telling you is because you have every right to know. This is not me cornering you, but I hope that you understand that this sort of thing happens."

"You sound like you're about to give me bad news."

"It's hard news, but I'm going to do the best I can here. Henry…again, I just want you to know. I'm pregnant."

# ELEVEN
## DO THE RIGHT THING

After Mary dropped the truth on Henry Atkins, there was a pause over the phone.

We all looked at each other, prepared for anything and everything.

"Henry?" Mary said. "Are you still there?"

Pause.

"Yeah," he replied, his tone deeper and much heavier.

I could only assume that he was still in shock, and that he was responding on autopilot. I can't blame him really, because this must be the most astounding thing in the world, and that he had no choice but to be horrified.

Parenthood, after all, is a blessing for those who are expecting it. But for him, the world must feel as if it fell on the wrong side up.

"Yeah," Henry Atkins repeated, his voice still hollow. "I am still here."

There was a pause over the phone again.

"Congratulations," Henry continued.

"Thank you, but I admit that I am—I did not intend this."

"Exactly. Last time we talked, we spent a whole hour competing with who knew more about WWII jets."

"Yeah, the FD-1D Corsair is a totally underrated plane," Mary uttered, laughing nervously.

"Yeah, it is," he replied, equally nervous in his tone.

"They are deflecting," Lydia whispered in Kitty's and my ear. I flinched, unaware that she had come back into the room. "They are using their military experience to avoid the topic."

"Yeah," Kitty said, also quietly, "they are in shock. That being said, the Corsair was a fantastic fighter jet."

"It was," I concurred, whispering, "It was brilliantly built. I wrote a whole paper on their construction and how affective they were on the Japanese kamikazes."

I blinked, wondering how quick we all were on adding side-notes to the comment. I think, deep down, we also were a little apprehensive about how this conversation was unfolding. I think we were afraid of how this was going to end.

"Mary?" Henry asked.

"Yes?"

"Who's the father?"

Mary rubbed her lips, giving a despairing look at us all, and she continued.

"You. It's your child."

Another pause.

"Oh, god," he grunted on the other end, clearly overwhelmed.

Mary remained silent, letting him react how he wished. Looking at dad, I saw a vein pulsing in his neck. Henry's reaction did nothing to feel endearing, but I was patient. After all, this was not easy news to hear.

"Mary," Henry Atkins said, "are you sure? It could always be another guy, and you're just saying it was me."

While I was prepared for this reaction, Dad was not in the mood.

Without thinking, he reacted.

"My daughter is telling the truth!" he roared.

Embarrassed, Mary's cheeks turned red, with Henry knowing that there was an audience.

"Who was that?" Henry asked, his tone harder.

"My dad," Mary responded, "he's here to help me through this. Henry, don't be angry, please."

"I'm not angry!" Henry said.

"Excuse me!" Dad continued. "Are you screaming at my daughter?"

"Dad," Mary whispered, trying to shift the topic back to her and Henry.

"I'm sorry," Henry rushed out, "I didn't mean to—I'm just freaking out, sir. That's all. I just had to ask. I didn't mean to be offensive."

Dad looked at me, instinctively, as Jane began to tiptoe down the stairs.

I nodded to him, and put my finger on my mouth, indicating for him to be quiet until Mary and this Henry guy finished talking.

Grinding his teeth, he moved away, leaned against the wall, and breathed out and in heavily. This was very hard for him, but Mary had to carry this on her own now.

"Henry," Mary continued, "I know that this is not easy. And I get why you would ask that. But it's impossible for it to be anyone else—since you're the only man that I've been with in the last three years."

"Three years?" Henry repeated. "We've only been together for a few weeks. I'm the only—"

"Yeah. You remember that I told you that I was not very much interested in relationships. I was kind of too focused on my work."

"Exactly. Mary? You still wanted to go through with this? Not to sound like a jerk or anything…"

"You're not being horrible for thinking in that direction. I thought of it too, and I almost did go in a different direction."

"Mary…you love being in the Airforce."

"I know. I went back and forth on it for too long. But I will get this all figured out, and here I am. Look, I know that this is the last thing that you wanted, and that we are in a hard place. And I'm not going to tie you down to this. I just want you to know that you have a kid out there in the world, and that you're a father. You have the right to know that. Telling you was the right thing. You understand that, right?"

I heard Henry shifting around, by the sound of it.

"Yeah, it was," he replied, his tone still heavy. "It's just that, no matter what, I'm in a bind. Knowing about it puts me in a terrible position, either way. If I stay away, then I'm a father who abandoned his kid. And if I stay, then I'm in a place where I will be a bad father. I have no idea how to do this. After all, it's not like we planned on doing anything else except for being casual with each other. Your dad is still listening, isn't he?"

"Yeah," Dad grunted, "he is. And it's time that I take control of this situation."

"Dad?" Mary interrupted, but he overrode her.

"Mary, this is where I have to get in the middle. Because this is the moment where men should talk about this with other men."

Dad walked up to the table, and leaned on it, placing his hands on the countertop. "Mr. Atkins, here are the facts. You had some fun with my daughter, and this is the reaction that can occur. Now, I admit that I don't know how frightening it is to hear news like this and to be totally unprepared for being a father. I was prepared. So, I must ask, and I need an honest answer. Are you scared right now?"

Henry did not respond.

"You don't look like less of a man for admitting it. The plain truth is that, if all goes according to plan, you're going to be a father. Out there, in the world, will be a child that you helped create. And a woman who brought your child in the world. Are you scared, my boy?"

"Yes," Henry acknowledged, "I am. This is scary to me."

"I get it. But here's where I need you to rise above that fear and confront things. Now we don't know what's going to happen. We don't know if you and Mary will want to continue a relationship. But we have the right to know the man who will be my grandchild's father. When Christmas comes, will you be on leave from your fort?"

"Yes, I will."

"Good. Now this is the only time that I order you around. During Christmas, this is the time of the year where most of the family are getting together. We need you to come visit, so that you get to know us. When there, we will discuss future plans, whether you both will want to have a go at wanting to be in my daughter's life, how you can assist financially, and what will work for both of you? This is the best course of action, and I think you know that. And these next few weeks will give you time to get used to the idea."

"I think I can do that. It does make sense. I really just need time to get used to this idea—and still, yeah, I am very scared."

"Good. We'll let you know what day you can come and visit."

"Thank you."

"Thank you, Henry," Mary echoed. "Thanks for being okay with this."

"I..."

He trailed off, and it was obvious that he was speechless.

"I just need time," he continued. "I still don't know what to say."

"I get it. I do. But it would be nice to see you at Christmastime. And, if you don't mind, can I call you every now and then, up until the holidays? Just to keep in touch. That's all."

"Of course. That's only natural."

After a few more awkward sentences between them, they said goodbye and hung up. At the fall of the conversation, Mary continued to look at her phone.

"Dad," she said, her body deflating.

"I know, dear, I know," he said, holding her. She wept into his arms.

"Thank you," Mary spoke, "thank you so much!"

―――

"Well," I said, sitting next to Dad, in our guestroom, "that was very well done."

"I have my moments," he said, sitting upright, against the headboard. "I can't believe it. Another of my little girls is going to be a mother."

"Yeah," I replied, smiling, "strange, isn't it? I mean... what's it like seeing your daughters grow up and then make kids of their own?"

"It's freaky," Dad replied, "you can't believe it. But you also are happy about it for many reasons. Among them is it teaches them to be sympathetic to us."

"What do you mean?"

"Well, when you become a parent, there's no manual on what to do. People can give you advice all that they want, but it's a plane that you're flying blind. Even when Lydia was born, I still wasn't sure of what to do, because you all were so different. And that meant that no matter what I did, I would make mistakes. I would do something wrong that would hurt you all and stunt your growth process. But when your kids have kids of their own, they understand what you were going through the entire time. You learn to realize that, like you, we were doing the best that we could."

"To be flying blind," I empathized, "even though I might never have a kid, I do know a little bit about that."

I took his hand.

"Thanks for coming, Dad. Things feel more stable now that you're here."

He chuckled.

"You know what's strange. A part of me hopes that this Henry Atkins guy does not marry Mary."

"Really? I get it since they don't know each other very well. That could easily lead to disaster."

"Yes, but my reason is a selfish one."

"What?"

"When Mary delivers, and if the baby comes out healthy, then it will have my last name. The kid will be a Bennet."

I laughed hysterically.

"Are you serious? My father, the classicist!"

"I can't help it. I like the idea that my name will continue. If this Henry guy helps, that's great. But Mary could easily learn to be a single mom. She has it in her." He smiled sadly. "I'm going to be a grandad again. Isn't that something?"'

I kissed his cheek, said goodnight to him and prepared for bed.

———

When I lay in my bed, watching an episode of 'Brooklyn Nine-Nine', my mind drifted to Dad, who was lying asleep in his guestroom.

After years of service, being married for decades, raising five daughters, and where was he now? In a guestroom to a house that he no longer is part of, rents a small suite in Oklahoma, has no property to his name anymore, and this is what he has to show for it.

You don't always wonder, at his age, what he's thinking? How he's feeling about this being the result of his life's work. One day I will have the heart to ask him. But today was not that day.

If time could be rewound, did he remember what it was like when he married Mama, of when Jane was born, then myself, Mary, Kitty and Lydia.

To have a child!

What is the sensation like, for when you first hear that you will produce life, spend endless hours, looking after that life, raising it, getting little sleep as you hold the child in your arms, to rock it to sleep, to work to make sure that it does not want for anything, knowing that one day, it will break your heart. Children have no choice but to do that to their parents, eventually.

I know I broke my mother's heart.

I am sure that I broke Father's. He just loves me too much to talk about it very much.

Jane has undergone it.

Kitty might.

And now, Mary definitely will, and she will spend her life trying to raise a child that will inevitably break her heart in turn.

I don't know how many people do it! Yet somehow, through all the sleepless nights, picking the child up from school, helping them with homework that you can't remember well yourself, teaching it principles, punishing it when it does something wrong, praising it when it is right, avoiding teaching it the wrong lessons, and knowing that, and hope that it will not ever grow to hate you—I suppose you can only do one thing. Accept it, and just keep going.

I fell asleep.

# TWELVE
# ALLOWED TO EXHALE

Friday came around, I got dressed comfortably, but respectfully, rushed down the steps and into the kitchen to grab a water bottle. Jane, Lydia, Mary, Dad, and the kids were eating breakfast, when I was a burst of frantic energy that had come dashing in.

"Morning?" Dad said as I swiftly kissed him on the cheek.

"Morning," I responded.

"What's the hurry?"

"I have a tour this morning," I said, "this group comes from Tennessee, and they specifically wanted an early tour."

I threw the water bottle in my bag, told them that I was going to grab some breakfast along the way, and I was out of the door.

The tour was to begin at Alexandria's Christ Church, and the Tennessee group arrived, all wearing the same patriot hats. I liked them immediately, gave them some brief history of the building from the exterior, we were able to go inside, and I gave a little more information of what was within. Then we went to Wood-lawn and Pope-Leighey House, a couple more locations before I ended the tour at Gadsby's Tavern, and finished my tour with a brief history of the founding fathers who dined there.

Since they had requested to end their tour where food could be found, I entered with them so that I could recommend the best appetizers to eat. As the host told them where to be seated, I said goodbye to them and was about to leave, when I spotted a familiar face from one of the booths.

Looking over, I chuckled at the coincidence.

Darcy was sitting there, with a plate of half-eaten food in front of him.

He waved at me nervously.

"Well," I said, grinning, "How did a guy like you end up in a place like this?"

When seeing that I was in a 'gaming' mood, Darcy's shoulders relaxed.

"I'm like a bad penny," he declared. "I can turn up at the oddest of moments."

"Clearly. How are you doing today?"

"So far, so good." He gestured to his food. "I took a gamble when I chose this meal, but it's pretty good."

"Are you kidding?" I said, walking up to him a bit, "This is Gadsby's; they gotta be perfect, or they won't live up to their name. Back when I was still in the Airforce, I couldn't afford to eat out like I always wanted to, so now I get to appreciate the place."

"Am I going mad?" Darcy asked. "Or are we making small talk?"

"Yeah," I realized, "I guess we are. Am I making you uncomfortable? I probably should go, huh?"

"No," Darcy rushed out, "I'm fine with it." He gestured to the other side of the booth. "Care to join me?"

I looked at the empty seat and threw caution to the winds.

"Oh, what the hell."

I sat down on the other side, facing him.

"I'll treat you to lunch," Darcy said.

"Thanks, but I'm specifically starving myself actually. I'm meeting up with a friend later, and she's making a lot of cool food for me. I can't pronounce it, because I've never been very good at learning Mexican and Spanish food terms. Which is sad because I've gone to quite a few Mexican and Spanish ceremonies. But I can't crack memorizing their entrees. I just know that it tastes good, so I stuff my plate, and let ignorance wash over me."

"Your friend is Spanish?"

"Puerto Rican, actually. Her kids were born in the States. Quite frankly, I don't even know if I have the right to call her a friend. I met her on the plane ride here, and we've only seen each other once since then." I tapped my head, indicating my brain. "That's what happens when you are one of those people who drifts around. You come, you make relationships quickly, but they don't last long."

"That's what you do?"

"Yeah, and I'm not afraid to admit that about myself."

"I get it. I just don't understand it."

"How can't you? You know how you can rotate from one base to another, and then get deployed at any time."

"Well, yeah, but there's a structure to it all. I'm a soldier; I know where my place is. But for you, to go from one place to another, and just pick up on where to go next, is scary to me. I guess that I'm the kind of a guy that likes foundations. I don't know how to drift."

"It's okay. Some of us need stability. Others of us tend to migrate."

"I can't even wrap my brain around it."

"There's nothing wrong with adapting to a new perspective. Different people can live in different ways. You'll learn to get it."

I shifted around in my seat.

"So," I asked, "how are you feeling after when we last saw each other?"

"Oh, so now we're getting to the heart of the matter."

"We both did a good job of dancing around the subject for as long as we could. Conversationally speaking, we did quite well at the waltz."

Darcy laughed gently at my joke. I found myself liking that.

"But now, I think we are ready," I furthered. "How are you doing? And I know that I dropped a lot of bombs on you, but I really did need to do that. Are you mad?"

"No, I'm not. Especially since it's clearly helped us."

"Yeah, I think it has." I groaned. "Why didn't I stand up to you earlier?"

"Honestly," Darcy admitted, "I don't think it would have made a difference, Liz. I was what I was at the time. No lecturing would have helped. If anything, I would have probably just been even harder on you. We were kids; at that time, no one could tell me anything. I didn't learn that whole 'maybe I was wrong about something' until much later."

"When you went into the army," I determined.

Darcy looked at me, surprised, and I thought it was better to explain.

"If you're thinking that I'm really perceptive," I explained, "I'm not. I heard about your time in the army from Bingley."

Darcy closed his eyes, taking another bite of his food.

"Bingley didn't say anything to hurt you," I pointed out, "He talked about how you became friends."

"And that's where he mentioned Marsters?" Darcy asked gently.

"Oh yeah, he told me all about your drill sergeant."

Darcy nodded slowly. In his eyes was much, despite his ability to mask it. As someone who had been trained in the army as well, I had to go through everything that he would have. As a result, I saw what he was remembering.

Bad memories.

A history where he was molded into shape by a bully, and he was the victim.

I leaned forward, thoroughly engaged.

Now he knew… now he could fully understand.

And that explained everything.

"I went through the same training that you went through," I asserted, "so I know what you're remembering. Your drill sergeant was meant to be hard on you, for a reason. To be in the military, you gotta have strong stuff to you, or at least the ability to learn how to be strong. They must harden us, because if they don't, then what kind of soldiers would we make?"

Darcy nodded and ate some more.

"Marsters really was harsh on you, wasn't he?" I asked. "You can't forget it, and so it eats you up?"

Darcy put down his fork and looked out of the window.

"Let me guess," I said, "you kept talking back to him."

"I still hadn't learned."

"I see."

Darcy smiled sadly.

"I still have some of the bruises that he gave me."

I closed my eyes, frustrated.

"A drill sergeant would only go that far if you attacked them. Did you?"

He rubbed his face.

"He just wouldn't leave me alone. He just—"

"Hurt you?" I asked, "I did it for four years. How long did you suffer?"

"You're making me feel guilty again."

"No, I'm looking for a connection. And I found one. You were in a bad place and your drill sergeant didn't stop until he broke your bad side. In other cases, I see why the sergeant's behavior doesn't work, but when we're training, we have to know how to follow orders, and not talk back when we are not doing the right thing. And now, look what happened. You're nicer. Kinder. And more empathetic because you were humbled."

I leaned back in my chair.

"You were bullied," I added, "and you didn't like it. So, at what point did you become me?"

He looked back at me, rubbing his cheek.

"You punched Marsters, didn't you?" I furthered, realizing that I had hit a dark spot. "You punched your drill sergeant. And that's why you got those bruises."

"Yeah, I did."

Leaning back, I laughed.

"Darce, that's on you, man. And you know that it's all on you."

He laughed with me.

"Yeah, it was a little bit on me."

"We soldiers are not politicians, and that's the beauty of it," I added, "we don't have to deal with all that stuff. We obey because we are there to protect. You can think for yourself all that you want, but first, we all got to be a unit."

"I know that now. I've gotten better at keeping my independence, but also understanding the point of being a team. And—" Darcy squinted, leaning forward, and looking at me quizzically.

"What?" I asked him. "Is there a fly on my face?"

"No, it's about what you said."

"I just realized that I gave you a lecture on soldier-etiquette." I chuckled. "Whoops!"

"No, it's not that. I can take a casual lecture. You said 'we soldiers are not politicians. But you haven't been a pilot for years, right? You just talked about it like you still are. You used present tense, and not past tense."

I bit my lip, surprised at my verbal slip. I had done it...again.

"Oh, I said that?" I asked, slight discomfort in my voice.

"Yeah, you did."

"My bad," I excused, "I don't know why I said that. Old habit, I guess."

Darcy's expression changed from introspective to inquisitive.

"Liz, have you ever heard of that thing called 'verbal slip'?"

I ground my teeth, annoyed at his sense of superiority.

"Yeah, I did, you scum bucket; we both went to the same high school."

He grinned, just as some more of his food came.

I closed my eyes, happy that the food arrived. This gave me the chance to change the subject.

"You ordered correctly," I said as Darcy bit into his food, "that's one of the best meals they got here."

"Yeah, this is the third time that I ordered it."

"You're a regular?" I asked, amused.

"I think that I can call myself such." Between bites, his eyes grew more casual, as did his voice. "Is it me, or are we exchanging small talk more comfortably?"

"I think that we are getting better at it," I said. "How am I doing?"

"How am I doing?" he repeated.

"Sorry, that was a premature question. We need more time before we give each other grades on casual conversations."

Darcy's eyes twinkled.

"I like this."

"Well, I don't," I stressed.

"You don't?" he asked, with a raised eyebrow.

"Yeah. You see, I've grown to despise you for so long that I've grown fond of disliking you."

"Seriously?"

"Oh yeah. You see, hate is as addictive an emotion as love. When you love something, it sucks when you no longer have that sensation. And when you hate something, it sucks when the thing you hate changes, and you can't hate it anymore. It is such a spur to one's genius, such an opening for wit, to have a dislike of that kind. One may be continually abusive without saying anything just, but one cannot be always laughing at a man without now and then stumbling on something witty. I know that what I am saying is not logical—"

"But it is, nevertheless, true."

"Precisely." I chuckled. "Now you sound like Spock from 'Amok Time'."

Darcy's eyes brightened.

"You watch 'Star Trek'?"

"Not watch it. I freakin' love it."

"Me too."

"Yeah, our whole family was raised on it. I like the new shows, especially 'Strange New Worlds', but despite popular opinion, I like the original show too."

"So do I. People judge it too harshly."

"It came out in the 60s. It was groundbreaking at the time, and look what it led to? A franchise that has gone on for over half a decade. You like Trek too?"

"Yeah, but I hate the new shows that are out."

"I can understand why they are not your thing, and I'm not going to bully you into liking something that you don't like. When it comes to us fans, it's easy to not like change, and be angry when people mess with the things that we love. It's also easy to not like something when you first see it. Things take a little getting used to. But time always helps, and in a year or two, watch the new stuff again, and maybe you might see something you like about it."

I tapped the table, just as a habit.

"Again, I'm not trying to push you into liking something that you don't like. I'm just saying, give things a chance over time, and see how you get on."

"Yeah," Darcy said, "I'm not against changing my mind every now and again."

"I'm not trying to be judgmental, don't get me wrong. Heck, I used to be the sort who totally believed in first impressions. Sometimes, I treated my first assessment of stuff as rule for how things always are. That bit me in the butt enough times for me to get the message, that maybe I should rethink that philosophy."

"Is that why you miss the idea of hating me?"

"Yeah. You're creating a better second impression. Or third impression. Or fourth impression. Or fifth impression."

Darcy chuckled, between bites.

"I forget what impression we are on now," I admitted, "so I'll leave the number to you."

"You got witty in your older years," he acknowledged.

"I better have. If I didn't, that would be stupid."

Sighing inwardly, I rolled my lips in between my teeth and studied Darcy's face most acutely.

"You really have changed a lot."

"It would be stupid if I didn't." He repeated my words. Clever.

Darcy finished his food and asked for the check.

"After all," Darcy continued, "I wasn't used to being the one who was bullied, I guess. Then I was. I had no choice but to grow."

Somehow, I felt a strong notion to be direct, and introspective. I just wasn't in the mood to beat around the bush—again. What about Darcy brought out the honest savage in me?

"What is it like for you?" I asked him. "To be me."

Darcy grinned casually, and then he sighed.

"It felt like—like I was alone. And that I would be in pain for a very long time. It passed eventually."

"But while you were still in the middle of it, it felt like it would never end."

"Exactly."

I tapped his hand!

I was more astonished at the gesture than he would have been. I neither knew why or what had prompted me to do that. Not thinking at all about it, but rather, it had been an impulse.

There was no thought to it.

Just action.

"You got out," I said, "that's all that we can say. You got out of it. Now you can say that you're not lost anymore."

Looking at me in wonderment, Darcy put down his wallet.

"You felt lost all that time?"

"Yes. But the truth is, I'm still a little lost. Some of us just stay that way, so we get used to it."

"You think I stopped being lost?" he asked, his strong voice innocent.

"You seem stable now."

"I just look it. But underneath…who knows, eh?"

"Whoever does know?"

I checked the time.

"Oh, crap. I gotta go. I'm going to be late."

"Sorry," he rushed out.

"It's fine. This wasn't awkward, so thank you for that."

As I stood up, I put on my coat and began to tie my scarf around my neck.

"Um," Darcy said, "since Richard's leave is over, I was wondering if maybe you might want to hang out sometime."

The surprise must've been clear as day on my face because Darcy immediately rushed his next sentence.

"No pressure or anything. I just—"

"It's fine," I overrode him. "I don't feel like you're pushing your company on me. I'm just surprised that you want to see me again. I just thought that seeing me would be uncomfortable for you."

"Well, if you don't feel uncomfortable around me, then I can get over myself. If you're up for us meeting up every now and again, that would be cool."

"You know that I can't take Richard's place, right?"

Darcy grinned.

"Liz, I don't want you to act like my cousin."

"I know," I replied, lightheartedly. "I'm just saying that, of all the people in the world that you want to hang out with, why in the world would you want to be around me more?"

Darcy rolled his head, looked away, and for a second, I thought that he was not going to give me an answer. Fortunately, he did not keep me waiting for long.

"Some bullies spend their whole lives being loved. Then there are the rest of us. We wizen up and realize that people don't want to put up with us. Let's just say that, over time, you realize that you don't have as many friends as you thought that you did. Or you realize that you don't really have any friends at all."

"Oh," I uttered, willing to not push the matter more. I had a feeling that he didn't want to say much else. "Sorry if I pulled the truth out of you."

"No. I just figured that I'd be honest. That was always a problem of mine, wasn't it?"

"Too damn honest."

"Yeah. Too damn honest."

"Fine."

I gave him my number, kindly told him that he could contact me whenever, and then I was off.

As I exited the tavern, I turned around and stole a glance at Darcy as he tipped the waiter. Taking in his tall and strong frame, I couldn't help but wonder at the man. Between him and Wickham's betrayal, once more, there were too many changes happening to me at once.

But I would weather them—come what may, eh?

I dashed off.

# THIRTEEN
# MOTHER WHO IS NOT YOUR MOTHER

When I arrived at Delores's House, she already had all the food laid out for me to pig out on.

After kissing her on the cheek when I first arrived, she ushered me into the house and let me dive into the food when she saw my mouth water.

"This totally beats ice cream as a 'pick-me-up food'." I said, as she piled food on my plate.

"Good," Delores said, "eat up, because in half an hour, you're coming with me to a bridal salon."

My eyes widened at the news.

"Bridal salon?" I gasped.

"Yeah, one of my nieces, Consuela, is getting married, and I've offered to pay for the gown. But I hate shopping with her because she never knows what she wants. And you're built just like her. I'm going to need you to try on some gowns. It will help me a lot."

I put down my fork.

"Did you trap me into this?" I asked. "For reasons that I can't get on why."

"Actually, I thought that you would love this. Sometimes, after suffering a large disappointment, two things occur. First, you retreat from the world for a bit, and don't want to see another man at all. Then secondly, you turn from isolation completely, and you want to get really social, showing the person who broke your heart that you have the strength to get along with life and aren't thinking of them at all. Did you do the first stage yet, and retreated from the world?"

I know that it must be strange how easily it was to talk about this to Delores, but I actually loved it. She made everything so easy.

"To be honest, I was never given the time. It all happened so fast, and the next day, I had to get on with life."

"Did you listen to any sad music?"

"I listened to Sade."

Delores rolled her eyes, angry.

"Oh, God! Wickham really did hurt you badly. I'll kill him."

"You would do that for me?" I asked, amazed.

"Yes. Well, not kill him, because I am sure that I would get caught. But I'm very good at ruining evil people's lives. It's my skill. I'm sorry, Lizzy. When I introduced you at the birthday, I just thought he would be a casual sort of thing, where you both just kept each other company that night. I had no idea that he would pursue you at all."

"I'm not mad at you. I didn't forget how you told me to stay away from him."

"I suppose you wonder why we know him. He's friends with the men in my family and you know that he can be very charming, so, he always gets invited to things. But we always tell women what he is."

"Don't worry, I'm not the type who thinks you should cut someone out of your family's life because *I* have a problem with him. I'm not that shallow."

As Delores bit into some tostones, she saw that I was not eating my food.

"You don't like it?"

"Of course, I like it," I said, "but I can't eat and then try on gowns. I'd have a food belly, and the dresses wouldn't fit right."

"You'll be fine. Just suck it in whenever you put the gowns on. And stop thinking you're not pretty. I won't put up with that."

"And why did you choose me? There clearly could have been someone else for it."

"For your own good. When you texted me, I had a thought." Delores swallowed her food and poured me something to drink. "Liz, you texted me about what Wickham did. And you've only seen me twice. I deduced that maybe, the reason why, is because you don't have many others to talk to about it. Am I wrong?"

I bit my lip, and bit into a coquito.

"I'm right, aren't I?" Delores furthered.

I nodded.

"You didn't even tell your mother, or Jane?" Delores asked.

"I wasn't ready," I explained, heavily. Lydia knew, but only because she figured it out on her own. "With Jane, eventually, I will. But Mom wouldn't understand."

"By what you told me about your family on the plane, I figured as much. You just didn't seem like the sort who felt safe in confiding in your family. That's why I've been so pushy. It's time to talk about it, and I got the feeling of what happens when you don't have someone. What you went through was awful, but I don't want you falling away from humanity, Lizzy. I get the sense that when you do retreat from life, you retreat hard. And you do it for too long. Well, I'm not your family, and there's nothing for you to be afraid of, because there's nothing to lose by talking to me. So, what did that pile of horse crap do to you?"

The longer that Delores talked, the more my resolve was shaken.

You know, like so many of us, how when we break, we don't want the world to see that we are broken. We don't want people to see us as weak. And then that person comes along who can strip our pretenses from us and bear our souls to them. Those sorts are our kryptonite. Delores was many people's kryptonite. The more she talked, the more that I felt all my defense's layers strip away, and I felt so bare, in the face of shame.

When she finished, I began to weep, and my heartbreak was brought forward again. All the pain that I had been suppressing, that I had been willing to push to the wayside, had resurfaced. I could not tell, in that moment, if that was a good thing or a bad one. But it was happening, no matter what.

"He broke me, De," I cried, "he broke my heart so much."

Instinctively, Delores folded her arms around me, and I buried my face into her shoulder, barely audible.

"I don't get it," I cried. "Why me?"

"It's not you," Delores assured me. "It's him. It will always be him."

She cradled me in her arms, like I was a child again.

And no wonder.

When suffering under the agonies of being heartbroken, we are all children. Aren't we?

———

"So," Delores said as I delved even more into the food that she made. "Wickham hasn't even texted or called you, to apologize?"

"No," I said, after telling her everything, from the beginning of dating Wickham to the end of it. "And I can't help but wonder if I prefer it that way. A part of me wants revenge, but another part of me prefers just to never see him again."

"I get it. But I like the revenge instinct. People can call it irrational all that they want. But truth is, there is nothing wrong at being angry with someone when they have done everything to make you angry with them."

"Thanks, but I've seen what happens whenever I want revenge; it makes me happy for a little while. But then the satisfaction doesn't last long, and sometimes, I fall even harder from it."

"My dear, you're too good for him. And please, promise me that you will never doubt yourself over this. You did nothing wrong. Some people just have no sense of how they are the worst. Wickham is that, in a charming wrapper."

"I should have listened to you."

"You had no way of knowing. All I could do was advise you, but there are some things that you can only learn from by going through it. This is one of those times."

"Lydia said the same thing. I thought it was real. Too much of my life is built on things not being real. And I want real."

"Count your blessings."

"My blessings?" I repeated, flabbergasted. "What's good about this?"

"You found out before it was too late. Before you were knee-deep in this situation. You see, right now, you're at the beginning, where you are not so in love with him yet that you would forgive him for anything. Many a woman and many a man would suffer being the 'other person' in the relationship, because they fell in love with a cheating hussy."

"Don't worry. I won't fall for that."

"That's what we all say, and then bing-bang-boom, we meet someone, they are wonderful and everything we asked for. And then, a few months in, we find out that they are either dating someone else, are engaged, or married. By that point, we are so hooked into the relationship that we forgive that person—we tell ourselves that life is complicated. Love blinds us. That's what happened with me and my second husband."

My eyes widened.

"What?"

"Yeah. When I met my second husband, he was already married. I didn't know when we met, or when we got together. He waited till after we were intimate, to tell me. You would think that I hated him on the spot for being deceptive. I should have, but I didn't. I was so crazy about him that I forgave him and gave him the benefit of the doubt. He was not worth it. And I made a mistake."

She put her hand on mine.

"Do you hate me?"

"No," I acknowledged, "you were in love, and it blinded you, didn't it?"

"Yes. I was wrong, and I have no excuse for letting my emotions override my logic. But it does that, from time to time. As it might have done with you, if you dated Wickham for too long. You would have accepted any excuse he would have made for why he could not hang out with you for a couple of nights.

You would have seen many signs to show you what he was, but you would have looked away. And when he did tell you the truth and said that he just needs a little time to break up with the other woman, you might have been so in love with him, that you would have given him that time. Liz, I am so sorry for what he put you through. But I'm so happy that you found out. Now, you can get over him sooner, the heartbreak is not as bad as it would have been months from now, and you can recover. And he was never good enough for you. And never will be. I'm right; because I've been wrong before, and now I know what wrong is. So, you really ought to believe me, because now I am right about everything."

I ate into her food.

"I got out," I repeated what she said, "I got out."

"Yes, you did. And now, you can stay out. You're free of that trash. Let him stir in his own jerk-juices, while you've got friends, family, and clearly, more of a life than he does."

"Thanks." I closed my eyes. "But there's another problem."

"What's that?"

"What about Mary King? Wickham did a good job lying to her. I mean, it was so obvious that my shouting at him implied that he was cheating on her, with me. And yet, she still believed him."

"And she always will. Like I said before, she's been with him for so long that she's in love with him. And she'll either forgive everything, or willingly overlook anything about him that might be suspicious."

"Love."

"It's blinding. See? You escaped that. And she's right in the thick of it."

"But what comes next? What I mean is, what do I do? Should I tell her?"

"That's the only problem!" She put a piece of pernil on my plate and I bit into it happily. Heartbreak really does create a bottomless pit in your stomach.

"What sort of woman is Mary King?" Delores asked.

"She heard me say that Wickham was a cheating pile of trash, and she still believed him. That doesn't speak much for her common sense, now does it?"

"Like I said, love makes you stupid."

"Yeah, but with her, I felt like she's trying to convince herself that Wickham is not a bad guy. But maybe she's willing to look past that self-deception. Maybe, if I did tell her, she might eventually realize that he's been unfaithful to her."

"I'm not so sure. When a person deceives themselves, they will do everything to avoid the truth. You have no idea how far they will sink to the depths. I've been there."

"So have I, now that I come to think of it," I acknowledged. "To quote the song, everybody plays the fool, huh?"

"There's no exception to the rule," Delores agreed by citing the next lyric. "If I met this Mary King girl, I could make heads or tails of the woman, but that's the problem. If you do tell her, she could eventually realize it and thank you. Or she could always not believe you, and then turn around and hate you. Or come after you, looking for revenge. Usually, it's the other woman who suffers, despite being as much a victim as the first woman."

"That's the problem. Nothing is worse than being torn. I want to tell her, but I know that it could all be for nothing, and it falls on me. After all, ignorance is bliss, but the truth matters a lot. Usually, I always know what to do. So, why am I confused over this?"

"Because it's confusing. See her again and get to know her a little better. If you think she can handle it, without her blaming you, then give it a chance. But then you might get lucky."

"How?"

"Maybe you might never see her again."

I rolled my eyes.

"De, I'm me; I'm never *that* lucky." I looked at myself in the mirror. "And are you sure that you want me to help with this gown-seeking day? I look terrible."

"You look like no such thing. This is good. You need to be around more women now who are fussy and will make a big deal over you. I also get the sense that you're the sort who will have fun playing dress up *after a* dress down."

Our conversation had gone on for half an hour, and I actually did feel better. That was the way that it was with her; she exuded a comfortable presence, or a cloud of security. Either way, I felt safe in it.

Eventually, I found myself being driven to a bridal salon, meeting with Delore's sisters, and trying on wedding gowns. This event, by definition, should have been absurd. Why was I, this little outsider, amidst a horde of family women, being poked, prodded, made to dress and undress, looked after by the salon employees, for a ceremony that I had nothing to do with. All things considered, it should be regarded as outlandish.

And, ironically, I was having a jolly old time.

"It's strange," I whispered to Delores as another assistant brought me another gown to try on, "I should be weeping. Especially since I'm planning for someone else's wedding and being her model."

"But you're not," Delores acknowledged.

"Not even a little bit. In fact, am I laughing?"

"Oh yeah. Like I said, I didn't want you falling away from humanity. Liz, whether you like it or not, you're not the kind to sit around and mope, and do the whole 'wo is me', kind of thing."

"No, I'm not. I was like that once, but now, I think I'm getting to the point where I laugh myself out of things."

"Had a feeling."

Delores looked at the gown that the assistant gave us, nodded her approval, and began to unzip it for me.

"And that's why this was good for you. You need to be pampered right now, and to be made a fuss over. And since I was the one who got you and Wickham together, it's kind of my responsibility to bring you out of any funk."

"You didn't do anything," she said, "we would have dated no matter what you did."

I took the dress, went into the dressing room, and got suited up by the assistants. As I was being put into the gown, and marveling at myself in the mirror, I had more time to think about it all.

I was with friends, who cared about me.

I had family.

I had a life.

And I was not weeping, even though I still felt betrayed.

And wearing wedding gowns. By rights, I should have felt listless and forlorn. But instead of feeling like romantic love had let me down, I was recovering. Quicker than I thought I ever would.

And now, it made me wonder. Why was I getting over it so quickly?

I had my cry out and now I was getting back into the swing of things. It reached the point where I wondered if...did I really like Wickham, or was I simply in love with the *idea* of him? Or rather, was I in love with the memory of him? He was a good man in the past. I like good men, and he displayed all the signs of still being like that. But his past virtues clearly led to a place of pride, and that pride led to him thinking that he was God's gift to women. He was clearly high on himself—or narcissistic. And those are the kind of people that cannot be reasoned with. They will spend their entire lives getting what they want, hurting others in the process, and everyone else is a victim of being run over by them.

And now that past Wickham and present Wickham were two different men, I guess I could now separate the two identities and forget the present one.

I had fallen in love with a dream.

The dream turned into a nightmare.

And now I've woken up from the nightmare, hitting the ground hard, and the fall was immense. It was painful, relentless, and overwhelming, but once the shock faded away, and the moment, hours and days gave way to so many other changes that unveiled themselves, thus I was opened, to becoming fortified. I could reflect, observe, and consider that I would never fully know myself, and that this was just a bridge I would have to keep crossing in my life.

I was getting stronger. And I was proud of myself for it.

I twirled around and looked at myself in the wedding gown.

"So," the assistant asked, "you look lovely."

"Thanks, but it's really the gown that is lovely. I hope they choose this one for the bride."

"What does she look like?"

"I have no idea." The woman gave me a strange look. "I was roped into it. That's the best explanation that I've got. Just roll with it. I've learned to do that, especially with Delores in my life."

"Well, it's no skin off my back," she replied, "so, do you have a special person in your life? Or perhaps I'm being offensive for asking."

"Don't worry. I'm not that kind of woman who feels stupid when she admits that she's single. I was dating a guy, but it turns out that it was not serious, and he didn't really care about me at all."

"Oh! I am so sorry."

"Thanks. But, somehow, despite the romantic forces that be, I'm getting over it. I don't know how, but I am."

"That's good. Don't waste your time on a man who does not love you. That's what my mother always told me."

"I heard that advice too, but in a lyric from the song 'Too Many Fish in the Sea', by the Marvelettes."

"I love that song!"

"So do I?" Then I began to sing. "Too many fish in the sea!"

"Too many fish in the sea!" She sung with me.

"Oh, we're singing now?" Delores's sister said, "we love that song!"

Suddenly, all Delores's family were singing the song, from beginning to end, showing how they do that sort of thing often.

We looked at the assistant, smiled, and began to sing along as well.

"My mother once told me something and every word is true. Don't waste your time on a fella who doesn't' love you!"

We kept singing, as more gowns were brought forth.

While I tried on three more gowns, I was still sold on the one that I had started with. Mind you, even if I voted, it still was up to Delores and her sisters.

Once I took off the last gown, I still marveled at how one's fortune could change so quickly. Life was like a basketball: it bounced up and down so randomly.

My past crush turned out to be a lush.

My past enemy turned out to be friendly.

Darcy!

I know what happened to you, but I still wish that I knew more. Between his own confession, Richard's comments, and Bingley's information, his transformation must be true and complete.

I was now becoming curious about him. Since he was better, and we had reached a comfortable place—much to my surprise, well—what then? What was going to happen now?

I still could not believe that I had such a great time.

When it was over, Delores said that she wanted to quickly show me the church that the wedding would take place in and promised that it would not take long.

Since her incredible habit of being intuitive had helped me a lot, I was willing to be amenable to a visit that was a little longer.

We drove along and there was some construction that was taking place on the side of a road. A new building was being built and the men were clearly ending their work shift and were filing out.

Wickham was in construction!

I swallowed hard and put two and two together. Especially after I realized that Delores was slowing her car down and parking in front of the half-built structure.

"Delores," I uttered.

"Yes?" she replied, proudly, and boldly. I could not believe it! No, she didn't! But she did.

"Are you serious?" I realized.

"Ah," she said, "so you know what I'm about to do, eh? You're really good at being deductive."

"I know that Wickham is in construction, and on our dates, he talked about a new building that he was working on. He's here, isn't he?"

"Oh yeah," one of her sister's said, "since he's one of the coordinators, he is one of the last to always leave the site. He'll be coming out in a couple of minutes."

Delores turned and looked at me. I read the look in her eyes.

"You planned this!" I gasped.

"Yes, I might have definitely done that. I knew that you would not want to see him, or confront him, so I figured that this whole wedding thing was a good way of tricking you into seeing him again."

"De! I refuse to patch things up with him."

"Oh, that's not why I arranged this all. We're going to confront him."

Discomfort and anger was swelling up in me.

"I'm not ready because I know that I'm going to explode. Remember, girls, that he may be larger than me, but I'm a trained soldier. I will kill Wickham."

"Don't worry," Delores said, with a knowing eye, "I didn't say that *you* were going to confront him. I said that *we're* going to confront him."

I looked around at the other women, who had a conspiratorial look to them.

"Don't talk to him," another woman said, "he's not worth it. But we're here."

They were going to gang up on Wickham.

Suddenly, Wickham emerged from the site, talking to Guan as he was leaving, and talking about how he was going to meet up with Mary King later.

"It's showtime," Delores said.

This was awesome!

————

All at once, Delores and all the women jumped out of the cars and approached Wickham viciously. When seeing them, he was initially smiling, but when seeing them angry, his smile faded.

"Hey!" Delores called. "If it isn't the cheating tramp!"

"Delores!" Guan said. "What are you doing?"

Not one to be on the sidelines for too long, I also emerged

from the crowd and got closer to the scene. Usually, I did not want to be the kind of person who didn't fight her own battles. But this was a group of angry women who were large, intimidating, and maternal. It's moments like this that make you enjoy that this is what life is all about. Retribution with a slice of womanly fire.

"We're throwing out the trash," Delores cried. "He cheated on Lizzy!"

Guan looked at Wickham.

"What? Wick, you did what?"

"It's complicated," Wickham rushed out. "It's just a misunderstanding. We can clearly—"

He froze when he saw my face, in the background.

He had Guan, who clearly was not going to support him, now that Delores had enlightened her boyfriend about his 'friend'.

I had an entourage of overpowering ladies.

I had the stronger army. That swelled my confidence, and when seeing him, any past affection was now fleeting. His beautiful face left me cold. His charming voice was hollow and weak. I was now really getting past him in every way. And that indifference, that refusal to care for him, to exercise compassion, was gone. He had no ally with me, and his charm could not save him. As such, expression gave nothing away but coldness and a slice of ruthlessness that I refused to apologize for.

"Hello, George," I said, my voice like ice and my eyes firm and steely.

"Lizzy," he said, his voice shaking and bereft of any confidence that he had cultivated.

I had nothing else to say, but one thing. Without even looking at Delores and her sisters, and other family members, I spoke simply and casually.

"Just don't break any bones."

Delores and the other women ganged up on Wickham and started screaming at him, in Spanish! I wish that I had focused more on my Spanish classes in high school, because I wished that I could understand what they were saying. But it didn't matter because we got their meaning quite well. In fact, their cries perhaps were better than they were in a language that had more punch to its tones.

I just stood back and watched, flattered beyond means. If you wish for me to apologize about my mean thoughts, I shall never do that. Retribution and reckonings are good things to exert, every now and then.

Wickham was outnumbered and outvoiced. In fact, with all these women screaming at him, and beating at him, all he could do was back up and be horrified.

It was glorious.

They scared him so much that they pursued him towards a six-foot deed hole in the ground that had been dug up, to create foundations.

Without seeing where he was walking backwards, he fell into the hole, butt first.

Crying out, Wickham rolled over, groaning out in pain, holding his backside.

I moved to the front of the crowd and looked down at him.

When seeing me, he stopped moaning out, and just looked at me as he held the parts of his body that were bruised and hurt.

Our eyes locked.

In his was the shock of knowing that he could not rise out of this embarrassment.

"This is where we say goodbye," I said simply. "If you see me walking down the street, walk on the other side. You will never enter my life again, and never walk back into it. And if you do, I will destroy your life, because I do believe in that thing called revenge. Don't speak because I can't stand the sound of your voice. Just nod. Do you agree with my terms?"

Wickham nodded.

Smiling sardonically, I walked away, with the women behind me. Walking up to Guan, I tapped his arm.

"Make him stay down there for two hours, and then help him out," I ordered.

"Do as she says," Delores added, supporting me.

There were too many women for Guan to be anything else but helpless and compliant.

"Okay," was all that he could muster up.

"Ladies!" Delores declared, "we go!"

Like a flock of birds, we all left the construction site.

Thanking the ladies, I approached Delores and kissed her cheek.

"If it weren't for you and your excellent scheming," I said, "I never would have faced him again."

"I felt like you needed that, and that you needed backup."

"I did. You know what?"

"What?"

"You must be one heck of a mother."

"Oh, we're the type who are made for it."

And that was the day that I fully walked out of Wickham's life, and he would not walk into mine. The door was closed on that chapter of my life, and it was final. Now, I could turn down another path.

# FOURTEEN
## MOVING ON

"That really happened?" Charlotte said over the phone.

I was on the bus, headed back home, and on the ride there, I had called Charlotte Lucas and told her everything that had happened.

"Yeah, it did," I replied, "it was brilliant."

"You sound happy."

"I am. In ways that you can't imagine. At first, I was content with just forgetting about Wickham, and just letting it all fade away gently. But you know what? I really think that I needed that."

"Revenge is something that is hard for us all to know how to do correctly. You got lucky, Liz. Delores and her family knew exactly how to do it."

"I know, right? I didn't even have to try. It's nice when people care and do the job for you."

I leaned back against the bus seat and sighed

"It's over. I can fully move on. Now and completely. And I have other things to wonder about."

"Like your mom and my dad? And your dad and your mom's cousin?"

"I'm pushing that to the back of my mind right now. It's about something else. It's about Darcy."

"What about him?"

"Char, I think I did something strange."

"What?"

"I gave him my number."

There was a pause on the phone.

"You didn't?"

"Yeah, I did. I wonder what that was about."

"So, you like him now?"

I almost choked on my own spit.

"What? No. No, no, no, no, no." I paused. "And no."

Charlotte took a beat.

"So, I am guessing that's a no," Charlotte said at last.

"Gee, you think?"

"But you gave him your number for non-liking reasons."

"Shut up."

I heard Charlotte laughing on the phone.

"Call it a 'turning over a new leaf' moment. The fact is Darcy is here, his cousin is dating my sister, and it's pretty official. And I think that he's lonely. Maybe, it's better just to get around to being friends. And this might help."

"You're past being angry with him."

"I stood up to him. I can't believe that I found that remarkable thing called closure. That *like* never happens in real life."

"Usually, people only obtain closure in movies and books."

"Precisely. But as for us real-lifers, all we can do is walk away and make up a moment of closure in our heads. Then again, a made-up moment of obtaining catharsis will always be better than any apology that a real person can provide. The made-up apology that my evil college roommate gave me, in my imagination, really helped me move on from how she ruined my sophomore year."

"I hear ya. The made-up apology that I thought up my first two ex-boyfriends gave me for breaking my heart also helped me not have an emotional breakdown."

We both paused as we thought over what we just said.

"Are we normal?" I asked.

"No. Being normal is overrated."

"True. After all, what is normal anyway?"

"We're getting too philosophical for my brain to process while I'm making my kids some lunch. So, Darcy has your number."

"Yeah. Now here's where I get stereotypical."

"And how?"

"Well, if I gave Darcy my number, and I want him to be friends with the family, then should I call him first, to make the first gesture? Or should I wait for him to call me to see if he wants to socialize? Or was it one of those, 'I gave him my number, but it's more of a formality, and we don't expect to call each other', and I don't have to worry about that? I'm just afraid of trying too little or trying too hard. Do I have the right not to care? Or should I care? Am I overthinking this?"

"Whoa, you are going full on stereotypical here."

"I know!" I exclaimed, exasperated. Apparently, I did it so loudly that I disturbed the passengers near me on the bus. I whispered the word 'sorry' to them.

———

When I arrived at Longbourn, I went into the house to a scene that had every reason not to be surprised by: mom and dad shouting at each other.

"I hope that you die alone and that your kidneys fail on you!" Mom said, storming out of the room.

"Good luck with that, Ari," Dad jabbed back. "You gave me one of your kidneys, remember? Watch it be the organ that leads to me outliving you!"

He turned to me just as I closed the front door.

"Hey, Liz!" Dad said pleasantly.

"Hey," I sing-songed. "By any chance, was that because you both talked about each other's love lives."

"We thought it was better just to get it out of the way."

I nodded, walking out of the room. Then I jerked backwards, turning back to him.

"How long have you and Mom been talking? What I mean is, how long has it been since you saw each other again, and you began an argument?"

Dad looked upward, trying to remember the exact time that he and mom met, and their argument began.

"By chance," I continued, "that it's been an hour between you both meeting again and the fight began?"

Out of nowhere, Lydia entered—almost magically. Actually, she probably came from the kitchen, because she had a popsicle in her hand. But it felt magical.

"Maybe an hour," she clarified. "Possibly an hour. Oh, that's right! *Definitely an* hour."

Sighing, I turned to Dad.

"You proved Lydia right!" I gasped. "Dad, come on. She literally told you precisely what you were going to do. And you did it?"

Dad rolled his eyes, and Lydia's eyes glowed.

"On that note," she proclaimed, "time to head back to my dorm."

She left the room, as magical as she came.

She probably just went upstairs to get her luggage, but you know what I mean.

# FIFTEEN

# MAKING THE FIRST MOVE...OR THE SECOND?

The next day, I had another tour, and luckily, it went well again. That group was from Japan, and it was nice to see that they were returning to Virginia, considering their fears of traveling to America after the COVID pandemic.

After another fortunate day at the 'office-that's-not-an-office', I went back to Meryton Manor Tours, to get briefed on how the Christmas events would proceed in Alexandria.

Mr. King was there—and I confess that it was a little awkward seeing him, while knowing that his niece was dating a guy who was the worst.

And that was when it hit me!

Mary King naturally would not believe me. Even when it was obvious that Wickham was not all that he seemed, she was so crazy about him that she was suffering from full-on self-deception. But would she listen to her family?

"You really don't like getting things electronically, do you?" Mr. King asked me as he handed me all the information on the Christmas schedule.

"Sorry, I know that I must be a pain," I said, taking the documents, "but you know that there's always one of us who prefers all the clang and clutter of hardcopy piling up in our rooms rather than read stuff on a computer screen. It's not that I'm against progress, because I am. It's just always easier for me to stick with holding things in my hand."

"Still got a flip phone?" He smirked.

"Still got one," I responded, flipping through the first page, and then looking up in surprise.

"Oh! I forgot about the Mount Vernon Salutes Veterans Day."

"Yeah, it's in two days." He removed his glasses to clean them, and he remembered the connection. "Oh, that's right. It should be free for you, right? Since you're retired from the Airforce."

"Yeah, it would be." Considering, as we humans are oft to do, how long it's been since I had seen an old site, I wondered if it would be as I had remembered it. "I haven't been to Mount Vernon in years."

"Well, it's now the perfect time to go back."

"I probably should. You know how easy it is to get in a rut? What I mean is that you work, go home, prepare for the next day, and that's all that there is to your life. And then you kind of start living your life through other people's stories and their adventures."

"Story of my life." He responded.

"Well, it's an ongoing saga of mine too. And when I moved here, I've been so much wrapped in getting settled that I missed out on everything in October. I missed out on the Art Festival, the Halloween Howl, and the Del Ray Halloween Parade."

"Oh, you totally missed out! The Halloween Parade was a big hit this year."

"I was preoccupied with some of the wrong things," I said, rolling my eyes as I thought of Wickham, "but now I really want to get in the thick of things. I think that I will go to Mount Vernon."

"Also, it will get you back into the mix of relearning the history of the place."

I looked at the itinerary and smiled.

"Meryton Manor is going to help out with the Christmas Market and Holiday Craft Show?"

"Yeah. They need some supervisors on site to help the crafters and businesses set up their booths."

"Well, count me in," I replied merrily, "if you need more people at it."

"Good. Because we need more people."

"When do we start assisting with the Scottish Walk parade?"

"Next Thursday. Still up for that too?"

"You bet," I said. "I like parades. Again, that's the old-fashioned side of me. Even though we are still living in the better times."

"We all love the past, even though it was harder. By the way, Mary has been asking after you."

Uh oh.

When hearing him referencing Mary King, I was frightened.

For about two seconds. After all, surprise was only natural. Although, the speed of the human mind is as quick as the speed of sound. We can jump from alarm, to wonder, to acceptance, and then to inspiration in the rise and fall of a couple seconds. Light, sound, and emotion; all things whose speed works in tandem.

Rather than dwell in fright, quickly I adapted and realized that this was precisely what I wanted. And I didn't even have to bring it up, because Mr. King brought it up for me.

"Has she?" I asked, nonchalantly, as I put all the information in a folder, and placed it in my bag. "I gotta admit that I'm surprised by that. From what I remember about our meeting, I thought she wasn't crazy about me."

"She actually felt bad about how she talked to you. She realized that she didn't make the best impression. She told me that she didn't know why."

In amazement, I looked up at him.

"She wants to apologize?"

"Yeah, she does."

Will wonders never cease?

"Tell her that I don't hate her. I'm guessing that's what she worries about, isn't it? Sorry if I'm getting her character wrong, but is Mary that kind of person who doesn't like it when she's scared that people don't like her?"

"Well, aren't we all that way? A little."

"True. We are, but at some point, it's okay if someone doesn't like you, because sometimes, it's okay to only care about those people who are worth caring about. If someone is not worth caring about, then you don't have to bend over backwards to make them like you. Sometimes, having an enemy, an enemy who is the worst, can show that you are willing to take a stand."

"You sound like Alexander Hamilton now."

I chuckled.

"Despite his flaws, I'm fine with the connection. Then again, back then, they were politicians building a nation during terrible times. No one was perfect. Especially if you cared about things. Sorry, I'm going off on tangents. We were talking about Mary. Tell her that I appreciate that she wanted to make a good impression, and that I'm not against her at all."

"Thanks. She'll want to hear that."

Buttoning up my bag, I felt the heaviness of having to confess something disconcerting.

"That's good because I've got to tell you something. And I'll leave it to you to tell her if you want. But Mary King will probably fully hate me after this."

Mr. King stopped giving me casual side glances, and now was heavily enthralled by what I had to say. After all, our conversations had always been surface-level, until now. While we were talking, he had been arranging papers on his desk, and that stopped him.

"Why?" he asked, shutting a drawer in his desk, and sitting down. "Did you do something?"

"Consciously, no."

At last, I faced him, and I refused to sound shaky.

"Mr. King, what I am about to tell you, please believe me that I don't want to shake up the pot. I don't want to cause problems, and I don't want you to tell anyone else this. Except if you want to tell Mary, you can. But I know that she might believe you if this comes from you. If I told her myself, either of three things would happen. First, she would not believe me. Second, she would take her anger out on me. Or third, it would ruin so much, especially since the Christmas play is right around the corner. It's about the guy she's dating. George Wickham."

Mr. King leaned back in his chair.

"What did he do?"

I sighed inwardly, happy that he was directing his attention toward the mistake being in Wickham's direction. I should not have been surprised, because, despite the history of the world being sexist towards us women, when it comes to romance, men usually never side with other men anymore. They are too aware of each other's behavior.

"I met Wickham a few weeks ago. We were friends when I grew up in Oklahoma. Soon after seeing him again, we started dating. And I was crazy about him. Then I found out that he was dating Mary King."

Mr. King's eyes were like ice, and I felt a subtle venom radiating from him.

"Please," I urged, "I'm not lying. I'm not here to be a drama queen. I found this out the hard way."

"That's why you were shocked when you saw Mary?" he asked.

"Yeah. I first saw her when she was with Wickham, and didn't know who she was at the time, until you introduced us. This is all a mess. I accused him of cheating, right in front of her, and if you speak to her, she can verify that. But she clearly likes him enough to have let him make some stupid excuse. It's not her fault. I get why she would not believe me, and still clings to him. But the fact is that he was not cheating on me, because nothing about us was real. What really happened was that he had been cheating on her, with me. I promise that I am telling the truth."

Mr. King leaned back in his seat and looked at the wall.

"I'm not saying that you have to tell Mary," I continued, "but I told you this so that you can decide what you want to do. And if you do believe me, then it would be better if it came from a family member."

"Well," he stated, his tone deep but a little hollow. "This is terrible. This whole situation is *terrible*."

"Yes," I answered, slowly, "it is."

He rubbed his lips, nervously.

"I want to believe that there is a mistake, and that you are wrong. But I get the feeling that you are not a liar. And you seem like you are always teetering on wanting roots somewhere. You are not the type who is looking for problems."

"Thank you," I responded, "and believe me, I went back and forth about this. I didn't know what to do, and so this is the best that I could come up with."

"Yeah, this must have been hard for you. And Mary is in love with him. A lot. To the point where I could see how she would not believe you, and even blame you. And I've met Wickham. In the few times that I talked to him, he has seemed great to her. But sometimes, a person can be a little too great. When it comes to love, we all get lied to a little."

"Wickham lies a lot. Believe me, *he lies a lot*."

"That's the difficulty. I have a feeling that you are right, but Mary would want proof."

Sighing, I removed my cell phone.

"Thank god for these." I smiled. "These are all the proof that a modern-day romantic needs."

Opening my phone, I brought up all the texts that transpired between Wickham and me, and then showed it to Mr. King. As he scrolled through our conversations, I saw his cold expression change to rage.

"He cheated on her," he uttered quietly as he finished. "I should kill him."

"Steps were already taken to ruin him just enough," I said, thinking of Delores. "All Mary has to do is being told the truth, accepting it as true, and if she wants to leave him, that's her call."

"I'll convince her. He's not worth a damn, is he?"

"He was a better man once. But now, no he's not."

"I'll make sure that Mary believes this. Thank you, Liz."

"Happy to help."

"And sorry that you had to go through this."

"So am I. But sadly, I think I needed this."

He looked at me strangely, and I realized that I had to explain.

"If I didn't learn this now, think of how much longer I would have been seeing him?" I explained. "He has ruined Mary's life, but if I had dated him longer, he would have ruined mine, and I might have been resigned to accept his cheating side, like we humans sometimes are dumb for doing—I'm human too. Sometimes we accept the unacceptable and become just as guilty. I got out in time. With Mary, it might be harder."

"True. I never would have looked at it that way. You're wise."

"A side-effect to making every mistake in the book." I grinned. "Now I admit to being a little stupid; it's helped me become self-aware and see things clearer."

———

That evening, I went to rehearsal for the Christmas play, and luckily Mary King was not there. That boded well because that was one bit of awkwardness that I didn't have to face.

Jane, Josie, Killian, and I went home to find our parents doing their best to be peaceful.

It was awkward to say the least.

But since Mary was there, in the throes of a pregnancy that unrooted her life, their disagreements were not what she needed. And they knew it.

"By the way, for Christmas," Mom said over dinner, "I thought it would be a good idea to invite your uncle and Aunt Miriam here. It would be fun since I have all my daughters near home at the same time. And with Bingley coming back, this is the perfect time."

"You're asking Edward to come travel all the way from Arizona?" Dad asked.

"Yes," she said, through slitted eyes, "after all, he is *my* brother."

Dad was about to argue, but I gave him an imploring look.

"Right. Well, if he wants to come, then I'll just sit here, not having any opinion."

"Sounds like the last few years of our marriage."

"It's how I survived," he responded.

"I'm pregnant and don't need this right now," Mary spoke. "Please, like each other for a little while."

Jane looked at Mom.

I looked at Dad.

Josie and Killian looked at their grandparents.

"She is right, you know?" Killian uttered.

I laughed.

———

"It is a good thing for Uncle Edward and Aunt Mir to come this Christmas," I said to Dad as he lay in bed. I came to speak to him as he was reading his usual bedtime material: the 'Jack Ryan' novel series. When I had entered, he removed his glasses, let his book rest on his side, and I attacked the subject immediately.

"Yes, it probably is," Dad acknowledged. "It's just that if it were me, I would not be crazy about my traveling to another side of the country, just for the holidays."

"That's because you are in two different states, 'librarian without a library'," I teased. "When you weren't deployed, you were always in your man-cave, reading. The idea of going too far for family events never was your thing. But you and Uncle Ed are two entirely different kinds of men. I think he would love to see us. Especially since Mary needs more family right now, Bingley's coming back, and I'm home again. Maybe they would like to see us."

"Yes," he admitted, "they probably would."

"Then what was that about?" I asked. "Why did you get angry with Mom about it?" When he didn't respond, I pinched his wrist. "Come now, old friend, you wanted to make mom angry on purpose. Be honest about it."

He chuckled.

"I guess that maybe I did want her to get a little riled up. I think that I enjoyed knowing that I have the power to still do that."

"That's wicked, but I can see why you would get your kicks that way; you like seeing her temper flair up, don't you?"

"I like knowing that she still cares about what I do."

"But it goes both ways, you know. You being angry still shows that you still care about what she does."

He nodded and pointed at me.

"That was the only drawback to my plan."

Squinting at him, I rolled my head, wondering about the ways and means of divorced people.

"Do you still love Mom?" I couldn't help but ask, because I couldn't stand not knowing—and I so much wanted to know.

"That's a hard question to answer."

"Oh, old friend! You can do better than that. I believe in you."

"Very few divorced people stop loving their exes completely," he confessed, his eyes growing misty, as he looked ahead. Naturally there would be a little bit of defensiveness to his tone because he was fortifying himself from reality. My dad was a strong man… a tough one. A soldier who learned how to swallow his emotions and keep them swallowed. As a result, whenever he would acknowledge his feelings, and his disappointments, I was quick to listen. Because I knew that it was fleeting.

"And with your mother and me," Dad continued, "we were intense when we got married. That was a violent and awesome kind of love. It was real. That kind of love doesn't die. It just… very few marriages fully work out like you plan when you walk down the aisle with each other and exchange vows. The love eventually grows stale, and it settles down to a calm indifference. But the love is still there."

"With you and Mom, the love went from hot to cold," I summarized.

"Precisely."

"You don't think that Jane and Bingley will go through that? I don't believe that they would."

"Jane and Bingley are different than your mom and me. When they met, their love was more moderate. But with your mom and me, it was a red-hot kind of thing. We had no choice but to burn out."

"And Kitty and Richard? What do you think will happen to them?"

Dad looked away from me and focused on an invisible horizon.

"I want to believe that they are different as well. They fit right now. I hope that they always will fit."

"So do I."

Out of nowhere, my dad tapped my hand.

"And what about my little Lizzy?" he asked.

I smiled.

"Still up for calling me little Lizzy, eh?"

"Always."

"But what is going on with me," I repeated the phrase, just in a different way. "Well, Dad, you are equally going to be happy and disappointed. I've noticed that it's hard for dads when their daughters date. But it's also hard when they notice that men do not find their daughters attractive."

"Yeah, we are ironic in that way. Curse the person who thinks their daughter is not worth looking at, but also how dare anyone think they are worthy of dating our daughter."

"Yeah, that must be hard," I acknowledged, "being a father to girls."

"It's to the point where I cannot imagine being a father to boys."

Looking at him sideways, I became curious.

"Did you ever want a son?" I asked, surprised that I had never considered that query before.

Dad rolled his head and looked up at the ceiling.

"At some point, you accept that it's never going to happen," he answered. "And yet, you are okay with it. But at some point, yes, I did want one. Mind you, I was never disappointed. I just wanted someone to carry on my name when I am gone. And by the looks of it, if Kitty and this Richard guy get hitched, she's probably going to take his last name."

"Thus leading to Mary being the opposite. She's your big chance."

"Yes, she is. I wish that it didn't have to be that way, but thanks for a silver lining." His eyes grew misty as he looked back at me. "I never was angry that none of you were boys, you know."

I shook my head, swiping the air with my hand, dismissively.

"I'm not offended, Dad," I said, "I know how you really feel about things. Even when you gloss over it with a witty comment."

I kissed his cheek.

"I still don't have a handle on this thing called 'Romantic Love', as it is," I continued, "who knows? Maybe it's better this way."

"Depends. Are you happy?"

"Who is ever fully happy?"

He raised an eyebrow, refusing to allow me to be elliptical, even when that is one of my chief talents.

"Yes," I continued, "I am happy. I think that this is the happiest that I've been since I went on my first flight. Though, nothing can fully eclipse flying over the Superbowl football game."

Dad laughed.

"No, I don't suppose anything could."

"And you really do like dating cousin Anna?" I asked him. "Are you sure that you're not dating her to spite Mom? Be honest with me."

He sighed as he leaned back in his bed.

"Well, I suppose that I was being a little vindictive," he admitted, "such is the way it is with 'Case of the Ex'; we always feel like we have to compete. I might have gotten too emotional."

"Welcome to the human race," I finalize, chuckling.

After taking a shower, and brushing my teeth, I still wondered about the ever-surprising question that was running through my mind: what to do about Darcy?

As I looked at my reflection in the mirror—as many of us are wont to do when we are flossing… on the occasion where we do have the energy to floss—I didn't understand why my mind still wandered over to him.

We were reconciling. That was definite.

But did that mean that I ought to go out of my way to include him in our lives? Or was it strange for me to even wonder if he wanted to? If he was just being polite to mend bridges, then perhaps that was as far as he wanted to take things. But if he did want to be in our lives, and I never took any action to help that, then what was I doing by being idle about it? To act, or not to act, that was the question?

I spit out the toothpaste, washed my mouth and looked at myself in the mirror.

"So many questions," I uttered to my reflection, "Lizzy, what are you doing?"

And just as soon as I asked the question to the face that was trapped in the mirror, I came up with the solution. Picking up my phone, I began to text Kitty:

> Hey Kitty, you better not be dead. Are you awake?

At that time, Kitty would be in her bunkbed, since dinner was well over at the Base. Since nighttime was the only time that she could be in contact with anyone in the outside world, she always had her phone on her. So, I knew that I didn't have to wait for long.

> Yeah, I'm awake. What's up?

Going back to my DVD bookshelf, I pulled out 'First Wives Club', and began to text Kitty back:

> Can you text me Richard's cell #? I need to ask him for some advice about Darcy, and it needs to be tonight.

Kitty's reply back was swift:

> I'll make it easy on you. Wait three minutes.

155

The text answered my question without answering it, which was good enough for me.

As I put the disk into the DVD player and skipped past the commercials, my phone rang. Opening it, I raised it to my ear.

"Hey Richard," I began.

"Hey Liz," Richard said on the other line. "Kitty told me that I should call you, because you wanted to ask me something."

"Yeah. Sorry to bother you. Did I interrupt you hanging out with your friends?"

"Not at all. We just finished playing cards and talking about our first times."

"First times that you went on a mission?" I said, which was common when you were at the base. Usually, you always had a way of retelling whenever you went on your first assignment.

"No," Richard said, chuckling, "the 'other' first time."

"Oh," I replied, amused, knowing what he meant. "I'm a big girl, Rich. Even we women talked about our first time whenever we were in our bunks."

"True. You know me."

"The gentleman."

"Yup, the gentleman. So, what's up?"

"It's about Darcy."

"Ah! Please tell me that he didn't do something stupid."

"He didn't. But I might."

"What are you about to do?"

"I just—Rich, I don't know how to handle this. I spoke to him a couple times, and it seems like he's doing everything in his power to mend things between us."

"He is, and I'm happy that you are open to the idea of noticing."

I swiped the air.

"Don't worry, I'm not so stubborn as to not see what's right in front of me." I lowered the volume on the tv so that I could hear Richard better. "But that's the thing. Where do I go from here? Should I start inviting him over for things, or was he just being polite. Sometimes people are just making gestures, and they don't want to do anything more than surface level. It's more like they are just friendly in passing. But I don't know much about Darcy, so he could always want me to want him to come to some things. And I don't want him to be uncomfortable. And I don't want to make him uncomfortable either. But I don't want either of us to feel obligated to hang out, when neither of us want to hang out with each other. But the fact is that you are his cousin, and he is going to be in our lives. What is Darcy like? Is he casual about things and likes to keep things light and breezy. Or is he the sincere type, where if he asks to hang out, then he expects me to be real about it. Does he want me to make the first step to us being more friendly, or does he not care at all." I pause, and then came to a revelation. "Or am I talking too much?"

"You think?"

I covered my eyes, a little red in the face as Richard laughed on the other side of the phone.

"On a scale of 1 to 10, how manic did I sound?" I asked, unafraid of hearing the truth and being exposed to my own uncertain paranoia.

"12," he answered. "Calm down, young whipper snapper."

"Calming to the point of bland," I responded, "but don't think that you have the right to order me around. Got it?"

"Aye, aye, captain."

"I'm just—well, I feel a little turned around, that's all. With you, it's different. With Bingley, it's different. You're the type of person that a girl knows where she stands, and what he wants. Darcy—he's a different kind of person."

"He's difficult to read."

"And what's sincere about him. When he was vicious to me, I still knew where I stood with him. And now…"

"The roles have changed," Richard finished my sentence. "He's not what you are used to envisioning him as, and that scares the hell out of you, doesn't it?"

A sudden cold overtook me, and I suspected that I knew what the source of it was. It was the way that a person usually feels when you must change your mind about something.

"Yes, it does," I acknowledged, "there was a time where I was so certain about things, and now it's all gone topsy turvy."

"Topsy turvy? I haven't heard anyone use that phrase in years."

"I'm trying to bring it back in fashion. What I mean is that I was thinking about going to Mount Vernon for the Veteran's Day celebration. And being in the army, I thought he would appreciate that."

"You want to invite him to it?"

"Yeah, but is that too much? I don't want to give him the opinion that I'm forcing a friendship on him. And I don't want to invite him to something that he doesn't want to do."

"Do you want to be friends with Darce?"

I chewed the inside of my cheek as I wondered if I did. Or if I didn't. And I was just putting myself through something that was not worth Darcy's, or my, time and energy.

"I don't know," I said. "And that's the problem. I'm not sure what I want, but I do want to know where I stand with him. And that I'm not going to act like he's not there when he is back in our circle. But I don't know how to proceed. And if he wants to be friends with the family, then I don't want him to always be the one to make the first steps all the time. I realize that it's got to be a two-way street with this kind of stuff. Perhaps I should try. So, I thought I would ask you if it's a good idea to start inviting him to things? Or would I make him uncomfortable to start doing that? And I am talking too much again, right? And I'm overthinking this."

"Actually, your tone does make sense. It's not easy to know how to proceed with things, when your relationship with Darcy is so weird, and has a lot of history to it."

"Darcy and I don't have a relationship."

"Relationship has many meanings to it."

"True. Relationship is a plural term and not singular."

"Exactly. And no, you're not overthinking it. This is a confusing situation, and it shows that you care."

I breathed out, relieved that he understood.

"I'm happy that you get it. Any chance that you have any advice for me. Mind you, at the end of the day, I'm going to follow my instincts."

"Naturally," he said, in a mock-serious tone.

"Naturally," I echoed, using my 'man' voice.

"Fortunately, I do have some advice."

Leaning forward, my attitude shifted as I heard that he had a lighthearted solution to this all.

"Go on," I said, "I'm in suspense."

Richard made a contemplative sound, humming through his lips, and then he came to a decision.

"I'm not going to tell you the advice. I think it would be more fun to show it to you."

I cocked my head to the side, a little frightened if he had a plan up his sleeve.

"What are you about to do?" I asked. "I get the sense that I might not like it."

"You asked me for advice, and now you have to pay the piper. I'll call or text you back in half an hour, to let you know if I was successful. Talk to you later."

He hung up.

Placing the phone on the desk, I raised the volume back up on the tv, and then pressed play.

The movie began and I watched it, but with my mind a little preoccupied. Naturally I was a little scared about what Richard was planning, but I was also determined not to get too nervous.

Right around the time that the three leading ladies in the movie were climbing out of the window and hilariocity was about to ensue, I got a text.

Eager to see what Richard had to tell me, I opened the phone, and practically dropped it on the floor when I saw who the text's sender was:

> Hey. It's Darcy. Rich said that I should call you, and that you would pick up.

Darcy!

Over and around me, the air felt like it was closing in, as if everything froze, and time was standing still.

We all know how you have those moments where it feels as if

the whole world falls away, because you fear the reaction to a small thing. A simple thing. And yet, we are still scared of it.

Every second must have felt interminable, and I was surprised when Manhattan jumped on the bed. Then I came down from reality, and the trivial became just that: the trivial. I was getting unnerved by something that was not that serious. But when you live a simple life, does not the mundane turn into a marvel?

I had to respond. So, respond, I did just that:

> Yes, I wanted to invite you to something. Would it be easier if I called you?

After the text was sent, a couple of minutes went by, and each second led to me making so many assumptions. This was a mistake, wasn't it? His silence said that much. Or he felt cornered, perhaps. Oh, what was I getting so nervous about?

Then the phone rang.

And I knew who it was.

Opening my phone, I accepted the call and raised it to my ear.

"Darce?" I asked.

"Hey," he said, on the other end, "since we might be planning something, it's probably easier to talk about it. I like text messaging, but sometimes when a conversation takes a lot of replies, that much typing can be annoying."

"My thoughts exactly, despite that I am quite a serial texter."

"That was funny."

"Thank you. In a couple days, I was planning on going somewhere and I thought that you might be interested. It's late notice, but I figured that since we are trying to get along better, maybe I should try and make more of an effort. Or am I being annoying?"

"Depends on where you're inviting me. Either way, it does not matter, because Richard told me that I should say yes, no matter what."

I raised an eyebrow, amused a whole lot.

"He did?"

"Yeah, he did."

I had to chuckle.

"That is just like him."

"Yes, it is."

"Well, Rich has got nerve, I give him that. And maybe he made it easier on us both, because I think we are flying blind here."

"Yeah, I do believe that we are."

I thought it would be best to throw caution to the winds and just be honest, like him and I always had a way of being.

"Maybe it's better that way," I said, "for us both to admit that we are flying blind. Being honest makes it easier."

"Yes, I think it does. So, where are you inviting me?"

"Well, in a couple days, there's going to be the Veteran's Day at Mount Vernon, and I kind of want to go. Usually, I'm very good at going places on my own—make no mistake, I am not afraid of doing things alone."

"So have I," he said, shortly. His tone was not very inviting, but I deduced that he didn't mean anything by it. More and more, I was beginning to realize that *that* was just his way.

"Well, I was wondering, if you're not doing anything, then would you want to go with me?" Naturally, I did not want him to feel pressured. "Of course, if it's not your thing, and you really don't want to do it, then I won't take it personally. I just thought that you might like the idea."

"You do remember that no matter what, Rich told me that I had to accept, right?" he asked, his tone lighter.

"I like that he pressured you, but I am letting you off the hook. If there is one thing that I prize, is not making people do things that they don't want to do, socially."

"Actually," he countered, "I am not against the idea. First, I am available. And second, I've never been to George Washington's house."

"You haven't? Well, solitary soldier, this might be good for you."

"Well, then why not?"

"So, that's a yes. I think it will be interesting. And veterans have a way of being very good at talking and holding conversation, so even when we run out of things to say, they might help make up for it."

"Works for me."

"Brilliant. Do you want to drive, or should we hire a ride? If you drive, I'll cover half the bill for gas."

"Much obliged. I prefer to drive. I like having things in my control. Fine, it's a date."

"Right," I agreed happily, "and—" I halted when I realized the last thing that he said. "Wait, this is not a date."

"Of course not."

I was not entirely sure that he understood that I was serious.

"Darce, this is not a date."

"I know," he stressed. "It was just a term that I threw out there."

"Oh, sorry. I just read too deeply into something…again."

"You've really gotta give us a better chance of being casual."

"Mind your manners, soldier," I declared, lighthearted. "It's too early in our relationship for you to be thinking you to judge."

"Oh! So, we have a relationship?"

"No," I replied, throwing his remarks back at him. "That was just a term I threw out there."

"Cheeky," he chastised me.

"Giving cheek is my specialty," I responded.

I gave him the time for when he was supposed to pick me up, our goodnights were a little clumsily given and we hung up.

As we spoke, the movie that I had watched had gone on and on. When I looked at the TV again, the movie was almost over.

As I sat there, wondering at what I had gotten myself into, I saw Manhattan looking up at me.

"Men," I said to him as he purred when I pet him behind the ears, "I will never understand the lot of you, will I? Then again, you probably don't understand us."

# SIXTEEN
# THE DATE THAT IS NOT A DATE

Veteran's Celebration Day arrived, and I was standing at the window in our living room, waiting for Darcy to pull up. The familiar Honda rolled down Longbourn, and parked a couple stops from our house.

"Who is that?" Mama asked, coming behind me. She was eating some ice cream and looking at who just stepped out of the car.

"Be prepared for a shock," I said, "In fact, I'm still amazed that this is about to happen."

Wearing a tweed coat, with a gray scarf draped over his shoulders, Darcy stepped out of the car.

Mom's eyes widened in disbelief. I confess that seeing the shock in her eyes was kind of fascinating.

"Wait?" she asked. "Is that…"

"Yeah. Darcy from back home."

"The idiot who was mean to you."

"Yup, *that* Darcy."

"He's coming toward the house." She gave me a quizzical look. "What are you not telling me?"

"If it helps, I'm just as confused myself. He's grown up a lot. He's trying to make things right between us."

"Or he could hurt you again."

My heart warmed at the idea of her being willing to defend me.

"Don't worry. I've grown up a little bit too. I can face him, and not break. But he's not going to hurt me."

"Let me be the judge of that."

She moved to the door, and I knew what she was about to do.

"You don't have to meet him, Ma," I said, rushing up behind her. "And he's been better to me."

"And I'm going to make sure that he keeps it that way."

Just as Darcy climbed the front steps, mom opened the door. I grabbed my coat, scarf, and hat and raced after her.

The look on Darcy's face was priceless as he saw my mother emerge, with me, red in the face, but I confess that I was very much a little amused.

"Liz?" he asked.

"Darce," I greeted. "Good morning."

"Morning," he said, apprehensive as he eyed my mother, suspecting who she was.

"Up for an adventure?" I asked, trying to sound positive. "This is my mom. Did you ever meet her?"

He looked down at my mother, whom he towered over, but it made no difference. Her small figure loomed large in his eyes and Darcy buckled at the very sight of her. His shoulders slouched, humbled as he almost mumbled through his words.

"Oh, Mrs. Bennet!" he uttered, anxiety in his voice. "It's nice to meet you."

"Thank you," she said, her voice confident and strong, "you and my daughter went to high school together."

"Yes, we did," he replied, sensing that maybe the mother of the woman he bullied might know a thing or two about that. "I was the worst back then. The side-effect to being a teenager, I guess."

"True. The wonder years are the hardest, and I'm happy that you are past that." Her eyes grew harder, though, despite the smile that was pasted across her face. "But my daughter's happiness means a lot to me. And for a while, she was not happy.

When you are around her, make sure not to do anything to upset or offend her. Do we understand each other?"

As I looked at my mother, I felt a mingled sense of embarrassment and admiration. Nothing is more humiliating than when your parents meet a guy that you are going to hang out with, but you also enjoy knowing that your mother is in your corner. My mother was *in my corner*, and he was flustered.

Darcy, like me, was also a little turned around. He looked at me briefly before he gave a humbled 'yes'."

I wanted to laugh and retreat at the same time. We humans can be such ironic things.

"We'll probably be at Mount Vernon for about an hour and a half," I said, "we'll be back by around 4."

"Good. Call me when you get there."

"I will," I replied, going down the stairs, with Darcy at my side. "Tell Dad where I went. I forgot to tell him in time."

"I will."

We didn't speak as we walked to the car.

"Get the door for her," my mother yelled at Darcy.

"Of course!" Darcy rushed out, still intimidated as he opened his door for me. As I got in, I looked in his eyes, gave him a 'I am enjoying this so much!' look, got in, and he closed the door behind me. He rushed around the other end of the car, trying to get in as quickly as possible, I opened the door for him, he got in, turned the car on and we were off.

———

Now that we were driving along, we finally had the time to speak.

"Penny for your thoughts?" I asked Darcy.

"Your mom hates me, doesn't she?" he asked.

"She can't help herself. Remember, she was the one who always saw me come home from school, crying. If it helps, I never told her to give you the 9th degree like that. *But*, if I were to be honest, boy did I like it!"

He chuckled as he stopped at a red light.

"I bet you did," he intoned.

"Oh, I did, I did, I did," I retorted, chuckling. "I cannot help it. Nothing is more terrifying to men than moms. There was a lot of fun in seeing you squirm."

"I admit that I do get scared around moms."

"It's okay to—believe me. Though I'm sure that dads are also frightening, under some circumstances. If it helps, moms can intimidate me too. Imagine if your mom was here with us. I would be scared, half the time, and would wonder if I was saying the wrong things. Of course, that would not stop me from saying those things. If I lose my courage to speak, then I lose everything."

Darcy gave me another side-glance, then the light turned green, and we were off.

"Everything?" he repeated.

"Yes, everything," I responded. "Well, you would understand better than anyone. Without our words, what are either of us?"

"First your mom puts the fear of god in me," he augmented, somewhat surprised, "and now you are being very philosophical."

"You're wondering how such different interactions can happen one after the other? Oh, come on, Darce. When has it ever been strange that a conversation can change, like an attitude can change."

"Be honest with me. Is your mom crazy?"

"Hey!" I gasped, and then I thought about it. "Well, maybe a little. Okay, more than a little. But she loves us all, and I appreciate that."

"Yeah. I wonder if I had met her in high school, she might have scared me from being mean to you, but who knows, eh?"

"What is your mom like?" I asked. "We already started this conversation in the middle, so I might try and steer us back to a little bit of normalcy. I thought you would like that."

"My mother is dead."

Dead!

Oh dear, now our conversation changed from strange to morbid.

"I'm sorry. I didn't know."

"Nothing to feel sorry over," he said, "she died a couple of years ago."

"Still miss her, don't you?"

"Every day." We turned on the highway. "She always made my lunch for me, until I started buying things at the cafeteria. And she would put little messages on the napkin that she put next to my sandwich. She would say things like 'I love you', or 'have a great day'. And she would put a sticker next to the words."

"My mom packed my lunch for a long time too," I added, happy to connect to him in some way. "How she had the energy to do it, I don't know. Then again, she graduated at the top of her class at the Academy and flew over fifty missions. After that, you learn how to survive from endurance alone."

"Richard told me that all five of you have been in the Airforce, in one way or another."

"We've all been pilots, except for Lydia, but that's just because she's still in school. She's also going to walk the same path that we did. We caught the 'military bug' from our parents, and they caught it from theirs. Truth is, it all goes back down to my grand-mother. She was the first woman in our family to go into the service during World War II."

"She was a WASP?"

"Yup. After Pearl Harbor was bombed, male pilots were in short supply. Twenty-eight women pilots volunteered to ferry airplanes that delivered trainer aircraft to flight schools, and they called themselves the WAFS."

"Women Auxiliary Ferrying Squadron."

"That's right. You get top marks there."

Darcy grinned as he switched lanes.

"After that, 1074 more women were trained to fly military aircraft," I continued. "They flew every aircraft in the Army's arsenal. She served on five different bases. Her first plane was a P-38 Lightning. She loved that plane. She liked her other ones, but she said that one worked the best under her. 'Love the plane that does what you want it to', she always would tell us."

Emotion tugged away at my insides as I recalled Granny, sitting there, with her bones old and she often didn't stand up when we were around, because of a condition that she developed when she got older. Sometimes, it's heartbreaking when you see pictures of a young woman, with the beauty of youth constantly cling to her, combined to all the strength that can come from training, and then for her to lose everything. I never asked her about how it made her feel, because you know that you can't, you see? In their minds, they must relive their glory days, but how can you ask them, out loud, if they miss it? Maybe you should ask them, because there's always a story there that they want to share, but you don't know if you ought to.

I must've turned reflective for too long because I had grown silent.

"What did she fly afterwards?" he asked me.

"Oh," I said, clearing my throat as I came back down to reality. Truly, I came down to reality quite hard. I may have been sitting in the car, but I felt like I had been transported to another stage of mind, which we all call memories. "She flew an AT-6 Texan. That was another pretty bird. If you ever see any of those WASP Calendars that get sent in the mail to people who give donations, usually our mom's picture is in the November month."

"I saw that calendar!" His eyes widened as he attempted to remember her image, and then his face relaxed when he found it. "I remember her now. She looked like you, actually."

"Yeah. I do look like her a lot."

"Your grandmother was lovely."

"Thanks. Many of those women pilots were, when you come to think of it. And she was built on her stories. Old age took her legs, and so all that she had was her history, and being a pilot was the highlight of her life."

"Did you ever get angry at her?"

I scratched my ear as I looked at him in astonishment.

"About what?" I asked her.

"Well, her legend kind of shaped your lives. To the point where it seems like you were born into a dream. But was that ever all of your dreams to begin with?"

I looked ahead at the highway that stretched in front of me. *Of us.* There were other cars in the lanes, who like us, were all headed in a direction that guaranteed a destination that we believed that we were going to arrive at. And where was I going? To a Veteran's celebration. Nothing about it felt foreign to me, until I thought about it, more in depth. I was driving back to my past.

A past, that had already been written for me. All our lives, it was just a given. A destination that we all knew that we were heading towards. Should I have been angry at my grandmother? Should I be enraged that I woke up to a fate that just felt right, but did I ever fully ask myself why I was on it?

And here is where I had a deep revelation…

No, I was not angry. Not angry at all.

Finally, I could answer Darcy.

"Until this moment, I never thought about it that much. It just seemed natural that we'd all go into the service. You would think that the burden of that legacy would be hard to feel. And yet, I'm not angry at all. I think…that there is nothing wrong with walking down a path when it's so much like your own wants and needs. I was born to be a pilot. So, it was natural that I became one. Even if Grandma didn't do it, I probably would have signed up and was another soldier flying in the air, at some point."

I felt a grin spread across my face.

"Hot damn," I declared. "I think you forced me to confront another side of myself. You, sir, are either a very incredible inspiration, or you are a donkey's behind."

Darcy chuckled, and I found myself liking it.

"I make you laugh," I said, "that's good. Laughing is good."

"Do I ever make you laugh?" he said, switching lanes.

"I don't know," I said, "but don't try."

"Don't try what?"

"Making me laugh. Trying to be an amusement system for someone can get exhausting very quickly. And you will have no choice but to let me down. And then you'll grow to hate the sight of me. Besides, I'm getting used to you."

"Then this was a good trip?"

I looked at Darcy, taking in his sharp jawline, and intense eyes.

"Yes, it is. Well, it depends on our destination."

"I think Mount Vernon will be kind to us."

"It has a way of doing that. I see why Washington always wanted to go back home, especially after he won the revolution."

"It makes me wonder," He began. "You're a tour guide. How does it feel talking about Washington when you discovered what he really was?"

I perked up, happy that we had shifted our conversation to something that required me not wearing my heart on my sleeve.

"You would think it was hard, but not really."

"Oh, really?"

"Yeah. It's the same way that I can talk about Benedict Arnold, and how he was a very good war hero for the Americans, and then also how he was turncoat who betrayed all the people who trusted him. I think it's because I've come to accept how complicated we humans can be. Even though we are all complex, we humans still have a hard time reconciling how contradictory we can be, within ourselves. We are built to have two different aspects of our character. But people have a hard time accepting this conflict. And with historic characters, I take in the good and the bad, weigh out the pros and the cons, and try to find the balance—and I also take in how people were raised.

"George Washington did not have the luxury of being raised in a good environment that we do today. He was given good principles but was left to practice them in pride and conceit. He was raised in a toxic environment and was told that was the only way to be, and how life was. He was never given the chance to see some higher virtues. That was not fair to anyone back then. And he kept making the same mistake for a very long time.

"However", I continued, "I also admit that he was the right person to be our first President. He fought for years, in a war that it seemed like he would never win. If you proved to be loyal to him, he didn't care if you were nationally born or a foreigner. And when he won, he refused to turn our country into a dictatorship. He stepped down as a citizen. He tried to reconcile our conflicts with the Native Americans, while being torn left and right in a political quagmire that never gave him any peace. He always came back to serve, he respected freedom of the press, and other nations respected him. And when his term was over, he peacefully handed his power over to another. And that set a precedence that must *always* be maintained. And when he gave his farewell speech, like it is said in the musical, 'Hamilton'—"

"We're going to teach them how to say goodbye," Darcy said the song lyric from the musical that George Washington sang.

"Precisely. George Washington taught us how to say goodbye, and how to move on. He also was very aware that he failed to do certain things and did not abolish evil practices that ought to be abolished. From a moral standpoint, he failed. But from a national standpoint, he succeeded. And from a self-awareness standpoint, he got straight A's. And he got better and wiser as he got older. So, no I never have a hard time talking about him, because I can see both sides of him: the man he was raised to be, and the man that was always fighting to overcome what he was raised to be."

"So, you can forgive a person's present way of being, while still acknowledging what they were like in the past?"

I gave him a side glance. Then I felt—saw—felt—and saw the connection that he was wishing for me to arrive at. Darcy, despite my hopes and wishes, was always smarter than he let on. He was deductive, and innocently manipulative in how he could steer a conversation. I had to learn to remember that.

"You are clever," I allowed, "very clever."

Darcy did not grin, but his eyes twinkled. Rather than leave it there, I was a glutton for punishment and just couldn't help but elaborate on what I realized.

"Once I started explaining the duality of human nature," I theorized, "you saw your opening. You knew that hearing my philosophy, it was like our history. And if I could accept the complicated lives of historical characters, I would have no choice but to accept our lives—our past. And live even more in the present than ever."

Darcy slowed down his car as he was turning onto the exit.

"Fine," he gave in, "you got me. I plead guilty to doing that. What's my punishment?"

"I'm not paying for gas."

Darcy laughed again.

"Don't worry," I added, swinging the air with my hand, "I am paying for gas. That was such an empty threat."

"It was? You should never have said that. Now I know that all your threats are empty, and I don't have anything to fear."

"Just because this threat is hollow does not mean that all my threats will be hollow. Don't underestimate women; we always come back and bite you in the bum."

"My mom taught me that already. She always had a way of wearing my dad down, and he spent their entire marriage just saying yes to everything she did."

"Oh, your mom was a genius. I'm not in the way of getting married, but I've got to give her credit. She had it *made*."

"You wouldn't put me through that, would you?"

"We're not married; you're safe from me."

"True." Darcy was staring straight ahead at the road, and his eyes were set, and lost all amusement. I wonder what that was about. "True."

———

Eventually, we arrived at Mount Vernon and found quite a great number of Veterans walking around the grounds, some single, and others with their families. Those who were retired just wore their Veteran's caps, and those who were still in active duty, wore their uniforms.

It turns out that the Veteran's Day ceremonies had already begun. And we missed the first part.

"Do you feel terrible for being late?" Darcy whispered to me. "Because I do."

We showed our military cards to get free admission.

"Don't worry," I assured him, "the first part of a celebration is almost never the best part. People like it when things build, so the best is yet to come."

We had just arrived at 11 am and were told that there were two historic reenactors portraying George and Martha Washington in the Interpretive Center.

"Let's power walk or run," I suggested.

"Power walking is overrated," Darcy retorted, starting to jog.

"You are such a soldier," I jabbed, jogging beside him as we dashed to the Interpretive Center, to a bunch of people cheering as a tall actor and small actress entered, in picture perfect colonial attire, and looking impressive in every way.

Darcy and I said excuse me as we found two seats next to each other, and placed ourselves near the back, to avoid being disruptive.

When looking at the two reenactors, I couldn't help but get a little giddy.

"It's them!" I whispered, excited, "I mean that I know it's not really George and Martha Washington, but I'm still excited."

"Me too," Darcy said, his voice still a little stoic. I guess that was his version of excited. "Why are we excited, despite them not being the real ones?"

"Simple," I said, matter-of-factually. "Because it's our past."

George and Martha Washington gave a presentation, and then we were allowed to meet them and ask them any questions.

Darcy, to my surprise, asked George Washington what his favorite section of his Farewell address was when he stepped down from being President. When hearing that, the reenactor grew animated, despite Washington being genuinely known for his calmer demeanor.

"Actually, there are two sections that I cherished so much, that I memorized them," the Washington look-a-like declared. "If you all kind people would be so humble as to let an old general become sentimental, then I appreciate it, and it will not be a long recitation. It will only be a couple of minutes."

We all agreed to this.

"Do you need a paper, George?" the Martha Washington look-a-like offered.

"Thank you, my dear Martha," he responded, "but I do believe that I can recall it all with perfect clarity."

'Martha' stood beside 'George', as he stood with his hands placed behind his back and began to recite his favorite passage.

When he finished, we all clapped. I had to hand it to this actor; he took his role seriously, delivered it well, and he did something more: he made us feel. He made us understand what it meant to believe. Not think or theorize… just believe.

———

After that, we were led to the Smith Auditorium to listen to some Colonial Singers of Williamsburg.

Afterwards, we went to Washington's Tomb, where the Sons of the American Revolution and the Daughters of the American Revolution, did a ceremony. If I had the skill to describe every event with incredible detail, rendering it in a way that you would find it compelling, then I would do that, in a heartbeat.

But I can't do that, and my reason is simple: it's because I'm not good at it.

Needless to say, that Darcy and I were having a good time, and what's more, we had achieved something else. We had learned how to be silent around each other, but comfortable. Naturally, conversation is like everything else in life; it can run dry quickly. Eventually you run out of things to say, and you are left making your company feel very awkward, because there's nothing else to contribute. This is natural. Painful, yes. But natural.

And all you can do is hope that the silence is organic, it was properly arrived at, and it was naturally arrived at. And neither party don't feel the anxieties of having to supply more topics in a forceful way, because you arrived at a good balance. It was not said in words, but was felt, related to, and complete.

Darcy and I sometimes didn't have anything to say to each other. And it was not because we were awkward. We simply had nothing to say, and it never felt strained, or tense. It just felt… comfortable.

I wonder why that was.

And when did this transition occur?

From us being enemies.

To us being forced acquaintances.

Then to us confronting who we were, versus who we are now.

Next, to us tolerating each other.

And then, to us hanging out.

Lastly, to us finding a proper comfort around each other.

I never felt like this with Wickham!

Wickham... I should still be heartbroken. I should still be crying.

But I'm not.

In fact, I didn't even feel anything anymore.

How is that possible?

How did the man, who once stirred so much in me, quickly fade to obscurity and romantic oblivion?

Was I ever in love with Wickham at all? Or was it just an infatuation? A flame that burned hot but was quickly extinguished.

And with Darcy, I now... cared. Not romantically, of course, because that would just be stupid. After all, our past was too turbulent for us to ever feel anything else but casual comfort.

The times really are 'a-changing'.

———

At 2:00 p.m. was one of the final events for Veteran's Day. It was the U.S. Airforce Strings Orchestra Concert in the Smith Auditorium again.

At this stage, I was so comfortable and much at ease that I suppose that should have been the first sign. As time would go on to show, this was one of those instances where it showed the time-honored maxim: it's a small world after all.

As we went to get our seats, I heard someone calling my name.

"Liz!"

I turned to who said my name, and my eyes lifted as I saw a face from my past.

"Princess!"

Princess, one of my fellow pilots in the Airforce, was only a few seats down from me. And just as soon as I had said her name, I saw her flinch and I tried to cover myself.

"Sorry," I apologized, "Hey Pres."

"I'm happy that you didn't forget," she said as we got out of our seats and hugged. "It's good to see you."

"It's great to see you too," I said, then we looked at each other.

"I love your hair," we both said, in unison. Then we laughed together.

Darcy approached me. I introduced them both, and it turned out that she was not here alone.

"My boyfriend, Jacob Long, is in the orchestra," she said, "I came with him."

"Oh, which one is he?"

Princess pointed to the man who was sitting at the cello, and he waved at her.

"He's cute," I said to her.

"Thanks," she said, eyeing Darcy. "But I see that you are doing pretty well for yourself."

Sadly, I had to correct her. Wait, why was I sad to correct her?

"Oh, it's not like that. Darcy and I are friends."

"Oh, sorry, I jumped the gun there."

"It's fine. Natural mistake. You look great, Pres."

"So do you?"

"Still in the Service?"

"You know me. If I can take being bullied because of what my name is, then I'm in this for the long run." She rolled her head, slightly, looking at me from a different angle. "Still not open to coming back?"

And once more, I knew that no matter what I said, Princess would never understand.

"It's hard to explain," I said, "I like where I've been, but I also like where I am now. Don't get me wrong. Walking away was hard for a time."

"We tried to tell you," Princess said, with genuine concern in her voice, "repeatedly. Anne de Bourgh would not want you to go your entire life hating yourself for what happened."

"What?"

It wasn't me who said that word, but rather we turned to Darcy, who had asked the question.

"Darce?" I questioned. "What?"

"Did you say Anne de Bourgh?" he asked.

"Yeah," I said, "Anne was in our unit. You know her?"

"Yes. She was my cousin."

————

My insides froze as my mind was becoming fuzzy over this revelation.

Cousin?

Anne de Bourgh was Darcy's cousin!

Oh. My. God.

"She was?"

"Yes, she was. We were told that she was killed overseas. It was after she had been stationed over in Finland. We were told that she was shot down, and the attacker was unidentified."

When a reality catches up with you, in the way that you never could have expected, the sharpness of that *reality* will knock you off any sense of security that you began to establish.

Princess and I looked at each other, apprehensive, awkward, and anxious. Within my eyes was the worry of now knowing that I had to face the music, the grim melody of acknowledging what had broken me, what had shaken my resolve, and confronting a mistake to someone who I knew would be angry at the truth.

The truth that had been hidden for too long. Not for me. Not for Princess. For she and I were there when the great unraveling had occurred.

But for Darcy, this was frightening. And for me, it was even more terrifying, because I had to tell him what happened.

"Lizzy?" Darcy asked me. His voice was so close and yet it seemed like it was also so far away.

I felt as if we were all in a moment where we were moving and speaking in slow motion, like time had drawn itself out, savoring a bad moment, that we would be forced to endure.

"Yes," I said, slowly, with embarrassment filling my eyes. No, not embarrassment! It was more than embarrassment. It was mortification.

Darcy's eyes narrowed. The pleasant scene had faded, giving way to bleak background that I knew had ruined the experience. His tone switched from casual to subtle bitterness.

"Were you there?" he asked. "Were you there when Anne—"

"Not here," I rushed out, quietly. "I can't talk about this here, because I promised." I looked at Princess, for help, and she picked up on the cue.

"Yeah," Princess added, for support. "It was declared classified. We can't talk about it in public. We're not even allowed to talk about it at all."

"She was my cousin," Darcy said strongly and with a fierceness in his eyes.

I touched his shoulder, and Darcy flinched, moving his body away from my gesture.

I saw the coldness wash over him as he was clearly upset with me.

A side of my brain was angry at him for daring to believe that he had any right to be angry with me, given our past together.

But another side of my brain acknowledged that I was looking up at Anne's cousin, someone who was probably never told what truly happened to her. He was just told that she was shot down and that was it.

He wanted to know.

He had the right to know.

"Not here," I urged him. "Not here. Not right now."

"Then when?" he asked me. "I need to know."

Realizing that the excursion was over, I turned to Princess.

"I think we have to go."

"I get it," Princess uttered, and I could tell that she felt very bad for being the source to bring up the subject that clearly ruined the day for me. "I'm sorry, Liz."

"It's fine," I assured her. "This is not your fault. Really, it's not."

I could clearly tell that she was not convinced that I was not angry, but she also was eager to make a hasty retreat.

"It was nice to meet you, Darcy," Princess said, diplomatically.

"Likewise," Darcy said, his voice was like stone.

I didn't like that, and I was not going to let that slide.

"He does think it was nice to meet you," I smoothed over, and turned to leave. As Darcy and I walked away, I whispered my disapproval. "You didn't have to sound like that when she said goodbye. It's not her fault about what just happened."

"I don't care how I looked."

"Well, I do," I said, "be nice."

He pulled my shoulder and wielded me around to face him. The gesture was too hard, so it hurt me a little, and I had no qualms yanking his hand off me.

"What are you doing?" I gasped.

"I want to know what happened." His expression changed from wrath to being humbled. "I'm sorry. I just realized how I behaved. But Liz, you know what happened to Anne?"

"Yes," I said, shifting my attitude from being offensive, to understanding. He was angry, and it clouded his judgment. "I get it. But make no mistake; do not mistreat me at all. I won't stand it, and I'd rather walk back to Alexandria if you're going to act like that."

"I was being insensitive again. I'm sorry. It won't happen again."

I gave him a look, and he was even more humbled.

"I promise," he assured me, "I'll speak better. Cross my heart. But I just really want to know. And I think I deserve an answer. And so does my aunt."

"Your aunt?"

"My aunt Catherine," he said, "she was never told the real story either. We weren't given any information, so help me to understand. And she has a right to know too."

I rubbed my hand over my mouth. Like it was with Princess, everything had been made confidential. I made a promise. I signed contracts, confirming my silence. When looking at Darcy, I had to make a decision.

Break the silence?

Or keep it secret and leave Darcy never knowing what happened to his cousin?

I had to make a choice.

———

Choice!

The action that determines our entire lives.

It can bring everything together.

Or make everything fall apart.

Putting my hands in my pockets, I knew what had to be done. Even if it was against my better judgment.

"I will tell you what happened, on the ride back to Alexandria," I answered. "But only once we are in the car, and if you promise that you won't tell anyone else. I respect your aunt, but you can't tell her either."

"Liz—"

"I'm serious, and I mean it. You can't tell your Aunt Catherine. It's classified. If you tell her, and she tells someone else, I will get in trouble."

Hearing the sincerity in my voice, he nodded.

"Okay."

Not speaking, we walked back to Darcy's car and drove off.

I turned around and watched Mount Vernon get smaller in the distance as we rode away from it. It can be odd how your mind wanders to stranger concepts that span over the course of centuries. Your mind journeys across time and space, and you ask yourself, 'was it always this strange? Was life always this hard?'

And considering Mount Vernon, and the iconic man who once lived there, I thought of him. And thus, I could not help but ask:

*President George Washington, did you ever have to go through this? When you were a General, did you ever have to sit there and tell someone about how you were responsible for their loved ones being gone? That, when entering a conflict, you made a mistake, and it led to a life being lost?*

*Of course, you did. You made many mistakes. You were young once and had no choice but to fail and lead your men into a massacre. How did you face it? What words did you use? How did you learn the best way to phrase it? To put your hand on their shoulder and say, 'I am sorry, but this is what happened...'*

…And then I return to the present, and am sitting in a car, driving back to Alexandria, and being taken by the man who everything might get even worse than before?

And George Washington was dead and gone and there was no chance of asking him anything. Of ever wondering if he could conceive what I was about to experience. After all, I was centuries away from the man behind the legend. So, what was the point of me wandering, but for the fact that we all do look on our past, be it recent or distant, and seek connection there, to help connect the dots to why we act the way that we do now.

Such was the way that we humans are. And I always will be.

"So," Darcy said as we drove along, "do you want to talk about it?"

I sighed, resigned.

"I was hoping to tell you everything when we got closer to Alexandria, because I was wondering that you might not want to see me after I tell you. The closest that we get home, the less time that we have together before you drop me off and can rush away."

"You think that I'm going to want to get away from you?"

"People do weird things when they are angry."

Darcy ran his hands through his hair, apprehensive and wary.

"I'm braced for the truth," he stated simply.

"First," I began, "I want you to know something. Anne and I were friends. We faced a lot together and we had each other's back so much. And if I could trade my life for hers, I would."

"I appreciate that," he said, his tone softer, "it doesn't change the fact that she's still gone. But I do appreciate it, Liz. I really do."

"Good," I said, "then I can begin."

Breathing in heavily, here came the truth.

———

"Anne and I were both excited," I began, "when we found out that we both got stationed together, and we were deployed overseas to Rosings Park. It was a base over in Finland. It was brilliant because it was the time of the year when we would get to see the Northern Lights. It was a magical experience, and we knew that we were going to a base that had no action. It was more like working at a base where you could have a vacation. I suppose it's always those moments where you put your guard down, and when the worst thing happens. Which it did.

"One day, Anne and I were out doing surveillance. We flew across the Baltic Sea, and we were told that we were going to rendezvous with another pilot, who was checking in from a neighboring country."

"What country?" Darcy asked. "Latvia? Estonia? Russia?"

"It's classified," I said. "On that part, I'm going to be silent about, because it doesn't matter where the pilot came from. No matter what, human error and negligence is pretty universal. It turns out that the pilot we were supposed to check in with had asked to be relieved from service. He was suffering from post-traumatic stress, from his last assignment. He had been experiencing delusions, quick spirts of depression, hysteria, panic, and he was disturbed. His superiors rejected his request for resignation."

"What?" Darcy asked me. "They forced him to keep serving, despite his condition?"

"That is exactly what happened. Mind you, I didn't know about this until after the fact. When we went to the rendezvous, after we reported in with him…" suddenly, all the memories began to flood back in. I grew quiet as I remembered the events, slowed down to make sense of them in my mind. It was such a waste! Such a waste.

"Liz?" Darcy asked me, seeing how I must've looked sick, "are you okay?"

I could lie… or I could do something harder: I could tell the truth again. Oh well, in for a penny, in for a pound.

"No," I replied, my eyes still closed as I rubbed them, "I am not okay. I never was after that, for so long, and now I have to relive it. I know that you deserve to hear it, but it never will get easy."

Gathering my courage, I continued.

"The pilot shot Anne's plane, and it blew up," I said simply, "and she never was even given a chance to eject herself. Her plane went down in flames, and she went down with it. I didn't see Anne die, but she was gone."

———

Hearing it out loud did not make it easier, because it never *would be easier*. There was no joy, no sense of time helping things, but I would always feel pain over this all.

"That's what happened?" Darcy asked, at last, as he drove along.

"Yes. Anne was shot down by friendly fire, not by an enemy. No one deserves to die when they are young, but this was the worst way of it happening. To know that we were shot down by an ally."

"But why do you feel guilty over it?" he asked. "It wasn't like it was your fault."

Coldness and humiliation filled up my focus, because now I had to say everything. Say the secret that I avoided telling him.

"In some ways," I confessed, "it was. When we met up with the pilot, I got the sense that there was something off about him. As if he was wrong, in some way. My instincts told me to not trust him, and that he might be unstable. But I ignored the warning signs, I let my guard down… and now Anne is dead, because of me. Because I didn't trust my instincts. And if I had, Anne de Bourgh would be alive."

At last, I turned to Darcy, who was looking ahead. He was focused on the road, yes, but I knew that he was masking how he really felt.

"I'm sorry," I whispered, "I really am sorry."

"What happened to the pilot?" he asked, his tone dark and heavy.

"He's dead," I said, "after he shot down Anne, I shot him down. It wasn't till after he was dead that I was told about his condition. For the sake of not letting this become known, to cause no rifts between our allies, the mission was deemed classified, and soon after, I resigned from the Airforce."

"You were told to cover up the issue."

"I understood why eventually. Making the problem known could easily cause bad blood between our friends. This was a moment that all boils down to human nature, and it can easily happen. But truth is, at the time, I was angry. I was angry at the system that ordered the man to continue to serve, even when I knew there was something wrong with him. Because I did feel the bad blood. I wanted revenge for what happened. I don't think I could have let it go. And truth is, I was also angry at myself."

Darcy gave me a side glance.

"You felt like you could have done something."

"Yes, because I could have done something. Anything. Everything. In fact, I know, that if I had listened to my instincts, acted on how this man was behaving, then Anne would still be here. In the air, sometimes all that you have is two seconds to assess the situation. Sometimes even one second, and one second can make all the difference. When you're flying, thought can be the enemy of instincts, and instincts is your decision. I did not live up to that lesson. And so…Anne is dead. And I walked away."

———

Now the truth had come out. After all this time, it was all unveiled.

When releasing such a weight off your soul, you feel lighter. Yet, the air around you feels heavier. Bearing one's soul is a delight, and the reaction is the consequence of it. For after you close your eyes, happy that the truth was exposed, when you open them again, you must see the eyes on you. The eyes of the person who must take this all in. Who must receive this information and understand how to take it. And how will they take it? What will they react like?

I turned to Darcy.

There he sat, his tall and muscular form was against the setting sun that was outlining his figure as he drove along.

He was handsome, to be sure. Yet his looks had a ferocity to them. A severity. And in that moment, he was frozen in his posture, looking ahead at the road before him.

He didn't respond.

Because he did not want to.

And I was all too happy to not let him respond at that moment.

I think that he was angry, be it at me, or at the revelation of knowing what happened to his cousin. I knew that, no matter how he reacted, it was going to be hard for him. And for me as well.

Better to let silence reign.

Drive on, Mr. Darcy. Just keep driving.

That is the proper response.

———

Eventually we turned onto Longbourn Road. Once we arrived, I looked at my house and was never gladder to see it. Now, Darcy and I could part ways, and take some time away from each other. But, when all is said and done, no one can just simply say, 'see you later', and that would be the end of it. You have to say something else. *I had* to say something else.

"You don't know what to do now, do you?" I asked him. "You don't know what to say to me, or how to react."

At first, Darcy did not respond to me, but slowly, he started to open his mouth.

"You're right. I don't know what to say. I just need to be alone. I need to tell my aunt—"

"It's class—"

"Right. I can't even do that."

He rubbed his face and tapped at the steering wheel.

"You're mad at me?" I asked gently.

"Yes." he said it simply, but also effectively. That one word was enough, in every way to make me feel even colder inside than usual.

"All right then," was all that I could muster.

"I just... I'll see you later, alright?"

*I'll see you later.*

Those words were the kiss of death.

"Okay. Again, I am so sorry. Like I said, I would trade my life for Anne's, if I could."

All too happy that I was, to get out of the car and rush into my home, and away from anything that Darcy had to say.

As I closed the front door behind me, I heard Darcy's engine start up quickly as he drove down the street. There was urgency in his departure, and I knew why.

When I leaned my back against the door, I was surprised to see Mom's head pop out of the doorway to the living room—and Lydia's head emerge behind hers.

"How did it go—" my mother asked, her words trailing off as she saw the look in my face.

"Judging by the fact that I heard his car drive off like the Road Runner from the Coyote," Lydia said, referencing to the Coyote cartoon who was always trying to chase down his prey, "Something happened to sour the evening."

With my head resting against the door and my eyes closed, I didn't even need to look at her.

"Yes," I answered simply.

"And you're not even getting mad at me for pointing that out." Her tone was cheery—she had a puzzle to solve, and I was not going to be saucy about it. "That means that you are exhausted. If he did something to ruin the night, you would be animated and willing to snap at me. But you're not, so that leaves me with only one deduction: you said something or did something to bring it all come crashing down."

I looked at her slowly out of the side of my eye.

"Maybe you're right," I gave in.

Lydia perked up.

"Well, that's new."

I looked at Mom.

"You were right to tell me that it would be a bad idea for me to go out with him," I said to her.

Mom perked up.

"You're saying that I was right?" Mom questioned.

"And you're saying that I was right?" Lydia echoed.

"Tell me everything," Lydia and mom said together.

"Anne de Bourgh," was all that I could say. When hearing her name, their expressions went from exhilarating, to apprehension, and worry. After all, they knew her. I told them about Anne quite a few times.

"What about her?" Mom asked. "What does she have to do with you and him?"

"She was his cousin." I crouched down at the door. "Anne was Darcy's cousin."

When hearing that, they both were shocked, in a quiet sort of way. They didn't speak because they didn't have to speak. They knew how difficult it was for me to talk about my past. So, for it to come back and bite me in the butt now, was even more intense. For now, Darcy was connected. They understood what I was going through, and I appreciated that.

"I decided to be proud and not a coward," I furthered, "and I told him what really happened."

And much to my incredible surprise, Mom and Lydia didn't start crowing at me, and showing how superior they must've felt.

Mom walked forward, sat down beside me, and wrapped her arm around me. Feeling the warmth that comes from comfort, I rested my head on her shoulder, and I almost wept.

"I should have looked after Anne better," I whispered, my voice hoarse. "If only I trusted my instincts. If only I had listened to myself."

Mom hushed me, using soothing tones.

"Lizzy, I know that you feel terrible when you can't control the world, but that's just what happens whenever any of us takes to the air. We all run that risk. And you forget that Anne also didn't suspect the threat. You both didn't know, and this is you putting the weight of the world on your shoulders. Again. And you walked away from the world because it got too heavy. But you never had to carry it all on yourself. And now you can reconcile with that."

"Is that what I do?" I asked, still weeping into her arm, "Is that what I..." I trailed off, too overcome.

As mom and I sat there, cradling each other, dad came from around the corner and stood behind Lydia.

"What's happening?" He asked.

"Lizzy just came to a revelation," Lydia uttered, watching us like she was watching the climactic scene in an indie film and the lead characters just had a breakthrough. "She is now showing signs of life."

"Ah. Wait, what does that mean?"

"She's confronted the darker sides of her past. In other words, she's being awkward."

––––––

"So, that was the date from hell, huh?" Mary asked.

I was in my bedroom, lying down, with my head pressed firmly against my pillow.

Mary was lying on my bed as well, in the reverse direction, with her feet near my head and my head near her feet. She was eating some beef jerky, a cucumber, and two butterscotch crumpets—those food cravings were really kicking into gear.

"Actually, I have had some pretty bad dates in my life," I said, "can't think of any of them right now. Besides, it wasn't a date. It was the beginning of me patching things up. Sewing some holes from my past, but it led to the past turning into pandora's box once it got opened. No good deed goes unpunished, eh?"

Mary drummed her hand against her stomach pouch.

"I can second that emotion."

Feeling immediately ashamed of wallowing in my self-pity when she had worse problems to face humbled me.

"I'm sorry, young grasshopper."

"No, don't do that," Mary said. "I like that you confided in me about this. It's just…" she rolled her head so that I could get a better look at her expression. "We're all told that it doesn't do any good to dream, and then forget to live. I decided to live and do the right thing by it… and this happened. I suppose that maybe that's the side effect to life: things get messy. But you don't have to suffer under it." Her tone changed from reflective to authoritative. "It happened. You second-guessed yourself, but Anne did the same thing. Risking yourself is part of the job of when you go into the service."

"But Anne died for a stupid reason."

"I know. And life is not fair. But you need to stop putting that burden on your shoulders. It was the other pilot who committed the crime. And once you saw what happened, you fought back. Then, as penance, you left the only job that you felt fully comfortable in."

"I am happy as a tour guide, and I was not afraid to work at the Shakespeare Festival," I responded.

"I know; you've never been afraid to make a new path for yourself. But I know you. You loved being in the air. You like living another day so that you can fight the next week. I'm just saying that you don't have to be angry with yourself for telling this Darcy guy. In fact, he has no reason to be angry with you!"

Blinking, I looked down at her, astonished at her tonal change.

"Really?" I asked, rolling over on my side and placing my head on the side of my pillow.

"Yes, really."

I sighed, hopeful.

"Well, thank goodness for your resolute tones," I said, perking up.

"And I'm not saying this because it's just easy advice, but I mean it. You told Darcy the truth, you admitted what happened, you took responsibility for something that you were never responsible for. Even though you blame yourself for it. He has no right to be angry with you because it's not his place. And I'm sorry, but he better get over it. And if not, you're better off without him in your life. Even as an acquaintance."

"So, I shouldn't do anything to go out of my way to make things up to him."

"Hell no," Mary responded. "If he wants to patch things up with you, he needs to understand you and get over his pride. I get it that he is upset, so I'll give him the benefit of the doubt. But only for a short time. At some point, he needs to get over it, and it's his job to make it all right again." With a deep reflective look, her voice changed into a bit of a whisper. "Do you want to see him again?"

"I was hoping that I could put our past behind us, and I liked the idea. A part of me does want to know that we are friendly. But I've seen what happens whenever we women make the first move to resolving things. Even though it makes sense for us to do that..."

"Sometimes guys like it when they make the first move."

I rolled my eyes as I turned on my back and looked up at the ceiling.

"Don't you ever hate that?" I asked. "That we women cannot make the first move when it comes to these sorts of things. When we do, the guy gets uncomfortable. Mind you, I am making generalizations and generalizations have a right to be taken with a grain of sand. But they are fun to make."

"It's an easy generalization to make. Be it true or not, let's just roll with it for the moment."

"And then take it back when we meet a guy who is different."

"Yes. When that happens, we can take it back."

"But if I don't try to contact him," I said, "he might think that I am just forgetting about it all. But if I do call him, he might get uncomfortable, and then get cold that I took the first step. Nothing is more annoying that being in this state of limbo."

"That's always the dilemma that I must face."

Suddenly, an idea came to me! It popped into my head without any prompting, and it was marvelous. To live in the ever-constant purgatory of 'don't call him but want to call him' could now be remedied.

"I just realized something," I remarked, with a sense of relief that I could get closure. "And if he doesn't take me up on it, then the problem is all on him."

"Ah!" Mary remarked, interested. "Do tell."

I told her everything, Mary agreed that was the best plan, and I was resolved.

# SEVENTEEN
# MY WAY BACK

The next day, I had nothing planned except for rehearsal for *The Goblin Who Stole a Sexton*. Therefore, that gave me the opportunity to go to the basement and look through some of the storage boxes that I had brought from when I was living in Kentucky.

As I sifted through them, one box I had labeled as Knick knacks, was at the very bottom.

As I brushed off some dust that had gotten onto the surface, I opened the box and began to sift through it. Because I didn't have much, I knew precisely where to find what I was looking for:

WASHINGTON'S FAREWELL
ADDRESS

To the People of the United States

It was a book bound copy of George Washington's farewell address when he stepped down from the USA presidency and gave the first Presidential Farewell Address.

It had belonged to Anne de Bourgh. I had it custom made for her.

As I held the book in my hand, I felt a brief sorrow eclipse me, and I wiped the emotion away from my eyes.

A flood of memories washed over me, as I opened the book, fell back into my past, when Anne and I had been stationed at Lambton, a military base in Japan…

Excited that our last inspection on our planes had gone well, Tanya and I were running giddily into our sleeping quarters and found Princess and Anne de Bourgh laying on their bunks.

When seeing us rush in, past them, Anne nodded to us, but kept reading, while Princess was playing a game on her IPAD. Lowering it, she looked at us, laughing.

"You look happy?" Princess noted.

"Damn straight we do," Tanya replied as I began to take off my boots. "We just got to inspect the New Super Hornet model that came in."

"How does she fly?"

"Smooth ride and does what we want it to. I heard a rumor that they will also be flown over the Superbowl next year."

"They will," I confirmed, removing my socks, pants, and I began to put on my sweatpants and fluffy socks. "My sister told me. She's going to be in the flyover, and she gets to fly the Hornet."

"Congratulations," Tanya said, while also grinding her teeth. "We'll be stuck here when the football game happens. I would never get the chance to be chosen to fly over a sports event. Some people have all the luck."

"It's just a luck of the draw sometimes," I said, "and come on, T. Kitty worked hard to get there. I'm happy she did. Now she can find more to her than just being the middle kid."

"Which number is she?" Princess added.

"Fourth. She's the fourth sister."

"Did your parents ever want to have a boy?"

"I bet they did," I said, laughing, "why do you think they had five of us?"

"Because they liked having—"

"Eww" I cried, throwing my sock at Princess.

"What? We all have to understand, sometime, that the only

way our parents had us was if they made the beast with the two backs."

"Of course, we know it," Tanya responded, "we just don't talk about it because it's too gross. Just ill."

Before I put my dirty fatigues in the hamper, I was about to climb onto my top bunk, when I still noticed that Anne had not raised her eye from the book. Amused, and wishing to be a little mischievous, I snapped my fingers in front of her face. Anne still did not blink.

"Don't worry," Anne said, "I'm still here, and I do care about what you're talking about. But you know me when I get into studying mode."

I looked at the cover and saw that it was 'Washington's Farewell Address'.

"You've read it like five times," I said, going up to my bunk and plopping down on the bed. "Sometimes I wonder if I was wrong to give it to you. It's now become your best friend."

"I thought you never regretted anything you did," Anne said, chuckling. "That's something you're always telling me to do myself."

"Life shouldn't be wasted on regret," I said, "just call it experience and get on with your life."

"Precisely," she said, brandishing the book. "Don't regret this."

"What is the book?" Princess asked, also removing her boots.

"It's George Washington's farewell address," Tanya retorted. "Anne reads it a lot. Where do you go when she talks about it?"

"To my cloud," Princess responded, "we all have a right to retreat from life every now and again."

"Well, you're not in the atmosphere yet," Anne de Bourgh said. "I've highlighted some of my favorite parts. Listen to this."

"No, no, no," Tanya moaned, covering her ears with her pillow. "I don't like listening to politics. Especially from a bunch of older generations who all were so messed up."

"It was the 1700s," I interjected, taking out my copy of Neil Gaimain's novel, *Anansi Boys*. "Everyone was messed up back then. It was nearly impossible to find a person was born, lived, and died without their virtues being compromised."

"Precisely," Anne de Bourgh stressed, "if we don't learn the history of things because we don't like how things went down, then we won't learn about anyone. So, I take things for what they are: the good and bad of stuff. And don't worry about politics. I get it; politics is not something any of us like talking about; that's why we're soldiers. Our lives are simpler, and we understand loyalty better. But when Washington wrote this, it was after realizing the best and worst of his past, and he's not talking to the people like a politician, but as a person. I don't agree with all of it, but I definitely like much of it. Come on, let me read some of it to you."

I looked over my bunk and down at Anne.

"And this is why we call you the girl scout."

Anne smiled.

"That's me. Guilty as charged."

Taking that as an affirmation, Anne raised up the book and began to read us some of her favorite excerpts from America's first President's farewell after he stepped down from office. She cleared her throat and did her best to read. The thing is that none of us were orators:

"For this you have every inducement of sympathy and interest. Citizens by birth or choice of a common country, that country has a right to concentrate your affections. The name of American, which belongs to you in your national capacity, must always exalt the just pride of patriotism more than any appellation derived from local discriminations. With slight shades of difference, you have the same religion, manners, habits, and political principles. You have in a common cause fought and triumphed together. The independence and liberty you possess are the work of joint councils and joint efforts—of common dangers, sufferings, and successes."

Anne lowered the pamphlet and looked at us.

"See what he said," she stressed, "he said 'citizens by *birth* or by *choice*'. That's important. And, how any prejudices that we feel towards each other are not something that should get in the way of us all connecting. And how, what we are, should overcome any discriminations that we were raised to have."

Anne turned the page.

"Now, here's another bit," she said, beginning to read again.

"In this sense it is, that your Union ought to be considered as a main prop of your liberty, and that the love of the one ought to endear to you the preservation of the other."

Anne looked at us all again, to give her reaction to the term.

"Well, that's us," she declared. "All four of us are from different states, have different backgrounds, but we're all defending the same thing. We want to keep our nation alive, don't we?"

I looked over at Tanya and Princess, who all changed a color, a little naked under the philosophies that we were being made to face.

"Now don't worry," Anne said, "I'm just going to read you one more, because I know that if I go further, then you might kill me."

She read the last excerpt:

"The basis of our political systems is the right of the people to make and to *alter* their constitutions of government. But the Constitution, which at any time exists, until changed by an explicit and authentic act of the whole people, is sacredly obligatory upon all. The very idea of the power and the right of the people to establish government presupposes the duty of every individual to obey the established government...

"...All obstructions to the execution of the laws...are destructive of this fundamental principle and of fatal tendency. They serve to organize faction; to give it an artificial and extraordinary force; to put in the place of the delegated will of the nation the will of a party, often a small but artful and enterprising minority of the community; and, according to the alternate triumphs of different parties, to make the public administration the mirror of the ill concerted and incongruous projects of faction, rather than the organ of consistent and wholesome plans digested by common councils and modified by mutual interests. I have already intimated to you the danger of parties in the state...Let me now take a more comprehensive view and warn you in the most solemn manner against the baneful effects of the spirit of party, generally…The alternate domination of one faction over another, sharpened by the spirit of revenge natural to party dissension, which in different ages and countries has perpetrated the most horrid enormities, is itself a frightful despotism. But this leads at length to a more formal and permanent despotism. The disorders and miseries which result gradually incline the minds of men to seek security and repose in the absolute power of an individual; and sooner or later the chief of some prevailing faction, more able or more fortunate than his competitors, turns this disposition to the purposes of his own elevation on the ruins of public liberty…It serves always to distract the public councils and enfeeble the public administration. It agitates the community with ill-founded jealousies and false alarms, kindles the animosity of one part against another, foments occasionally riot and insurrection."

Anne lowered the pamphlet and looked at us.

"Washington thought the constitution could be changed?" Princess clarified.

"Yeah," Tanya said, "but by who? It's a good idea, and he was right, but who would write the new one? Those who were idealistic, or by those who were just trying to do things for their own ends."

"Yes," Anne said, "but the point is that, while Washington supported the Constitution, he also understood that naturally, more laws and changes would have to come over time, *for* the community. Considering the world that he was in, his past, and what was going on around him, it's wise. And he predicted the future. He warned us all about factions growing, and corrupt people using those factions to spread their agendas to subvert the power of the people, and that that minority of people, will use the majority to execute their behavior, which will lead to them destroying the very government that elected them to that spot."

I had this discussion with Anne before, so it wasn't me that she needed to convince, but the other two, so she directed her attention to Princess and Tanya.

"That's why I read it, a lot," Anne said, "it's because we're always living this. But we were warned about it."

"Warned about it by a man who made every mistake," Princess said, laughing.

"That doesn't mean that we have to ignore it," Anne overrode her. "And who doesn't make those mistakes? Who doesn't turn right when they should have turned left sometimes? Washington was like his farewell Address; flawed, but heroic. George Washington was dated, but also timeless."

Anne chuckled.

"I have a *cousin* who is like that," Anne added.

"You do?" I asked, my ears perking up.

"Yeah. He's the walking version of that: dated, but timeless. His past is littered with mistakes, but he's always moving forward. That's what makes me forgive him whenever he is being annoying. He always has a way of getting over himself, eventually, and then finds his way back to humanity again. I can't explain him better than that. You'd have to meet him, and then you'll get it."

"You know my code," I said, "I don't meet families. Things get too complicated."

"I know. And I get it."

"Oh, thank goodness," Tanya said, "we're returning to general topics. I couldn't stand any more political science, because when things get too moral, I can't stick around for too long before I hate myself."

"Ah," I remarked, "the natural tendency to not talk about virtues, because after a short amount of time, it will make you sick. What about imperfection that we prefer to read? Perfect images are provocative."

"That's probably why I don't have many friends," Anne said, "I'm always like this. How do you put up with me?"

"I think knowing you is a cross that I'm willing to bear."

Anne de Bourgh chuckled, continuing to read…

———

Looking down at her copy of Washington's Farewell Address, I swiped at my tears. Hurled out of my memories, I was back to the present, in our storage room.

Anne was too young. And she had so much life to her.

Putting the copy in my bag, I slung it over my shoulder, when I spied another box from out of the corner of my eye, that read:

## LIZZY'S FATIGUES

Curious, I walked over to it and began to open the box. My eyes glazed over in wonder as I saw all my army fatigues, my military uniform, and everything that I had during my time in the Airforce.

Never had I been so utterly sentimental, to the point where I let objects overwhelm my sensibilities, but now…the weight of memories, the pressing knowledge of sentimentality, of recalling hope and feeling, of the feeling of belonging, and better memories folding themselves around you.

All my flight training, all the friends I had made, all the joys of soaring through the air.

Freedom!

The one thing that we all seek but is hard to obtain.

Flying was freedom.

As I brought my fatigues close to my chest, smelling all the age that had been absorbed into them, I felt more than saw, a presence. Turning around, I saw my father standing in the doorway.

"Dad," I said, my voice a little hoarse from still being a little swept away.

"Yes," he said, "we kept them."

"All my stuff?"

"Yeah," he said, his tone soft, "we did. We know that you had walked away from it all, but we still thought that you might end up finding your way back."

"You know me very well," I replied.

Folding his arms over his chest, dad looked at me, kind-hearted.

"I'll always know my little Lizzy. So, when will you forgive yourself for something that was not your fault?"

Looking down at my fatigues and presents that my fellow pilots gave me on my birthday, I had felt my heart wake up, perhaps even more than it had before.

"I think that I'm starting to."

"Good."

Smiling at me one last time, he turned around and left.

No more tears, Lizzy.

No more tears.

# EIGHTEEN
# FINDING COMMON GROUND

Sitting in John Carlyle Square, during my lunchbreak, I waited for what might never happen. I texted Darcy to meet him here, at this part of the green. Things were being brought in for the Alexandria Christmas Market and Holiday Craft Show, so I was still on the clock.

While it made sense to be nervous, surprisingly I was not. Despite the fact that I didn't like the idea of him being out there somewhere, and thinking badly about me, I was not going to be too upset about it. After all, I had been honest with him, the whole time, and I had done the right thing. If he didn't show, then that only confirmed that he hadn't changed as much as he thought. Or I thought.

I rested my elbows on my knees, leaned forward and placing my fists under my chin, deep in thought.

This could either go very well, or very poorly, as I played out every scenario that could occur. So deep was I, in thought, that I didn't even notice footsteps approaching.

"Liz?"

Starting, I looked up and saw Darcy standing there, in surprise.

"Darce."

"Did I scare you?"

"I'm fine," I assured him. "Actually, I needed a little jolt, because I'm a little on the sleepy side of things today."

"Oh," he said, awkwardly. "Well, I'm happy to help."

Seeing that we began in a strange place, I thought it would be nice to help him on.

"Sorry," I said. "I began this in a weird place."

He was wearing a long wool scarf that looked handmade, a knit hat, a long warm coat that fitted him well, and he had a thermos in his hand, probably with some coffee or hot chocolate.

"How are you?" I asked.

"Fine," he said, simply, taking a drink from his thermos. "And you?"

"How do you think I am?"

This question caught his attention, and he lowered his thermos. Putting it down on the bench, he sat down next to me.

"Why did you want to meet me here?" he asked.

"I have something to give you."

He raised an eyebrow, apprehensively.

"Don't worry," I assured him, "It's not like a present for you or anything. Believe me, I've learned my lesson about giving guys things randomly. It drives you all up a wall."

"Yeah, for some reason, whenever a woman gives us something randomly, our knee-jerk reaction is to freak out. I don't know why we're built like that. It's instinct, I guess."

"Well, time gave me experience there. It's something that I gave to Anne de Bourgh, and I think her mother would want to have it."

I took out the copy of 'Washington's Farewell Address' and handed it to Darcy. After reading the title, he looked at me.

"She must've read it a dozen times," I said, "to the point that she could memorize certain parts of it. She also wrote notes in the margins, about her opinions on some sections."

"You brought this for her?"

"Yes. At first, I felt that I opened a can of worms when I gave it to her, but it was in a good sort of way. She couldn't stop talking about it. She connected to most parts of it."

I looked him in the eye. "She believed in why she served. You see, when we soldiers go off, fight, and then come back, we wonder if anyone cares? Do people see what we are constantly putting our lives on the line for? Do they see what we do? It's not their fault that they can't, because they are not on the field or in the air with us. Well, I think Anne loved this book, because it reminded her of why we mattered. It led to her being called the Girl Scout a lot. She laughed at that, and sometimes, her virtue made her hard to talk to: after all, who can stand talking to a goody-too-shoes for a long time. But we were good friends, and she meant a lot to me."

Darcy put the book into his inside coat pocket.

"Thank you," he said. "I'll see that my Aunt Catherine gets it. She will appreciate it."

"Good. Well, I'll see you later, because I've got to get back to work."

"Right. See ya."

"See ya."

Turning to walk away, I just realized that I didn't want to end it there.

"For the longest time," I said, "I blamed myself for Anne's death. Then I realized something. She would've hated that. Especially since there really was nothing that I could do. And she never would have wanted you to make me feel wrong either. I don't need this. I don't need your anger. I just needed understanding. Someone to be there for me. And that person was not you. I'll find a friend who it would be."

I nodded goodbye to him and left before he could say anything else.

Like I said before, I got my courage back. And no one would take it from me again.

———

After getting back from dress rehearsal for the Christmas play, I was making dinner for the family, when the doorbell rang.

"Killian, can you see who it is?" I asked, because Josie and

Killian were in the living room, watching tv while they were playing on their I Pads.

"Yes!" Killian replied, going to the door. "It's a guy, Aunt Liz."

"What kind of guy?"

"Uncle Fitzwilliam's cousin."

The surprise was enough. Darcy was at the door. Nervous, at last, I told Killian that it was okay to let him in.

From the kitchen, I heard Darcy's voice as he said some polite things to Killian. Killian told Darcy that he could find me in the kitchen, and soon, his tall figure was framed in the doorway.

I looked at him as I put steak in the oven to broil.

"Good evening," I began.

"Good evening," he echoed. "Nice apron."

I was wearing an apron over my clothes that said 'Halloween or Christmas; don't pick. Just choose both'.

"Thank you," I replied, "sometimes, I have my moments."

Opening a pan on the stove, I began to stir the red beans and rice.

"If you are here because you are angry with me," I said, "I'm not going to apologize."

"I knew that you wouldn't, and it's because you were right. I'm sorry that I put my anger out on you. It was a quick reaction, and I hope that you can forgive me."

Closing the pot again, I looked at him, earnest.

"You mean it?"

"Oh yeah, I mean it. And you know me; I hate apologizing for things. Apologies hurt."

"Darn straight they do. I know the feeling. But I like hearing it."

Darcy smiled.

"I had a feeling that you would. Do you need help with the cooking?"

"Depends. Are you going to stay for dinner?"

"If there's enough food."

"We've got two kids to feed; there's always enough food. You remember that age. You could eat a horse and not gain a pound."

"Yeah," Darcy said, chuckling, "those were the days."

"Well, if you want to make yourself useful, then you can set the table. And remove your jacket, for starters."

Chuckling, Darcy removed his outerwear, hung it up and began to put the dishes and silverware on the table.

"You do know that you can come here for dinner whenever you want, right?" I offered. "Your cousin is not here, so I feel like you need company. I know that being a single man, you want your nights to yourself sometimes, but we're here, you know."

When hearing my offer, Darcy smiled.

"You really are okay with that?"

"Yes, I am. Despite it all, I have one fatal problem."

"And what's that?"

I smiled at him.

"I've grown accustomed to your face."

I threw a dish towel at him, leading to him laughing.

———

Dinner went by easily, and Darcy was happy to know that Bingley would be home in time for Christmas.

"We always managed to get along," Darcy said to me as we were putting away the dishes. "It would be nice to see him again."

"Yeah, Bingley is sure of making friends wherever he goes," I summed up. "Do you ever get a little jealous of those types of people? Those who can dance through life, when the rest of us are walking, and sometimes trudging through the mud?"

"A little," Darcy admitted. "But life is not about being fair, is it?"

"No, it's not. But don't worry. We don't have to be sad about it. People like us serve a purpose."

"Do we? I'm not arguing with you. I just want to know what theory you have come up with about that."

"Well, the way that I see it," I theorized, "curmudgeons like us are like foils that complement easygoing people. We're like the red to their green, the orange to their blue, or the yellow to their purple. We're the complementary color. How could those people be valued without others like us?"

"A sound theory. So, you think that we're curmudgeons?"

"I'm not putting it past me, and that's for sure," I said, "I can be a little curmudgeon-y. You don't think you are?"

"I can be a little curmudgeon, I don't deny."

"There, you see? We complete those expert talkers. We are the other part of the picture."

Josie and Killian dashed into the room, wearing their costumes for the Christmas play. They were singing one of the songs that had been written for the musical. They dashed around us, I sang the song with them, and they rushed into the living room, where they would put on a brief little sketch version of the real show to our parents, Jane, and Mary.

"Remember when we were that tall?" Darcy asked me as I handed him another dish to put in the dishwasher.

"Oh yeah. Back then, Barbie and Polly Pockets reigned supreme in my house. And the American Girl dolls. How about you?"

"I was straight up into video games. I had a few action figures that I played with, but Nintendo was my life."

"Did Richard tell you about the kids Christmas play?"

"Yes, he did. Charles Dickens's lesser-known Christmas story."

"Are you going to come?"

Darcy's eyes shifted, in what looked like confusion.

"Sorry if you don't want to go," I said, "I just thought that I'd offer it."

"It's not that," he said, "I just never thought that I would get invited. Do you want me to go?"

"Well, I think the kids would appreciate it."

"Liz," he said, his eyes intense as he looked at me. "Do you want me to go?"

I looked at him, but found his gaze too direct, so I looked back down at the sink.

"I would like it," I said simply.

"If it makes you comfortable," he declared, "then yes, I would like to go."

I hung the dishtowel over the rack.

"You do know that I'm not afraid of you anymore, right?" I stressed. "I don't want you to feel like I'm going to break around you because I'm not. My courage is here, and I'm not alarmed by you being near me. I just want you to know that, because being worried about you being around me is no way to start a friendship."

When hearing that, Darcy's shoulders slackened, in the manner that Atlas, the Greek Titan, would feel like if the world was taken off his shoulders.

"Thanks. I like that burden being lifted *off my shoulders*."

"I hope you enjoy the play," I said, going into the living room and him following me. "I can't sing for my life, but my voice gets drowned out by the parents in the chorus."

"I'm sure that you'll sound fine."

"Thanks. I need all the encouragement that I can get, and—"

I was interrupted when I got a text message. It was from Delores. When reading it, I smiled to myself.

"What is it?" Darcy asked.

"It's from a friend, O' Curious one. You're coming here for Thanksgiving dinner, right?"

"Yes, unless the plan changed."

I lowered my phone, with an arched expression on my face.

"Now tell me your feelings about going to a pre-Thanksgiving dinner that has food that you probably never tried before."

Darcy raised one of his eyebrows.

"Come again?"

―――

"This is ridiculous," Darcy said as he was driving me to Delores's house. The day had come when I was attending Delores's pre-Thanksgiving dinner and managed to rope Darcy into coming along with me. "This woman doesn't even know me."

"I told her that you would be coming, and you'll like her.

Trust me, she's good at making people feel comfortable. It's her superpower."

"How did I let you talk me into this?"

"Guilt," I answered, smug. "You still feel bad for how you treated me before, and you wanted to make up for it. So, I asked you at a time where you were in a vulnerable place."

Despite driving, Darcy couldn't resist giving me a passioned look.

"You took advantage of me?" he scoffed.

"Yup." I grinned. "It was awesome."

Darcy's eyes shifted from bitterness to amusement.

"You've got a little mean streak in you," he noted.

"Uh huh," I agreed. "I really had a good time doing that. Besides, I could easily come alone, but I think I really did want you to come."

"Why?"

"Because," I admitted, "in a strange way, I like having you around."

Even though he had to focus on the road, I saw Darcy's eyes light up.

"You do?"

"Yes. I think it's because of our history. We've already been through hell and back, so there's nowhere to go but up, with us. We have a history, so we don't have to try and build up a relationship from scratch. And, I don't have to try around you. When you first meet someone, you're always presenting your best self, you know. And it's to the point where you wonder if you are deceiving the other person. You're not showing them your worse side, because you are scared that if you do, they will cut and run. But it's only a matter of time before you show your bad sides."

"But with us, it's different. We already know each other so well, and so the pretense is so low."

"Yeah, that's why I think that it was so easy to ask you to come with me. It's because there was nothing to be apprehensive about. Or do I sound like I'm not making any sense?"

"Yeah, you're a madwoman," Darcy said, with a mischievous look in his eye.

"So says the curmudgeon."

"You called us that."

"And I regret nothing."

We drove on.

———

"Ah, there she is!" Delores cried.

"Yes, here I am," I said, kissing Delores on the cheek. Darcy parked in front of the house, and Delores greeted us at the front door. Darcy hung behind me awkwardly. "And I've got a hang-nail behind me."

"Hangnail?" Darcy repeated.

"I thought we were still in the name-calling phase."

"Oh, right. Creature from the Black Lagoon."

Delores analyzed us both.

"You call each other names. It's decided. You both are on the way to a comfortable relationship."

Darcy looked confused, I told him to just roll with it, and we went inside.

"How is the wedding gown doing?" I asked.

"It's perfect. At first, she was against the choice, but then realized that I was right."

"You're like my youngest sister; can't you not be right for one day?"

"No. Being right all the time is brilliant."

Pulling Darcy close to me, I thought it better to explain.

"They were choosing a wedding gown for one of the women in their family, and I was used as the model who tried on the selections."

"Why were you chosen for it?"

"To this day, I still don't know. But I had fun with it, so I didn't fight the feeling."

"That's something that I've been wondering about. Do you ever see yourself getting married?"

"It all depends on the right man coming my way. But if he doesn't, I won't weep. And how about you?"

"Same, really. If I find the right woman, then totally. But until then, I'm good to go."

I turned to Delores.

"Are all your sisters and daughters here? I want them to meet Darcy."

"Why would they want to meet me?" Darcy asked. "I'm so boring that I'll embarrass you."

"Trust me, you'll have fun."

"Trust her," Delores agreed, "you'll have fun. Wait till you see the food."

"Yup. Wait till you see the food!"

We entered the dining room and there was barely any room because of how many people were there.

"Lizzy brought her new boyfriend!" Delores cried.

"He's not—," I began.

"I'm not—" Darcy overrode.

"Oh, shut up," Delores declared.

"Okay," I said, willing to give in.

"Right," Darcy conceded as well. Sometimes, it's not worth the fight.

"Come and meet everyone," I said, pulling Darcy along.

"You're enjoying this, aren't you?" he added. "Making me the center of attention."

"Yup. It's fun."

"I'm going to embarrass myself."

"Delores and I are here to save you. Right, Delores?"

"It's what I do," Delores said, pinching Darcy's cheek. "You're looking peaky. You need some enchiladas."

"Enchiladas?" Darcy's eyes perked up. "Oh, lead the way then."

Everyone laughed. Delores introduced him to everyone as she led us to the food. Along the way, I kissed every abuelas cheek because that was the custom to always kiss the grandmothers in the set. The family welcomed me with open arms, I felt the warmth of the moment, and Darcy had no choice but to relax a little bit. Delores had that effect on people.

Being a tall and handsome man, naturally the ladies present

must have found him impressive. That being said, they were not the type who were intimidated by intensely striking masculinity, so Darcy's natural awe-inspiring demeanor did not render them thunderstruck, or silent. They were verbose and eager to get to know him. It got to the point where I barely got near him, because Delores and her sisters were always moving around him, putting food on his plate, and telling him about which sister cooked it.

All I could do was sit on the other side of the table and watch Darcy be smothered by feminine attitudes; I loved it! Every now and again, he and I would steal a glance at each other before he was made to answer another question. Seriously, the ladies were hurling queries about his life like a tennis player serves a pitch. They wanted to know everything about him, and I found myself positively intrigued.

"He's different than Wickham," someone said next to me. I turned and saw Delores's daughter, Gloriana.

"Hey, Glor," I said, turning back to Darcy and watching the women faun over him. "Yeah, he is. I take it that you heard about how my relationship with Wickham ended, eh?"

"Yeah. My mom is good at bringing the gang together to bring down the trash."

"You're lucky, when it comes to having moms, you know."

"Oh, I know. Believe me," she said, also watching the women, "I know."

"Like Wickham," I elaborated, "I knew Darcy since I was in my teens. But here's where it gets weird. Wickham and I were always friendly, from the very beginning. And Darcy and I never were. He was always mean to me back in high school. Very mean."

"No way!"

"Oh yes, way. We were arch enemies."

"What changed?" Gloriana asked me, leaning into me, becoming intrigued. "What happened? I mean, you're bringing him here, now, so did you guys make up?"

"We did, by pure accident." I gave Gloriana a side glance. "You are interested in us? Why?"

Gloriana shrugged.

"There's this guy at school..."

My eyes widened, and it was my turn to become intrigued.

"What's his name?"

"Damon," she responded.

"How handsome is he?" I guessed.

"Very."

"And how big of a jerk is he?"

Gloriana rolled her eyes.

"He's so mean. And never smiles. It's like he's always kind of angry at life. And I don't get why. He's handsome and talented. So, what's he so mad about?"

"He's a teenager; during that time of our lives, we usually wake up that way. You're naturally happy, and that's good. But let me guess—despite that this guy is a lot of misery, you still can't help but stare at him sometimes, right? Or be curious about him."

"Yeah. I feel dumb and like a walking cliché."

"It's okay," I said, "I used to judge girls who were like that, but then I realized that I was being prejudiced. It's natural to be curious about those types because those type of guys invoke curiosity. And now you're thinking that this Damon guy is not so out of reach as you suspected, because I'm here with a man who was my high school archenemy." I grinned. "Did I hit the nail on the head?"

"Yeah," Gloriana replied, sighing. "I can't help it. For some reason, I can't help but like him."

"Does he show any interest in you?" I asked.

"No. I don't even register to him. In fact, I might as well not even exist."

"I only existed to Darcy, when he was making fun of me and laughing me out of the classroom. Glor, if you are okay with it, can I give you some advice?"

"Why not? I'm hopeless."

"You're not hopeless; you're just fifteen. First, it's natural to like someone, even when they don't like you back. It's not a sign of weakness. The world has turned and will always turn because we humans tend to fall in love with people who don't love us.

I've been there myself. But when Darcy and I were complete enemies, I didn't waste time liking him. The only reason that we are friends now is because time helped things. Lots and lots of time. But I didn't wait around, hoping his character could change, or for him to be the redeemed bad boy. Those types only change when they want to. The best advice that I could give is not to pay any attention to Damon. First, it will give you peace of mind. And secondly, you can still like him in secret, while keeping your options open. And third, usually those types of guys are actually more responsive to women who don't pay any attention to them. Some people are ironic that way."

"People who like those who do not like them back?"

"Precisely. This guy might be that type. I'm just saying this: like him, but don't waste time on him. If you both are meant to date, time will help it. And only flirt with him when he starts showing an interest."

"And if he doesn't? Like, what if he never comes around to liking me?"

"Then accept that you're going to like someone for a long time, but also let him go, and find someone else more worthwhile to flirt with."

"People make fun of flirts."

"Many people hate everything. But it's shameful flirts that get annoying to be around. But flirt with someone who you are inter-ested in, and that's okay. You're only young once, you know. But seriously, don't look at Darcy and me as an example that, one day, Damon is going to wake up and then realize that you are the girl of his dreams. That only happens in novels, which is why we love to read them so much. But if he is not going to show interest in you, find someone who does show interest. Believe me, it's better for your peace of mind."

"I just wish I could get passed him."

I sighed.

"Sorry. We can never click our fingers and then get passed an annoying crush that we have on someone. This is just something that you're going to have to wade through for a while. Is he in your school?"

"Yes."

"Oh boy. Is he in your grade?"

"Yup."

"Oh darn. Is he in many of your classes?"

"All of them."

I felt so sorry for her.

"By god!" I declared. "You can't catch a break, can you?"

"No, I can't. I turned around, and there he was. I walk in another direction, and there he is. I can't escape his face."

Truly, at that time of your life, there are no words to give the pained teenager. You can offer all the advice in the world, but at that time of life, love is like a knife that keeps stabbing you in the stomach and pulling at your insides to the point where it feels as if you are bleeding inwardly.

I am happy being older. My body is not as limber as it used to be, I fall asleep more, I get tired easily, and I must run to the restroom quite a bit, but it's better than the angst, the awkwardness and the sense of inadequacy of being in one's teens. Give me bills! Give me mortgage! Give me responsibility! But do not give me homework! Do not give me peer pressure! Do not give me sixteen-year-age acne!

I swear, how we humans survive adolescence will always be a miracle that bears no description.

Thus, all that I could do was pat Gloriana on the shoulder and offer her the only solace that I could give her.

We were interrupted by Guan, who told Gloriana to bring out the dish that she made for dinner. Now that some of the food was eaten, there was more room for other dishes to be brought out. When she went to the kitchen, Guan asked me if I was enjoying the food.

"Oh yeah," I said, with very little left on my plate. "I love food that has flavor. Thanks to you and Delores, I feel comfortable here. Thanks for that, Guan. I know that I'm an outsider."

"Outsider?" Guan repeated, with a raised eyebrow. "You know this family, Liz. You never were an outsider."

I smiled.

"Thanks. I suppose, the second that I sat down next to Delores on the plane, the writing was on the wall, wasn't it?"

"Yes, it very much was." When looking at Delores, I saw his love for her in his eyes. It was love. True love.

"You adore her, don't you?" I asked, even though I knew the answer.

"Yes. With all my heart."

How simple it was said. How easy and comfortable he was as he said it. A man who was not there to play safe with his heart, but had taken a gamble, put his heart out there for Delores to grab hold of it, hold fast to it, and he had won. He—had—won.

"That's the thing with me," I said, "I never really had that. I've dated, as you know, but I never had someone look at me the way that you look at Delores. I suppose that left me a little stale when it came to understanding true love."

"It's not you," Guan assured me. "Love—true love that is—is the one thing that we humans all need, but it's the hardest thing to obtain. Perhaps it should be hard, because if it was easy to get ahold of, we might get spoiled because of it. Also, you gotta remember that Delores and I didn't start dating until I was forty. And she's the main big love of my life. You young people need to remember that it's not over at your age. You're still right at the beginning of things. Love can be found later, you know."

How unique it can be to hear men talk in such a way! I'm sure that they all feel such things, but to talk about it, to give words to it, is another thing entirely.

"Which reminds me," Guan said, "I'm sorry… about George."

Ah, Wickham! I should have known that Guan was probably feeling a little guilty about what Wickham had done to me. Now was the moment where he had plucked up the courage to mention it.

"Thank you," I said, "but don't worry. I know that it was not your fault, and I will certainly not take my heartbreak out on you."

When hearing that, Guan's shoulders relaxed, and he obviously felt a great weight lift off his shoulders. Seeing that he might have needed me to say more, I decided to bear my soul.

"At first," I elaborated, "I blamed myself for not seeing what he was. But it was impossible to, as one of my sisters pointed out. So, I stopped getting angry, and just chalked it all up to another hard life lesson. But thank you for being nice about it and acknowledging what he was like. Especially since he is your friend."

"Oh, I've never let a friendship blind me from what someone is. That was another hard life lesson that I learned, too."

"When it comes to life lessons, there are so many of those, aren't they?"

"A list without end," Guan said, knowingly.

Smiling, I turned back to Darcy, just as one of Delores's sisters asked him about what his intentions were, regarding me.

Darcy's cheeks went pale, his eyes widened when he turned to me, and I couldn't help but laugh. That led to breaking the tension and Darcy couldn't help but laugh either.

"I don't know," was all that Darcy could utter. "I don't know, really."

––––––

The dinner proved to be very easy and fun. The food was great. The company was great, and Darcy and I ended up having a good time.

Just when it was time for us to leave, Delores approached me as Darcy was in the other room, getting his coat on.

"I like him," Delores stated her opinion, clear and sharp.

"You do, eh?" I said, giving her a sly look. "Well, I have every right to ask why you think so? Come on, tell me! I'm dying to know everything that you think about my friendship with him?"

"Friendship?" Delores echoed, with a knowing look. "That's all there is between you both?"

"Well, yeah," I declared, obstinate. "Of course, that's all there is. Our past is too complicated for it to be anything else."

"Actually, your past is perfect for the beginning of something greater."

I squinted, and then realized everything.

"Ah, so that's what you and your sisters were up to. You were asking Darcy about his entire life, and got every secret about his history with me, didn't you?"

"Guilty as charged," Delores answered, admitting that I was right. "But don't punish me for it."

"I'm not. You'll get no verdict from me. Now, tell me what your ultimate point is. I'm not afraid to hear it, even if I don't see the logic of it."

"Lizzy, look," Delores said, taking my hands in hers. "I know that you're not the type to rush into a romance just because another woman told you to, so I can tell you this, and know that you will do the right thing, in the right kind of way. I think you two might fall in love one day."

My eyes widened in alarm.

Darcy was handsome, that was true. And yet, his looks never reached me, because I had been scarred by everything underneath, for so long. To the point where the emotional wounds were permanent. Me and Darcy? That was impossible. From my head to my heart, it seemed like the least likely thing to ever happen.

"Del," I exclaimed, while still keeping my voice low. "You can't be serious."

"I'm smiling, but believe me, I'm very serious."

"You can't be."

"But I am."

"No, you're not."

"As serious as the grave."

"Graves aren't always serious."

"Yes, they are."

I groaned.

"Okay, yes, they are," I gave in, "but seriously!"

"I thought we were being serious."

"No, seriously, '*seriously*'. And be serious. There's no way that Darcy could like me, or me like him. There is too much water under the bridge. *Violent* water under the bridge."

"And that's why it's likely to happen," Delores continued, "I believe that men and women can be friends, and always be friends. But with you two, there's too much unity of looks between each other, of natural comfort around each other, and it's because of your past.

"With you and Wickham, you had a good past, and all the hell happened in your present. But with this Darcy guy, all your hardship is in your past, and now you both can move forward. Now, there's nowhere to go but 'up'. He's told me everything, and you feel comfort around each other, because of it. You've both suffered the worst, and so you can connect now. That level of connection can easily lead to love. But like I said, you're not the type to get confused about your relationship with Darcy just because I hinted that you might fall in love one day. I know that you will keep on going down the path that is natural to you."

I was a little flabbergasted, but Delores was right. The shock was temporary, and it gave way to me taking her advice from an observational standpoint, and not as law. Delores was making a prediction, but I now knew to always do things based on my instinct and what felt natural.

Right now, the idea of Darcy and I was not natural.

So, I would do nothing to alter the course of what was growing in between us.

"You know me very well," I said, kissing Delores on the cheek. "A little too well. I still don't believe that what you predict will ever come true. But I see the logic behind it."

"Good. Always keep an open mind but trust your instincts. That's the best way to live."

"Hey, Liz," Darcy said, getting my coat, "don't forget this."

"Forget my security blanket?" I said, bouncing up to him and taking my coat. "Never!"

"Well, my lady," Darcy said, "time to head out."

Darcy turned, thanked everyone for a great evening, I echoed the sentiments, and we left.

As we headed to his car, Darcy looked wonderfully happy.

"Penny for your cheeriness?" I asked.

"I just can't believe it," he remarked. "I had fun. I can't believe it. I actually had fun."

"Never doubt me," I replied, opening the car door.

"You know I'm a natural doubter," he replied, also opening his door.

"I know, Mr. Scrooge," I said, putting on my seatbelt. "But still, sometimes, you gotta take a little bit on faith."

"True," he said, starting the car. "True."

We drove back to Alexandria.

"It's bizarre," Darcy uttered as we drove onto a main road.

"I never met Delores—not until today. And yet, she's so—"

"Comfortable to be around and talk to," I finished his sentence.

"Exactly. I didn't think that I would be that way, and I'm not used to being around people that I haven't met before. I don't really have that talent, you see, of talking with strangers, easily. But with Delores, I didn't feel apprehensive. I was myself, and that was enough for her."

"It's her superpower. Did I tell you that I only knew her for a couple hours, before she invited me to her daughter's birthday party."

"Oh, yeah, Delores told me that you attended Gloriana's quinceanera. When she turned fifteen."

"Yeah, I did. And I felt like I would be evil for not going."

"You took a chance," he replied, giving me a side glance.

"Yeah, I took a chance, and this time, it did not shoot me in the foot. Don't you ever like when that happens? When chance doesn't shoot you in the foot?"

"I do. But, you see, there's too much risk with chance, and of giving other people *chances*."

"The fear of getting hurt," I deduced.

"Exactly. The fear of getting hurt."

"It's natural because you can easily get hurt. And the fear of letting the wrong person in is excruciating. It leads to us all closing ourselves off to people. There's safety in closing ourselves off. There's protection."

"Yeah, and I like being safe. I like protecting myself."

"Of course, you do," I assured him, "that's the only problem with remaining safe, we run the chance of not seeing what else is out there, that we might find pleasure in. We never see what might be coming, just around the riverbend."

Darcy's eyes lit up.

"Did you just quote the movie, 'Pocahontas'?"

"It's a darn good song, with a great message. Yes. I stand by that movie. You had a lead character who looked like a mature-looking woman, and who had actual conversations with the male hero, of her own choosing. And it ends with the two of them separating, showing that sometimes relationships don't always end with the people together. But the bond remains the same. That's life, in a nutshell. And it's a movie that has two people, from different cultures, fall in love. Pocahontas was a woman who was not afraid of being curious about difference, and the hero was a ruthless guy who had no problem in killing her people, and then changed over time."

"But the movie is historically inaccurate."

Despite the truth to this, I also accepted another truth, and that truth was something that I would always stick to.

"Historically inaccurate to who and what? Inaccurate to accounts of the colonizers who lied about their exploits and adventures, to get people to finance their expeditions, and to hide their cruelty and crimes? Inaccurate to what story? Secondly, I don't go to animated movies for history. I know, going into them, to expect inaccuracy. So, I go for the story, and it's a good one. And thirdly, those who criticized the film became like the people who never wanted to see a movie like that.

"Pocahontas is a movie about two people of different cultures, backgrounds, and ethnicities, falling in love. It's also about attacking difficult subject matter in a way that worked for kids. It's also about preaching to people to not fear difference, to make sure that you fall in love with someone over conversation, rather than only at first sight. It also teaches that you can fall in love with someone that you were raised to despise. You can overcome prejudice, and the pride that you once used to defend your prejudices."

As I said this, I turned to Darcy, and felt my confidence and inner peace stir within me. Taking in his tall frame, his strong countenance, I wondered about him, suddenly. But not in the usual way that I do, but in a whole different view. I was seeing another side of him, a different shade, or tint of the man who I had despised for so long. There was more to him now, as there ought to be. He had grown, in more ways than the physical, or mental. But the emotional…the side that matters most—he had changed.

"Liz?" he asked, noting how quizzically that I looked at him. "What is it?"

I jerked, in the way that a person jerks, when they have woken up from a daze or daydream, they flinch and then they look away from the direction that they were gazing at.

"Nothing," I rushed out, "I just realized that I fell into a bit of a rant, didn't I?"

"Yes, you did." Darcy chuckled. "But I kind of set you up for it, so that's on me, really."

"Thanks for understanding my right to talk about something I was asked about," I replied, lighthearted, "I'm just saying that how can I hate a film that is everything kids need to be exposed to and learn from? And as for the historically inaccurate stuff, well, until we have Pocahontas's actual story of what happened, from her own words, then we will never fully know what happened.

"Always remember, half of history is guessing, the other half is bias. And that the same people who wanted it not to happen, because of historic inaccuracy, ended up destroying a movie that promoted acceptance, and made all those who never wanted to see movies like that happen, satisfied. They scared studios from making movies like that happen again, and soured diversity, while claiming to care about diversity."

"Ah, the trapping of fandom: you kill the very thing that you are claiming to save."

"So true. But whether you like it or not, you gotta admit, 'Just Around the Riverbend' is a great song. I used to know all the lyrics by heart."

Darcy's eyes squinted, and I saw the mischief in his eyes. He was planning something.

"I dare you to try it."

"No way," I scoffed, rolling my eyes. For all the gold in the world, what was he asking me to do? How could I do it? I could sing in a chorus, but singing alone was a different thing entirely. I sounded like a screeching crow alone. "I can't sing, for my life. I can only carry a tune when I'm with other people, who drown out my voice."

"I'll sing it with you, if you like?"

Rolling my tongue behind my teeth, I was now very amused.

"You will sing it with me?"

"Well," he replied, his cheeks getting a little red. "I'll sing the parts I know."

"No," I grunted.

"Come on."

"No," I stressed.

"Seriously?"

"Come on…"

"I dare you!"

Now I was grinding my teeth. He dared me!

"Darn it," I hissed. "I've never been good at turning down a dare."

"I know. I had a feeling that would work."

"Fine." I sighed. "Promise me that you will not laugh at my singing voice?"

Darcy grinned wickedly.

"I will make no promise of the kind."

"Jerk."

"Dweeb."

Gathering my courage, I began to sing:

"What I love most about rivers is
you can't step in the same river twice.
The water's always changing, always flowing.
But people, I guess, can't live like that.
We all must pay a price,
To be safe, we lose our chance of ever knowing."

"What's around the riverbend," Darcy began to sing with me. When he joined in, our voices began to blend together. "I look once more, just around the riverbend." As he drove along, and we were closer to home, our voices began to blend together. "Beyond the shore, where the gulls fly free. Don't know what for. What I dream, the day might send, just around the riverbend."

"For me. Coming for me," I sang alone, when Darcy did not know the lyrics to that part.

We continued to sing the song, and as we neared the end, we turned onto Longbourn Road.

Should I choose the smoothest course?" I sang, "steady as the beating drum. Should I marry Kocoum? Is all my dreaming at an end?"

As the tune was coming to a close, Darcy remembered the last bit, so as he slowed down, at the front of our house, we finished the song together.

"Or do you still wait for me, dream giver?" he and I sang, looking into each other's eyes. "Just around the riverbend?"

Deeply…that was how far we fell into each other's eyes. I cannot tell any of you what I felt at that moment. Because some-times—words aren't there. They never can be, or ever would be. In some instances, and encounters, there can be no words for them. It is felt, and not spoken. It is lived, and not uttered. It is real. That much I do know. And I think he knew that, as did I.

"We really are friends now," I managed to get out. "I mean, I knew that we were getting along. But we really are friends now. In a big way."

"Yeah," Darcy said, leaning back in his car seat, equally as contemplative. "We really are."

I wanted to smile, but I didn't know how.

"Well, I'll be damned."

"I know, right?" he said simply.

The ending was awkward because it had no choice but for it to be.

"Well," I said, "I'll see you later. You're still coming for thanksgiving dinner, right?"

"Yeah. I am. See you in a couple days."

With one last knowing look between each other, I got out of the car, walked into the house, and saw Darcy drive off, down Longbourn, and back to his cousin's apartment. Once inside, I was happy to find out that no one was downstairs. That left me to walk upstairs, to my room, and find the peace there.

When alone, with just Vatalie on the rug by my nightstand, I collapsed on the bed, frustrated.

What was happening?

Delores could not be right!

But that was the problem.

Delores was always right.

No! I would not fall in love just because I was told to.

What was I feeling?

# NINETEEN
# THE THROES OF THANKSGIVING

So far, everything up until thanksgiving was uneventful. Wickham was out of my life for good, and there were no more thoughts to shed on that score. That part of my life was over, and I was glad over it.

As for Mary King, I would just avoid her like the plague. There was nothing for me to do, and we had every right to be perfect strangers.

Of course, I would naturally find myself to be wrong about that, and there were conflicts ahead of me…but now is not the time to discuss it.

After all, it was Thanksgiving!

In other words, it was the day that Henry Atkins was coming to meet the family for the first time and see Mary in the throes of her pregnancy.

Everyone was looking forward to it, while equally dreading it. Except for Lydia, who was just excited.

"I never thought Mary would be the sister who would give me the most excitement at the most boring holiday in this house," Lydia said as she was taking out the cranberry sauce from the can and putting it into one of our special potted bowls.

"Try to be less analytical," I advised her. "When this Henry Atkins man shows up, wait till you size him up."

"It's too late, I already have. Just like I already know what is going to happen."

"Already?" I asked, checking on the macaroni and cheese in the oven.

"I've known what's going to happen since Mary called him. First, this whole thing is going to be awkward for him. We can try and be nice, but there's no way that he can like any of us just yet. But he will stick with Mary, and stay in her life, for the sake of their kid. But they will never actually get together, until they have another kid. Which they will have."

"Why will they want another kid?"

"They are both in the military; they believe in strength in numbers and having a close friend. It's always better to have two kids, who can grow up together and never be lonely. Balance in numbers. And, when all is said and all is done, two is better than one, in the long run. And since Atkins is willing to meet us, him and Mary are going to get intimate again, even though they are afraid of each other right now."

"You think they are afraid of each other?" Jane asked as she began to open a can of mustard greens and poured them into a pot.

"They are going to have a kid together, and the kid was not planned," Lydia declared. "Of course, they are scared of each other."

"You're right," Jane said, "diving into parenting is like diving into the unknown."

"Well," I acknowledged, resigned. "What happens, will happen."

Mary called Lydia upstairs to choose what movie that we would watch for Thanksgiving, leaving Jane and I alone in the kitchen.

"You're being nicer to Lydia," Jane observed. "What brought that on?"

"I just realized that I had to accept that she will be right a lot, and that I should stop being mad at her because of it."

Jane smiled approvingly at me.

"Progress," she determined, tasting the mustard greens. "Almost done."

I was just removing the ham from the oven, just as the doorbell rang.

"Do you think that's Henry?" Jane asked.

"No, I think it's Darcy," I said, removing my apron. "He's bringing some mashed potatoes."

I walked through the dining room, around Josie and Killian as they were putting all the plates and silverware on the dining room table.

"It's looking good," I complimented them.

"Thanks, Aunt Liz," Josie replied as Killian pulled her hair.

At the front door, I looked out the window and saw Darcy standing there with a container in his hands. I opened the door and ushered Darcy into the house, took the mashed potatoes, while he took off his coat.

"Sorry for the plain clothes," he said, wearing some lounge pants, with a turtleneck, "but I like eating in comfortable clothes."

"No worries," I said, "we're eating a lot, so who wants to drop food on their nice clothes?"

"Precisely. Besides, when I eat a lot, my stomach expands, and I hate having to wear jeans, because they get too tight."

I arched an eyebrow, very amused.

"So, we've gotten to the part of our friendship where we can say anything to each other, no matter how weird?"

Darcy chuckled.

"It's okay," I said, "I like weird."

Josie and Killian said 'hey' to Darcy as he followed me into the kitchen.

"They like you, you know?" I observed.

"They do?" Darcy questioned, looking back at the kids.

"Yeah, they do. They think you are interesting."

"I can't think why. I'm no less boring than any other adult."

"You have a way about you," I said, "enjoy it. Jane, Darcy brought the mashed potatoes."

"Excellent," Jane said, "Darce, should I put the potatoes in the oven, or is it warm enough?"

"Nuke it in the oven," Darcy said, "it's warm, but not hot."

"Got it."

"I added some cheese, chives and bacon in the potatoes," Darcy said, "I hope that's okay."

"Don't worry," I assured him, "this family likes flavor."

"Good."

"I need to get changed for dinner," Jane said, who was wearing sweatpants.

I was wearing casual pants, that were stretchy, but Jane liked it when things looked just right for herself.

"Don't worry," I said, "Darcy and I will finish getting everything ready."

"Thanks," Jane said, going upstairs, leaving Darcy and I alone.

"She makes me feel inadequate," Darcy said.

"No," I assured him, "Jane is just one of those lovely women who believes in wearing the right thing at the right time. I refuse to try so hard."

"Me too," he said, conspiratorially. "Which is strange, because when I was younger, I was all about having the right look. Moving the right way and being impressive. But then, something changed."

"You realized that it's okay to be lazy sometimes," I wondered, understanding that way of thinking.

"Maybe, but it was more than that. When you are younger, you worry that everyone's eyes are on you, always commenting on you, and always judging you—which can be true. Usually, people are judging you, and so you base much of the way you are around that. Then I got older, and I realized that no one was looking at me that much anymore. And the older I got, I realized that no one was looking at me at all. So, what was the point of putting myself through much labor when I can just be comfortable with my own simple way?"

I transferred his potatoes to an oven safe pan and put it into the oven as it was warming up. I felt connected to him, because I seconded his emotion.

"And when you realized that you wasted so much of your

time worried about what others thought of you," I gathered, "what did you think?"

"That I regretted all that time I could have been doing other things than worry about what others thought," he realized. "I could have written a whole symphony with all the time that I wasted."

"And I could have written a whole series," I added, "but regret is natural, and so is wiping away the slate. So, you know what? How about we acknowledge that we wasted time on regret too much and move forward with it all? I regret what happened to Anne for years, but I can't change the past. So, I can go forward and let's look for the good times. And remember the past in a way that it makes us smile."

Darcy put his mashed potatoes container in the dishwasher, and then turned to me, leaning against the counter.

"I suppose that I could do that," he accepted, looking comfortably sensuous.

"So can I," I replied, grinning. "I think that I like this kind of arrangement. Don't you?"

"Very," he answered. Though he didn't smile, his eyes twinkled. That was good enough for me.

"We must try to remain friends," I finalized. "I like us being friends."

"So do I."

"And to think," I continued, "finally we got around to being better at this, and that's at the time where you will be going to Georgia soon."

"We can still see each other."

I shook my head.

"Life on a military base does not work at keeping friends outside of it," I said, "you know that secret rule, like I do. But if you ever come through Virginia, you can stay with us."

"You won't see yourself going down to Georgia to visit me," he offered, with a hint of a wish in his tone.

Astonishment was an understatement. I practically dropped the large spoon in my hands and turned to him. Clearly, he must have mistaken my surprise for discomfort.

"Sorry," he said, "I was being stupid for offering."

"No, it's fine," I replied, to assure him. "it's not that. I'm just surprised that you would even want me to come down and see you."

Despite myself, I couldn't help but start to chuckle. This led to Darcy giving a half grin.

"What's that about?" he asked.

"I'm just amused that we're friends. Isn't this fascinating?"

"Yes, I guess it is."

For a moment, we both just stared at each other, which left us to feel somewhat awkward. Our stare was keenly felt, and was so long that I believed, rather than knew, that something was passing between us, that was something like warmth.

It was frightening.

A strong bond is always frightening.

I suppose it's because it's real.

But no! It couldn't be…or could it?

Suddenly I felt a heat rise within me, and the tension was thick and overwhelming.

Just as I began to feel myself fall into his eyes, the doorbell rang.

To quote the famous TV show…saved by the bell!

I could very well believe that Darcy was equally happy for the interruption. For as I said that tension had grown too intense.

"Who could that be?" Darcy asked, taking a few steps toward the living room. "Isn't everyone here?"

"Except for one," I uttered, but it felt like my voice was coming from miles away, and not from myself. Then I realized who it could be, and my tone was light and amused. "Oh, I know who it is."

"Who?"

"Henry Atkins. The father of Mary's child."

When hearing that, Darcy's eyes widened.

"It is?"

"Oh yeah," I said, *my eyes* wide with interest. "This is going to be one very interesting thanksgiving dinner."

"Yes," Darcy replied, equally as interested. "Yes, it will."

I gave him a side glance.

"You're enjoying this, aren't you?" I asked.

"Yeah, actually."

I arched one of my eyebrows, willing to get in on a secret.

"I have a confession to make," I said, in hushed tones.

"What?" he asked, eating a string bean, which I smacked his hand away.

"I'm also enjoying this," I said, sharing his feeling.

Once again, our eyes seemed to link and the connection, that astonishingly delightful connection, found its way between us, and it was a hard thing to feel.

This was not my imagination.

Nor was it Delores pressing her advice on me.

Nothing could ever convince me to feel something that I did not feel. However, what is, is what is. Just like what was is what was. I cannot pretend, nor deny, what is self-evident, and what ought to be self-evident.

Something was growing between us.

Could it be attraction?

Could it be romance?

Or was it just still friendship?

No!

These questions are too hard to have, too hard to contemplate, and too hard to answer, then.

After all, it was Thanksgiving.

It was a time for family, and for awkward introductions.

Therefore, I must not think about this right now and should wait till the evening was over.

If there was one thing that I had not lost, it was my self-control.

Tearing my eyes away from Darcy, I removed my apron, and he followed me to the living room, where we were waiting for Henry Atkins to enter, followed by Mary, who had greeted him at the door.

"I got to see him!" Josie cried, rushing to the window in the living room and peeking out of it.

"Me too!" Killian said and joined her. The rest of us, being adults, had to wait until they came in.

"Poor guy," Darcy whispered in my ear. "He's literally been forced to make a grand entrance."

"There's nothing that he can do but disappoint everyone," I said, "because he can't possibly live up to expectations." I gave Darcy a side long glance. "Do you like making an entrance?"

"Not remotely," Darcy said, shaking his head, "give me the back of the room, any day, and I make a spectacular wallflower."

"There was a time where you were different, where you liked being the center of attention. We're all so different from the wonder years, aren't we?"

"We had better be."

"True. We had better be."

We were interrupted when the door opened again, and Mary entered. At this point, she was beginning to show. The man who entered with her was of medium height and average looks. He had long hair that he kept tied in the back and had high cheek-bones. His eyes widened at seeing so many people expecting him. He was evidently taken aback.

Due to the cold, he was wearing a long brown coat that came down to his knees, a handmade thick scarf, earmuffs, and gloves. Underneath were some corduroy pants, and boots.

"Oh, god," Henry Atkins replied, "everyone hates me already?"

We all moaned and exaggerated 'no', to reassure him, and Mary joined in as she began to take his coat from him.

"Don't worry," Mary assured him, putting his coat in the closet. "They want to meet you." When finished, she turned to us and stood by Henry. "Henry, I would like you to meet my family." She introduced us all, one by one, and then mentioned the ones that were absent. "I have another sister, Kitty, but she's not on leave and is back at the fort. Her fiancé, Richard, is also back on duty."

"Will they be here for Christmas?" Henry asked.

"Maybe," Mary replied, "they might get time off, because of their recent engagement. Their sergeants are friendly with them.

And Jane's husband, Bingley, is also coming home for the holidays."

"Oh, where is he stationed?"

"Japan," Jane answered. "He's stationed over in Japan, at Fort Netherfield."

"I was stationed there, before," Henry Atkins said, more at ease when seeing that he had something to contribute to the conversation. "It's one of the better places that I've been stationed at. The Japanese were nice to us when we were there."

"Bingley likes it," Jane said, "but he prefers being closer to home."

"By looking at your family, I can see why," Henry said, looking at Josie and Killian, who were still standing by the window. "You both were the first faces that I saw."

"We wondered if you would be ugly," Josie uttered, without thinking.

"Josie!" Jane cried. "I'm sorry, Mr. Atkins."

"It's okay," Henry smoothed over, "and please call me, Henry." He turned to the kids. "I know that I'm not the best-looking guy in the world, but hopefully you won't think that I'm very ugly."

"You're not very ugly."

We all suppressed a laugh.

"I'll call that a compliment then," Henry Atkins responded. At last, Henry turned to our parents, still standing next to Mary. "Mr. and Mrs. Bennet."

"Henry," Mama said, "it's nice to meet you."

Dad was silent. I knew what he was thinking, but Darcy couldn't help but acknowledge it.

"Your dad wants to kill him," Darcy whispered. "No matter what Henry does, he got Mary pregnant at the worst time. That's too hard for any father to forgive."

"You're right," I whispered back. "I'm not a father, but I get it."

"Henry," Dad uttered, his tone pleasant, but it held a slight malice under it. I understood it. My dad had every right to be a little off-putting. Fathers are much better at scaring men into treating their daughters well and chastising them for not protecting their daughters when a mistake is made. Protective dads do have their virtues, as you know.

"Mr. Bennet," Henry said, "I guess you have a reason to be angry with me."

"You bet I do."

Darcy leaned in, over my shoulder, watching the scene with interest. Since his face was close to mine, I felt his heat radiate from his body. I was enraged, secretly, at how affected I was by the proximity of his body to mine. With his face being so close, our eyes were no more than six inches apart.

I read his mind.

I sensed his thoughts.

"Dad," Mary began.

"It's okay, Mar," Henry said, "I get it." Henry turned back to Mom and Dad. "I really didn't mean for things to go so badly, and that I put Mary through this. But you need to understand, Mary and I were both pilots on the same base. And she was better than me, so naturally, she took me under her wing. I, kind of, had no choice but to get a little crazy about her, right?"

Dad sighed, a little resigned at that answer, but mom, who knew how to be the hostess, approached Henry and was welcoming to him.

"Now that's a good answer," she said, leading Henry into the dining room. "All my daughters are good pilots, and great women. You had no choice but to notice it, which is good. I cannot help but praise them for things. It's a mother's habit, you know."

"I get it," Henry said, "and that's precisely how it should be. I'm sorry that I didn't do things correctly."

"Well, the fact that you are here now, and protecting Mary now, is good. You're not running away, and that means a lot."

"Thanks."

"Great," Darcy said, rolling his eyes.

"What?" I asked, curious. "Unless he's a charming liar, he doesn't seem bad."

"That's the problem. Your mom likes him already because he's charming. Now I have no chance of getting her to completely like me, because she's got him as an example. He's a man who didn't protect Mary when they were together, but since he's making up for it, she thinks he's awesome."

Reading the emotion behind his words made me almost laugh.

"You're jealous," I augmented, amused.

"I am not," he retorted, obstinate.

"Oh, that is such a lie. Darce, you're irrationally jealous." I pursed my lips and teased him. "Yes, you are. Yes, you are."

Darcy rolled his head, and gave in.

"Okay, maybe I'm a little jealous," he said, "there goes hopes of your mom favoring me."

"You'll grow on her, and either way, it's going to be okay. We're friends now, and I like you. So, what everyone else thinks about you doesn't really matter to me."

Darcy couldn't resist smiling.

"I guess that's what's most important."

"It had better be. Now come on. It's Thanksgiving. Let's get stuffed."

"Until we hate the sight of food," Darcy inferred.

"Then give us a couple of days, and we'll like food again."

"True. It's a vicious cycle."

"Welcome to human nature, eh?" I pointed out.

"Yup. When will we learn?"

"Give us a few more centuries of existence. Then we'll get things right."

"Before we go the way of the dinosaur."

"Oh, we hope we don't go down that path," I declared. "That would be so inconvenient."

Darcy laughed.

I made him laugh again.

We were getting along better and better.

―――

Dinner was excellent, and Henry proved to be a very nice and consistent sort of man. Steady, if you could call it that. I know that word is rarely used nowadays, but it did seem to describe him well.

By the end of the dinner, our parents liked him.

"I don't think I could ever fully forgive him for ruining Mary's career," Dad secretly hissed to me. "But if there's one guy who would ruin it, he seems like the best one out of the rest of the male species."

"Ah, to be a Dad," I said, kissing his cheek. "And to have no choice but to hate men in general."

"It's our privilege." Dad looked at me, his eyes losing their wittiness and therefore having no choice but to turn to sincerity, and closeness. "Lizzy, promise me, that if you do ever get married, that he's a good guy and does most things right, and goes about it in the proper way. Because I don't think that I can do this again."

I pat his arm, lovingly.

"Dad, don't worry. First, there's a large chance that I'm never going to get married. But if I do, I promise: morally, the man I marry will be nothing short of a legend."

He kissed my forehead and moved to the other side of the room, to avoid Mom.

Believe me, they were once very much in love. Time is simply a cruel mistress; it either nourishes things, or tarnishes things.

When dinner came to an end, I was in the kitchen, putting everything in lock-in-lock containers. When I heard someone enter, I thought it was Darcy, who had remained close to me through most of the dinner.

"Coming to help me?" I asked, without looking over my shoulder to see who it was.

"If you want help," Henry Atkins said, "sure, I can. What goes where?"

Laying down a pan, I changed my tone.

"Oh, sorry! I thought you were Darcy."

"That makes sense. You and he are a cute couple."

My eyebrows felt like they shot up to the top of my forehead.

"We're not a couple," I denied. "We just are friends."

"Oh, sorry."

"It's not your fault. It's natural to jump from mere acquaintance to a romantic relationship fast. I'm more gradual than that. There must be varying degrees of relationships between men and women, or I'll feel like I'm on a winding road."

"That makes sense. Men and women can be friends with each other. No matter what some people say."

"Precisely. There are black, white, and gray areas to everything. Darcy and I are in the gray."

"I just came in here to get some more yams," Henry said, putting some more on his plate.

"Mary made the yams."

"Yeah, I know. I want her to know that I like her cooking. My dad always said, even if a woman can't cook, eat what she makes. Luckily, Mary seems good at it, so I don't have to act like I like it."

"It's nice when you don't have to pretend."

Now that I had him alone, I just realized that it was the best time to not pretend either.

"Speaking of the same topic," I began, "there's something that I have to be honest with you about." When I said this, I saw Henry Atkins's expression and stance shifted slightly. It was so subtle that only a soldier could detect it in another soldier.

"Don't worry," I said, "there's no need to get on the defense. I'm not taking you into a social battle. I'm Mary's older sister, so I have no choice but to protect her, and you in the process. It's my job. I'm not perfect, like Jane, so I'm the better one to lecture someone on."

"That's kind of true. Jane is so perfect that I have a hard time being around her. I just feel even more awkward than ever around her, because I feel evil just by being alive."

"I know how that is. That's what makes me the easier one to hear this all from. It goes back to what you said about not having to pretend. That's good because that's what I need you to be. Mary is going to have a baby. And it's yours. I know that's the hardest thing in the world. However, many people go through life, and their first child is a surprise. Does your world feel like it's upside down right now? Like a cruel trick has been played on you?"

When asked these questions, Henry dropped every attempt at looking strong and his posture deflated. Putting down his plate, he didn't respond at first.

"Put your plate in the microwave so that your yams do not get cold," I offered.

Obeying, he did what I instructed and stayed near the microwave.

"Am I right?" I asked.

"Yes," he answered quietly. "I am so...scared. This was not what I planned, what I meant for, and if I were to be honest, I never thought of having a child with Mary. If I had a kid, I would want to get married first and have known the woman longer than I knew your sister."

"I get it. And I appreciate that you are being honest with me. That's what I want. I also appreciate that you are trying your best to do the right thing. I always want you to try. Mary deserves it. It's important for the child to know that it has a father out there, who cares about it. I like that you are trying to be in their lives, and you ought to give it a go. But after a few months or years, if you reach a point where you are not certain that you can see yourself being with Mary—if you know that you both are not meant to be—I'd much rather you tell her gently, and wisely. Be nice and go about it in the right way. Don't just decide to up and leave one day. Give her time to adjust to the fairytale ending not how she wanted it to. And don't just eject yourself from your child's life. Work something out with Mary, where you can come back and see them, every now and then. You're not evil for walking away, when it's time to walk away. You're evil when you go about it viciously. Don't hurt Mary. Or I'll get angry."

"Now that," he acknowledged, "I can do very well."

"Good."

Henry Atkins chuckled.

"I think that I would fear you if you got angry with me. I think I might be a little afraid of you."

"Good," I responded, unashamedly. "There needs to be one

sister that you are afraid of. Jane is too perfect to be frightening. Kitty is always traveling to different bases on the globe and can't be in one place long enough for you to be intimidated, and Lydia is at the time of her life where she should be doing a lot. That leaves me, and it's right."

"Yes, it is. And it's true that Mary and I did not start this off in the right way, so it might not end in the right way. But I'm here… and I will do my best."

"Good. That's all that I ask of you."

Henry heated up his yams and then joined the rest of the family in the dining room.

Thinking I was alone, you could only imagine how much I jumped when I heard clapping behind me.

Turning around, I saw Lydia, who was standing on the back-steps that led the kitchen to the bedroom upstairs.

When Lydia finished clapping, I relaxed and finished putting the mustard greens in a container.

"How long were you listening in?" I asked her.

"Not my fault. I had to go to the bathroom upstairs, and so I had no choice but to hear everything. Much to my benefit."

"That reminds me," I said, covering up the ham in aluminum foil. "You were really quiet all through dinner."

"I needed time to study him. It's not like my family, where I have been studying you for my entire life. With this Henry Atkins guy, it's my first time meeting him. Even I need a few hours to predict what's going to happen. *Again*."

As I put the cranberry sauce in the refrigerator, I was open to her powers of deduction.

"What do you think will happen to them?" I asked her, innocently. "Now that you have met him, did you change your first theory?"

"Right now, they are not in love with each other," Lydia analyzed. "It's not their fault. There's a definite attraction between the two. But there's no way of knowing how long they will last. Although, one thing is definite. Henry will always stay in his child's life. He's the kind of guy who believes that, if you're a father, you don't abandon your kid. And he will always try and be kind to Mary."

Relieved, I picked up my cup of sparkling cider.

"Good. That's nice to know."

I joined the rest of the family, and Thanksgiving ended well. Henry promised that he would come by for Christmas dinner, and if everything went well, he wanted to introduce us to his parents, and Darcy was the last to leave.

"Should I bring a dish for Christmas dinner?" he asked.

"No," I said, "don't worry. We've got it covered."

Smiling, he put on his hat, coat, gloves, and left.

Watching him depart, I felt my spirit grow a little misty.

Mr. Darcy—what are you?

# TWENTY
## A WALK TO REMEMBER

After Thanksgiving, it was the official time to start looking for Christmas presents. I spent so much of my time zipping between my work, and helping set up the stalls so that merchants could sell their seasonal crafts. In an attempt to support local people, I brought all my presents from the vendors—except for Josie and Killian, who I knew to stop into Toys R Us store, to get them toys for presents.

There was only one person who I had problems finding the perfect present for.

"How is Delores and her family doing?" Darcy asked me, as we were walking through the Christmas vendors.

"They are doing great, except for Gloriana," I answered, taking out my wallet so that I could buy a handmade sweater for my mom. "It turns out that they prefer to go on vacations at Christmastime. They are going on a cruise through Greece and Turkey."

"Really?"

"Yeah. Not only do they get to have fun, but they get to see some family along the way. It turns out that one of Delores's grandfathers was from Istanbul, and one of her great-grand-mothers was from Santorini."

"Delores is Greek on one side of her family, and Turkish on the other side?"

"Yup. It just goes to show you, from a national standpoint, if you trace anyone's ancestry, you'll find out that we're all mutts."

"True. There's no such thing as anyone being 'one' anything anymore."

After I brought the sweater, I raised it up so that Darcy could see it.

"What do you think? Think Mom will like it?"

"You know your mom better than I do," Darcy said, "but it's pretty."

"I wanted to buy one for my Aunt Miriam, but I don't know her taste. So, I just settled for buying her and Uncle Edward a blanket from a catalogue."

"Your Aunt and Uncle are your mother's relatives, right?"

"Yes. My mom was Ariella Gardiner. Her brother was Edward, but we usually call him Uncle Eddie. And his wife is Miriam, who we usually call Mir. They will be staying till New Years Eve."

"And your dad is not bringing his girlfriend, right?"

"He wanted to bring her, but she didn't think now was the right time, so luckily, it's not happening yet. Since Mom's cousin agreed not to come, Charlotte's dad is also making himself scarce, and he's celebrating the holidays with his family. That's one problem that's lifted off our shoulders. We can save the drama for a next year. Better later than sooner is what I have to say."

The weather was nippy so Darcy adjusted his scarf to make it tighter around his neck. By doing so, he accidentally knocked his hat off his head, and it fell to the ground. Somehow the wind picked up and it blew his hat along. Instinctively, I rushed after it, with Darcy behind me. We moved around fellow shoppers, and eventually I got it.

I dusted it off and stood on my tiptoes as I placed it on his head.

Without apprehension, Darcy let me do so, and it resulted in our faces drawing closer to each other. Despite my keen awareness of this, I decidedly avoided his eyes as he looked down at me. Directing all my attention to placing his hat on his head just right, I continued the conversation.

"Life is nice when you can prolong a madness, eh?" I chuckled.

"When you look at how your parents' marriage ended, and how Delores also was divorced, how does that make you look at marriage? I'm just curious." Darcy was usually good at speaking slowly and confidently. But this time, his voice faltered a little, grew breathy, and was a little rushed.

"I'm not offended," I said, as we continued walking along. "It's a natural question. My mom is like Delores; she married the person she loved. Things end; that's the way of life. But they didn't stop living, which is what I can say for them both. They didn't shrivel up and put their lives on hold."

I became reflective, and suddenly felt willing to lay my life out before me, and in front of Darcy. For some reason, I felt that I could trust him, and as if he would never betray me. It was strange, considering our past, but maybe Delores was right: since our past was so turbulent, there was now nowhere to go, but up!

"I shriveled up," I confessed. "Love was something that I was never an expert at, so I was afraid of love, and the idea of it not working out. So, I bowed out quickly. And, whenever I opened myself up again, I did not prove to have the right kind of taste. And recently, that happened again."

"Recently?"

"I dated a man, and it turned out that he was already dating someone else. I turned out to be the *other* woman, if you will."

"Liz," he said, his tone heartfelt, "I am so sorry."

"Thanks."

"If it helps, try not to let it affect your self-worth. That scenario is more common than you know. I've made my share of mistakes and learned from them. So, do not let this bad time make you feel like you are not worthy of being the only woman in a man's life. And things always improve. Delores and your parents are proof of that.

"We humans are not always going to find that perfect one immediately. Sometimes we're meant to encounter the wrong ones at first, date the wrong people, and then the right one comes eventually. That's the real fairy tale of life: just around the corner, there might be something better, if the road you're on now is not a good one."

I wanted to laugh, to diminish the magnitude of his philosophy, but now was not the time for cold wit. Now was the time to accept that he had a point.

"Now that was a speech," I said. "I admit, that was very well done."

"Thank you," Darcy replied, puffing out his chest, a little. "That was quite good, if I will say it myself."

"We all wish things were perfect, and that love is supposed to be like that," I said, "so I really should accept that it's not."

"And that is the true fairy tale of it."

"Go into it for the journey, instead of just the destination."

"Precisely."

Grinning, I bumped my shoulders with him.

"You should not be wise so early in the day," I joked. "It's not right for you to be so wise this early at all."

"Fine," he agreed, equally as entertained. "I won't be if it doesn't work. We can start by me admitting that I have no idea what to bring to your house on Christmas?"

"You don't have to bring a present," I assured him, "it's too difficult for a family that you just got to know, and I'm not going to make you go through that."

"Thank you," he said, but his posture and countenance shifted awkwardly. Running his fingers through his hair, he looked ahead.

I cannot pretend to know everything in life, but one thing that I pride myself on is how to read some people.

As I looked at Darcy, I began to suspect what he was feeling.

"You're going to feel awkward if you don't bring something to our house," I said, "aren't you?"

"Heck yes," Darcy exclaimed quietly. "If I came, empty-handed, I'll feel stupid. Liz, thanks for being nice about it, but I won't be happy unless I bring something."

"Yeah, I sensed that."

"The only problem is, I have no idea what to bring."

An idea just came to me.

"Since I can't convince you that you coming to our house is present enough," I said, reaching into my bag, "what is the one thing that all humans like?"

"Financial security, without having to work much, or at all."

I blinked, seeing the logic behind that answer.

"Okay…what's the *other* thing that all humans like?" I decided to answer my own question. "Everyone loves good food."

"Ah."

I removed a holiday magazine from my purse and handed it to Darcy.

"This is where I ordered my aunt and uncle's blanket from. But they mainly specialize in food."

"The Swiss Colony," he said, reading the magazine cover.

"I learned about them from when I was working at the Shakespeare Festival when I was in Kentucky. They make cheese, sausage, nuts, and candy food platters. They are popular at businesses who buy them for their Christmas parties."

"Clearly," Darcy said, his eyes widening as he began to look through the magazine. "Oh, Lizzy, this is a tease. This one platter has cheddar, Colby jack cheese, Monterey jack cheese, and look at all the different type of sausages."

"Makes your mouth water, doesn't it?"

"And look at the bread! I love bread. That's why I could never go on a diet."

"Me too!"

"What should I order?"

"If you can afford it, buy a sausage, and cheese platter for the adults. But for Josie and Killian, buy a platter of chocolates or candy. Believe me, they will thank you."

"Perfect," he said, still looking through the magazine. "I can buy presents for my entire family this way, as well as yours. I can get all my Christmas shopping out of the way, without having to walk into a store. My prayers have been answered."

"Happy to oblige," I said, watching him keenly. He noted my expression and suspected that I was scrutinizing him.

"What?"

"I have a hunch. You're not just going to buy the food for your family, are you? You're also going to buy food for yourself!"

Darcy rolled his head backwards, knowing that he was found out.

"I'm a single man who can't cook. Sometimes, we just want finger food, and something that you can have for a fast breakfast."

I thoroughly enjoyed myself.

"I'm never going to get that magazine back, will I?"

He raised up 'The Swiss Colony' holiday magazine and then shoved it into his bag, with a mischievous look.

"Never," he declared. "It's mine now. So, good luck getting it back."

"Remember," I warned him, "I'm a fighter; I've now learned not to bow out from things. I'm a match for you."

"Clearly," he responded, looking deeply into my eyes. "And didn't you also say that my coming was 'present enough'?"

"Oh, no!" I declared. "I forbid you to remember that!"

"Too late. I already am."

"No, no, no!" I said, pinching his arm. "Don't remember that."

"I will remember," he said, running away from me.

Giving into the moment, I chased after him.

"Forget!" I cried.

"Never!"

I kept racing after him, until I caught him.

And caught him, I did.

———

The day of the Scottish Walk ended up falling on the same day as the Christmas play and it was a day of hecticness and mania. Meryton Manor tours provided much of the staff, and I was scrounging around, trying to make sure that everything would work out fine.

"I never adapted to the cold," I said to Darcy over the phone, rushing around everyone who was on the walk, tightening my scarf around my neck. "You would think that I got used to it every now and again."

"I like the cold," Darcy said on the other end. "During summertime, I sweat a lot and feel disgusting. Besides, wintertime is the time for wearing lots of cozy layers."

"And layers become you," I acknowledged, handing another coordinator a clipboard. "You promised that you would come to the Walk, and then take me to the school so that I can get ready for the play."

"I promise. Besides, I have no choice but to be here, and are you sure that we don't have time for dinner before you head off to the play."

"We might have to go the fast-food route, so that could work. It will be my treat."

"Cool. By the way, I have a surprise for you."

"Is it a good surprise, or a bad one? Because I can't handle any bad news right now. I'll faint—emotionally."

"I can see you," Darcy said, slyly. "But you can't see me."

"Stalker," I joked.

"Not stalker, just another attendee. Turn to your right and keep walking through the crowd."

I did as he bade me and managed to politely make my way through the crowd. As I sojourned onward, my curiosity grew, and I found myself looking forward to a bit of a surprise.

"What am I looking for?" I asked, slowly, drawing out my words to sound intrigued.

"What do you think?" Darcy asked. "Me!"

I heard his words both over the phone, and right in front of me. As a few men, dressed in their tartans, moved aside, Darcy appeared—wearing full Scotsman garb. He was wearing the entire ensemble of jacket, kilt, and the excess of his tartan was clasped over his right arm, with a sporin (purse) hung below his belt, and he rocked a cap with a crest on it.

The surprise was immense.

At first, all I could do was stand there, gazing at him. With full historical attire, he looked handsome and regal. How terrible it is to lose all one's self control and give into the sensation of feeling one's breath being taken away from them.

For indeed, I was speechless.

Without knowing what I was about, I felt my feet carry me a little forward, closer to the man who was once my arch enemy. And now—was my friend.

"You..." was all that I could muster. "You..."

All Darcy could do was look at me, with self-satisfaction in his eyes. If he wanted to astonish me, he succeeded. For that's what he intended, I surmise.

As I got close enough, I touched the tartan cloth that he had draped around his chest and over his shoulder.

"You are part Scottish?" I asked.

"Go far enough back, and I am," Darcy explained. "My great-great etc. grandmother from when Alexandria was founded. Her clan was Abercromby." He gestured to his family's crest, which was a Falcon rising. Above the falcon were the Latin words 'Petit Alta'."

"What does it mean?" I asked.

"He seeks high deeds," Darcy translated.

"You're going to be in the Scottish Walk."

"Yes. It's my first time, actually. Between being raised in Oklahoma, and then being in the army, I never had the time to do this. But, if I were to be honest, I never had the courage to."

"Never had the courage?" I scoffed, surprised. "You? Strong and hard-to-knock-down-Mr. Darcy was afraid? Will wonders never cease."

"But this year, I got the courage."

"What changed? Did time help you?"

"Well, it was you, if you must know."

I leaned away and looked at him, flabbergasted.

"Me? What about my constant misadventures helped inspire you?"

"When I found out that you were helping, I knew that I was not alone. So, I did it."

Amazed at him, I cupped his face with my hands.

"The joys of not being alone, eh?" I asked, lighthearted and with an arched eyebrow.

"Yup. The joys of not being alone."

"Lizzy!" Mr. King called me.

That was enough to break the spell.

"Coming," I said, and turned to continue my duties. Turning to Darcy, I began to leave. "Got to get back to work. I can't wait to see you. I'll know that you will be great."

Darcy blushed.

"I'm just walking," he called after me.

"Believe me, not everyone is good at walking," I replied over my shoulder. "With any luck, you will never see my graduation video when I received my diploma from Louisville. Worst walk ever!"

As I walked away, I spied Darcy out of the corner of my eye. He was watching me as I left. I couldn't help but be flattered.

———

The crowd was immense. The whole scene was complimented by all the Christmas decorations that filled the area, and the sky was cloudy, but with no hint of rain or snow. In many people's hands were hand-sized flags that we had arranged to be specially made.

The flags were all split in half:

The right side of the flags had the American design.

The left side of the flags had the Scottish flag design.

And then the ceremony began!

Drums sounded!

Bagpipes began to play, skillfully done, and sounding beautifully as the Walk began.

There were many participants, men and women descended from the original founders of their proud city, dressed in their different tartans, and progressing along.

The crowd raised their Scottish American flags as they waved to the walkers.

Despite the grandiosity of the event, I found myself impatient for only one face.

Where was Darcy?

I had to see him.

Searching every man in the procession, I wondered how I overlooked him—until there he was.

Near the end of the line, Darcy walked, his posture erect, and his appearance very dignified. His legs were perfect for wearing a kilt, which was of a green, blue, and black pattern.

When seeing me, our eyes locked again, I waved at him and raised my flag, to salute.

Darcy did not wave back, but he did not need to. In his gaze was comfort, connection, and congeniality.

Darcy had turned into a good man.

How many days I had wasted ignoring him, believing that the best thing to do was to reject him from my company.

How quickly we humans are to get in the way of ourselves—to be our own worst enemies. It felt as if, until now, I had never known myself.

I was beginning to feel deeply for him.

How could this happen?

I was not ready to fall in love again.

Especially when I didn't know if it was love at all.

But as I continued to get lost in my own musings, the Scottish Walk continued, leaving my emotions something I could keep behind, within myself.

One event went successfully.

Now it was time for the next trial to face.

# TWENTY-ONE
## MUSIC & MELODIES

"You were right," Darcy said as I rushed out of Wendys with our dinner. "We don't have much time."

I dashed into the car, and we headed off to George-Mason elementary school.

I felt like I had not eaten in three days.

"No, we don't," I said, "by the way, I am about to give you a word of warning."

"Oh boy." Darcy sighed.

"I have a feeling that, since Bingley still hasn't come home yet, Jane will want to have her own copy of the Christmas Show. If she asks you to record it, please say yes."

"Ah, that's it?" Darcy replied, sounding relieved. "Don't worry. I had a feeling that I would become the recorder of events."

"Thanks, me ole' son."

Eventually we arrived at George-Mason, entered with our food, and we ate in the auditorium while there was chaos all around us. Since it was only two hours before the show began, kids were entering with their costumes, parents were following after them to help them get into their make-up, the teachers and principal were arranging everything, the music teacher and audio techies were checking the microphones, and there was holiday excitement in the air.

"I'm nervous," I said to Darcy, between bites. "But also very happy. Does that make sense?"

"No, it doesn't, and you're insane," Darcy replied stoically, but he was actually just joking. I repaid his remark by pinching him.

As we finished, Jane approached me, a little winded from running around to make sure that Josie and Killian were ready.

"Liz—"

"Don't worry," I assured her, "I'm almost done eating."

"Thank you. And Darcy—sorry if it's too much for you but is there any chance that you will record the show for me? The school is taping it, but I can't help but want my own copy. I have my own camera if you would be so kind."

Darcy and I exchanged a look.

"Jane," he said, "I would love to."

"Thank you," Jane said, and then dashed off.

"Let me take this moment to go to the little boys' room," he said, and he headed off to the bathroom.

When he was gone, I took this as the opportunity to throw out our trash. When taking it all to a trashcan near the wall, I felt eyes on me.

Turning around, I saw that Mary King must've entered the auditorium. She was holding some props and must've stopped when she saw me. Great! This was the last thing that I needed right now.

"Hey, Miss King," I began, "are you looking forward to the Christmas play?"

"I am. I never read the story, so I am excited."

"Good. Hopefully it will surprise you."

She looked at the trash that I just threw away.

"You brought your new boyfriend to the show, huh?" Mary King announced. "You move fast."

"We're friends."

"You don't act like friends."

I was not in the mood for this. I could sense that she was fishing for an argument, but I was not going to take the bait.

"Miss King," I said, "not today."

"Pardon?"

"Whatever is about to happen, I won't let it happen today. Let's not argue, and if you got a problem with me, then I give you permission to do it after Christmas. But for tonight, please, make life easy on us both."

Mary didn't respond, but only walked away.

'Good,' I thought.

I knew that I merely put off our confrontation for a later date, but I was fine with that. This was Christmastime, and I was not going to let it be ruined by triviality.

I had a show to sing for, knowing that I was not a singer at all.

As I got into costume, looking creepy and goblin-like, I got a text from my phone. It was from Charlotte Lucas:

> We are here! My kids and I managed to get a
> seat in the front row. Good luck!

Smiling, I responded, 'I'll need all the luck that I can get' and was happy to know that she had come.

When I finished putting on my makeup, I looked at myself in the mirror.

*The measure of a person is not that they fall down—because we all fall down eventually. The point is all about getting up again.*

I was getting up again. And I was not running away from life anymore.

From now on, I will not run away from problems, but face them, and solve them in turn. I refuse to be afraid of life.

My courage will rise with every attempt to intimidate me.

From behind the curtain, I heard the increase in the size of the audience.

After the rise and fall of half an hour, the lights dimmed, and the music teacher walked on the stage and introduced the play.

"And now," the music teacher announced, "please enjoy our original adaptation of Charles Dickens's 'The Goblins Who Stole a Sexton'!

The lights fell black on the audience as they cheered, and now it was time for Jane, myself and the rest of the parents to come on the stage and sang the intro song.

We made it through without any mishaps, and we left the stage, with applause.

"Made it through the first one," Jane said to me, breathing heavily. "Now we just have to make it to the next number."

"Yup," I said, "one note at a time."

"You better give it your all!" Josie said, going past me. "Aunt Liz, promise me that you won't embarrass me?"

"Promise me that *you* won't embarrass *me*?" I repeated her question, tossing it right back at her. We both stuck our tongues out at each other, and then prepared for the next number.

Standing in the wings, I waited for the scene when the kid who played the lead character, Gabriel Grub, was cruel to another character, and sent the child running away from him, through the graveyard.

Now it was my time to come out. Sadly, each parent had two lines of a solo.

I had the first line to every stanza, and at the chorus, we all sang together. Stepping out, the music struck up and we all began:

> *Cruelty.*
> *Coldness.*
> *Malice.*
> *Soulless.*
>
> *The man of the graveyard, staring back.*
> *And who never thinks of giving back.*
> *A little bit of kindness*
> *A little bit of caring.*
> *A little bit of compassion.*
> *A soul willing to be daring.*
>
> *Gabriel Grub!*
> *A total rub!*

*Gabriel Grub!*
*A soul lost and undug!*

*But who will emerge*
*to challenge the heartless?*
*Who will change the heart*
*Of the gravedigger so worthless?*

*Gabriel Grub!*
*A total rub!*
*Gabriel Grub!*
*A soul lost and undug!*

The stage went black, we all clapped as we left the stage, for a scene change. The lead character, Gabriel Grub, was being played by a little girl, so she made her voice sound gruff and mannish.

Now it was Josie and Killian's moment. Them, alongside all the goblins who would steal the gravedigger, Gabriel, all rushed on stage, and began to swarm the actress, who let out a large scream.

My goodness, that girl knows how to scream!

The show progressed without any mishaps, which is a remarkable feat for an elementary show.

No one forgot their lines, no music got interrupted and when we all stood on stage for our curtain call, we had the luxury of deserving the thunderous applause.

We all bowed and now could kick off Christmas.

———

"You all were wonderful!" Charlotte Lucas said, with her children pulling at her dress, wanting to go home.

"Thank you," I said, hugging her. "And thank you for coming."

Deciding that the hug was the best time to whisper in her ear, I took advantage of the opportunity.

"And thanks for telling your dad not to come to Thanksgiving dinner," I whispered. "I know it was probably you who had convinced him not to go."

"What are friends for?" Charlotte asked. "But Lizzy, it's going to happen sometime. I think they are getting serious."

"I know. But I made a pact that I will wait till the new year to face those complications."

"Smart!"

"Thank you." Charlotte's kids kept pulling at her dress, begging for them to go home. She apologized because she didn't want them to cause a scene. I told her that it was alright. We gave our goodbyes, wished each other a happy holiday, and now I could approach Darcy, who had the camera still in his hands.

"How do I look?" I asked, gesturing to my makeup.

"Like you just walked out of the movie 'Labyrinth'," Darcy responded.

"Then that means that I succeeded. If you can't go full-on 1980s' creepy, then you are not doing things right." I held Darcy's arm. "Thanks for recording it."

"You were wonderful."

"Oh, please!"

"No, really, you were great."

"I was?"

"Yeah. I actually liked what everyone did with the story. I give you full marks."

"High praise coming from you. I appreciate it, Darce. I really do."

"Need a ride home?"

"If it won't be too much trouble."

"No problem. But since I don't really know anyone else, I'll just sit here, reading a book on my phone."

"That's what I would do."

Quickly, I got out of my costume, removed all my makeup, and asked Jane when we could leave.

She said that she had to stay behind and help the parents clean up the dressing room, but she gave me full permission to run away. Taking her up on it, I joined Darcy and left for our homes, a warm shower, tea or soup, and our beds.

When we turned onto Longbourn, I thanked him.

"Don't worry," I assured him, "I know better than to ask you to come in. You are exhausted, aren't you?"

"Today has been a long day. I'm wiped."

"You have every right to be. Good luck with getting my family a Christmas present."

"Thanks," he said, gesturing to the magazine that he nicked from me. "I think I can take it from here."

Once more, we looked at each other, and our eyes locked. There it was again—the moment. The moment where a connection was achieved, arrived at, and accepted—but I could not imagine. I could not fathom how it had occurred.

When did it begin?

Why did it begin?

And did it ever begin at all?

But it was there, nevertheless.

What was there to be done?

There was no right answer because there could be no answer for it at all.

A spell had been cast over us, and I felt Darcy's kindness, his understanding, and his friendship swell up within me, and I found myself unable to ignore the charm that radiated off him.

But such moments are meant to be felt, to marvel at, but not to last.

Almost as if we felt a snap, the connection was so intense, that Darcy and I looked away from each other simultaneously. We needed the break—or at least, I felt like I needed severance for it to happen.

"A week to Christmas," I said, opening the door, "let's promise to enjoy this holiday."

After I said it, Darcy looked at me again, but not with the misty-eyed expression that occurred when we were linked. Instead, it was in a casual and complacent way, that didn't say anything else but 'let's end this day pleasantly'.

"I promise. It is, after all, the most wonderful time of the year."

"Yes, it is," I said, opening the car door, and stepping out of it.

As I was about to close the door, a book fell out of my shoulder bag, and onto the passenger's seat. It was my copy of 'It Takes a Witch'.

Eager to be gallant about it, Darcy picked it up, and looked at the front.

"Nice cover," he said, flipping it over and reading the book description on the back.

"It's a nice book," I said, feeling the heat rise in the back of my neck. He was reading the book description! Why did I carry that book around with me? Now, I was about to be teased. Here we go!

"Wait?" Darcy said. "The lead character has my name?"

I took the book back from him.

"Oh, come on," I retaliated, prepared for him. "Darcy is a popular name?"

He looked at me, mischievously.

"Don't give me that look and think there is more to my motives than the fact that I like the book."

"Sure."

He kept giving me that look.

"I mean it, Darcy," I uttered. "Stop giving me that look."

He kept giving me that look.

"I mean it, Darcy. Stop it."

He kept giving me that look.

"You are incorrigible."

He kept giving me that look.

"Oh, shut up!"

Darcy laughed as I closed the door on him and dashed into the house.

I was fairly certain that, as Darcy was driving away, he was still guffawing. Unless I didn't know him at all, and I was wrong.

As I locked the door behind me, I looked at my copy of 'It Takes a Witch'.

"Well, Darcy Merriweather," I said, referring to the main character in the book. "You just got me into a bit of teasing. If your story was not so good, I would be very angry with you."

Putting the book back in my bag, I pat Vatalie and Manhattan behind their ears, went upstairs to immediately take a shower, get something to drink and jump into the bed.

When I had finally settled in for the night, I was lying in my bed, pretending to be asleep when the rest of the family came home, after the show.

I preferred to be dead to the world, to be honest. After all, it gave me time to look up at the ceiling and think in the darkness.

Delores told me that Darcy and I might become something more than friends.

I was not affected by her declaration, nor am I the kind of person to believe something will happen just because of another person's predictions on my life.

But I did believe in what was right in front of me. Also, when it comes to Darcy, I stopped thinking of my first impression of him a while ago. It was all in the past now, and I wasted too much time re-living that past.

But now, everything was changing. And this alteration of events led to such a turnover of everything that I expected.

Was I beginning to feel for Darcy?

How shocking a question—and how annoying a question.

It was most inconvenient, since I promised to never even like him at all.

And now, I had to ask myself if I was falling in love with him.

It couldn't be him because it was too soon and too irrational. Also, I refused to let Darcy be the victim to my own complications.

Wickham had betrayed me, and I did not want Darcy to be the reaction to my broken heart.

I would not let him be the rebound.

When I would look at him, I would see him, and him alone.

Finally, I went to sleep.

# TWENTY-TWO
# SHE KNEW SHE WAS RIGHT

The next day, I woke up before everyone else. Since everyone had a long night, I thought the best thing to do was to tiptoe through the house, to the bathroom.

After brushing my teeth, washing my face, and stashing my overnight tooth retainer in its case, I went back to my room, quietly made my bed, dressed in loungewear, and went down the stairs, just in time to hear someone put their key in the front door. Knowing who it could be, I opened the door before they could turn the doorknob and came face to face with Lydia, who had her duffel bags behind her.

When seeing me, her surprise did not last long, before she was back to being full-on Lydia, and raising her arms in the air, out to the side.

"Home for the holidays," she wailed, followed by me putting my finger over my mouth, indicating for her to be quiet.

"Everyone is still asleep," I whispered as I helped Lydia bring her stuff in.

"Couldn't help but make an entrance," Lydia responded, "or I wouldn't be who I am."

Closing the door behind her, I followed her into the living room.

"How was the play?" Lydia asked, in hushed tones, as she went and got some orange juice from the fridge. "I couldn't leave school until this morning. Believe me, I didn't want to miss it."

"It was great," I responded, handing her a cup so that she could pour the juice in. "Josie and Killian would have made you proud."

"They already do," Lydia said, "I've got the best niece and nephew in the world."

"Yeah, we do."

"So," Lydia said, "Let's talk Christmas presents."

"I'm not telling you what I got you," I declared, putting my foot down. "No matter how much you beg me."

"Don't worry," Lydia said, swiping the air, and looking into the cupboard for the bagel bag. "I stopped asking you that question in the tenth grade. You've got to let that go. I'm just bringing it up because I never was good at finding the right Christmas present for you, so try to be pretend to like my gift."

"I'm good at pretending that sort of stuff," I said, filling my glass. "But I'm sure that you found something that I will like."

Lydia gave me a side-glance.

"What do you want?" she asked me.

"What do you mean?" I asked, confused by that.

"You're being strangely nice to me. That must mean that you want something."

"I don't."

"Yes, you do. Spill it. What do you want?"

I closed my eyes,

"If it helps," I said, "it's a very small favor."

"Good. I have a group of friends who are always asking me to do big favors for them every week. A small favor is refreshing, and it will help me reboot myself."

"When Darcy comes to Christmas dinner, he's going to bring a food platter for a present."

"Food platter?"

"You know, those sausage and cheese platters that you get from magazines, that people often buy for office parties?"

"He got it from 'The Swiss Colony' magazine, that you probably showed him, didn't he?"

I wanted to throw my arms up in the air, out of resignation.

"How could you possibly have known that?" I asked, flabbergasted.

"Lucky guess," she replied, smug. "You love looking at those magazines, even though you never buy anything. And since you and him go out a lot, it was natural for him to ask you what to get us. I came up with a theory based on my past experiences: when you think of the obvious, and spot the obvious, then theorize the obvious. I just do it quicker than most."

Since I was the one asking for a favor, I was not going to belittle her own pride.

"The reason that I brought it up, was to ask you to promise me that you won't make any comments about his lack of originality on the present. I was the one who suggested it, and I don't want him to feel like we don't like the gesture."

"A big man like that shouldn't be so easy to offend with my jokes," Lydia wondered.

"Just because a man is big does not mean that he doesn't need to feel appreciated. Darcy wants us to like him, and I want us all to be there for him. So, promise me that you will say nice things about it? Please? For me."

Lydia rolled her head, looking at me queerly, while clearly studying me. I was not afraid, because she had every right to, I was coming to realize.

"Fine," Lydia said, "I'll be nice to him."

"Thank you."

"Also, if you could hint to him to get one of those food platters with the Summer Sausages, then I would be grateful."

I chuckled.

"I'll give it a try," I offered.

"Thank you," Lydia said, slicing the bagel and putting it into the toaster.

Turning around, about to go into the storage closet, to get the wrapping paper, Lydia spoke from behind me.

"So," she announced. "Have you accepted that you're in love with Darcy yet?"

I stood there, frozen.

I didn't turn to Lydia just yet but was doing my best to find out how to respond.

After all, perhaps I should have seen this coming. Since I needed time to form my thoughts, I hoped that Lydia would continue talking. Fortunately, I was right.

"Or," Lydia continued, "you aren't sure that you are falling in love with him. Or fear the day when you do."

"Lydia," I extolled, sighing, "I was hoping that you wouldn't say that."

"Well, I did."

"No, what I meant is that… Delores told me that. And now you are. And you both have a way of being correct. I was worried, that if you said it, then it would become a reality."

"But it is a reality."

I sighed.

"Yes," I accepted. "It is a *reality*. And now I have to be brave enough to face it."

"But you don't want to face it," Lydia continued, eager to be intuitive. "You want to run, to hide, from the fact that this is not what you expected, or how you planned for things to be."

"True," I accepted, "it wasn't. Also, you know what happened. Liking someone after experiencing what I went through is not the best way to enter anything."

"I see," Lydia said, folding her arms over her chest, looking even more contemplative. "You're afraid that your feelings for Darcy are manifested from your heartbreak of Wickham. And that your feelings aren't real but are a rebound."

"Yes," I said, "and I don't want to put Darcy through that."

Vexed, I knocked my hand against a countertop.

"This is not how I planned my life." I continued. "Do you know what it's like to try to organize everything, to go down the right path, and it always gets so confusing?"

"We're raised on the fairytale that is life," Lydia declared, "and that is do well at school, get a job, find stability, then find that certain someone, they will be the best one for you and then get married. That's the fairytale. And it's all well and good.

"But here's the problem: there's more than one definition of what fairytale is. Sometimes, the road to the fairytale, is bumpy and painful. It's filled with disappointment, heartbreak, betrayal, liking the wrong person, loving someone too soon after liking someone else before, and having the rug pulled up from underneath you. And people will tell you that it's all a nightmare.

"Well, I got news for you; that's all *PART* of the fairytale. It's not anything wrong. It's all one and the same. Now let's analyze your situation. You liked George Wickham. He was the angel from your past. And now, he's the biggest mistake you ever had. You hated Darcy, and now he's the better man and has become a light in your life. That's not a wrong fairytale. That's *another part of the happily ever after.* I won't push you any further than this."

"You sound like Darcy now," I realized. After all, he told me something very similar to that.

"That's got to be a first."

She tapped my shoulder and began to walk out of the kitchen.

"Always remember, there's more than one fairytale to life. And once you accept it, life gets so much more terrifying, so much more complicated, more alarming—and so much happier."

She left me standing there... accepting that she was right.

Again.

# TWENTY-THREE
## CURIOSITIES AT CHRISTMASTIME

C hristmastime had come at last!

Actually, it was Christmas eve, but that might as well be at Christmas day.

That morning, we found ourselves all rushing to our cars, to head to the DCA airport.

Since our parents were still there, we made sure to have them ride in different cars, to avoid any arguments.

When we arrived at Ronald Reagan airport, we had two planes to wait for.

Naturally, being Christmas Eve, the airport was packed with many people waiting for their relatives to arrive, to stay for the holidays.

The hustle and bustle of it was quite enjoyable actually. The great thing about Christmastime is that it was a moment of the year where you could look at a stranger, wish them a happy holiday, and they won't be creeped out about a stranger greeting them. Instead, they return the gesture and smile at you.

"To quote Charles Dickens," I said to Dad, as we all were waiting at a gate terminal, for a plane to arrive. "This is the time of year where men do open up their shut-up-hearts."

"And we all look at people as friends, instead of fellow travelers to the grave," Dad continued. "And then it all ends by New Year's Day, and we all get scared of each other again."

I laughed as a plane landed on the runway.

Jane, Josie, and Killian ran to the windows.

"I think it's Dad's plane!" Josie cried.

"Oh, it definitely is," Jane said, her eyes glossed over with happiness. "My husband is finally home."

The plane rolled around, close to the gate, and soon the passengers disembarked.

We all waited happily as people emerged from the walkway, and soon, through the throng, was a familiar face.

"Daddy!" Josie and Killian cried.

"Jo and Ki!"

Wearing his army fatigues, Charles Bingley had finally come back home.

———

Following her children, Jane ran up to Bingley, who dropped his bags, embraced his family, and began to kiss them all.

He crouched down to hug the children as much as his wife, and I marveled at the sight.

You are aware of those moments in time where happiness is found and kept. And those moments, though happening in real time, slow down to you, and you see it occurring in slow motion.

Bingley wrapped his arms around the love of his life, and the children who adored him.

They fell into his love, his smile, and his caring demeanor. Charles Bingley was born to be a husband, a father, and a family man.

After a few minutes of this, at last, he stood up and greeted us.

"Bennets," Bingley said, "I'm happy to see you. Please tell me that you are happy to see me."

"We are," Mom said, kissing him on the cheek. "It's nice to see you, Charles."

"You too, Mom."

Charles Bingley embraced the entire family, and then he turned to me.

"Merry Christmas, Liz," he began.

I smiled at his kind expression.

"And you too, Bing."

He laughed.

"Still calling me Bing, after all these years?"

"Your last name is Bingley; your family brought this on yourself."

"I'm told that I am the first arrival, and we've got another plane to wait for."

"Yup," Killian informed his dad, "Aunt and Uncle Gardiner are coming too. Their plane will be here in an hour."

"My boy calls them by their last name," Bingley said, roughing his hair. "You'll always be interesting."

"It's easier than calling them by their first names," Killian explained, "it takes less time."

"Don't worry," Bingley said, "as you all know, I know how to talk for an hour without getting exhausted."

"How does he do that?" Dad whispered to me. "I can't take more than a five-minute conversation."

"You always knew how to be economical with your words," I said. "So, that's where I get it from."

"I make no apologies," Dad said, tapping my shoulders.

"I know you don't, Dad. I know."

We headed to another terminal gate, and Bingley was true to his word and character.

He told us all about his time at Netherfield Base, in Japan. When in the air, he talked about all the times that he had to avoid hitting flocks of birds—at which point, I was able to add an anecdote about the times where I sadly could not avoid birds that flew into my plane. Mary also talked about her similar experiences, while drumming her hand against her significantly larger belly.

The conversation naturally drifted to Mary's expected baby and what names were being selected.

"I'm happy that you were wise enough not to throw out any of the stuff we had when Jo and Ki were babies," Bingley said to Jane. "Now Mary can use it all."

"Exactly," Mary said. "I literally don't have to buy many baby items at all because Jane preserved everything. That helped a lot."

"I had a feeling that we might have a kid again," Jane elaborated, "and that we would still need everything. See, my dear! There was a method to my madness. Or a method to my hoarder tendencies."

"Where's Lydia?" Bingley asked.

"She's at home, making Christmas Eve dinner."

Yes! Lydia was also a good cook. For the love of...

Next, the stories shifted to Kitty and Richard Fitzwilliam.

Afterwards, Lydia had her tales to tell.

So much was I hoping that the attention would not be shifted on me, because I felt like my stories were not grand enough for the return of our soldier.

Fortunately, I didn't have to share the little bit of my life that was a little bland, because Aunt and Uncle Gardiner's plane arrived.

Soon, they departed, and their eyes widened to see us all gathered to greet them.

"Now this is what I call a meeting!" Uncle Edward called.

"I'll say," Aunt Miriam agreed as we all rushed and hugged them.

Aunt Edward and Aunt Miriam Gardiner were the epitome of a happy marriage. They both were around the same height. Aunt Gardiner was a stout woman, and Uncle Gardiner was no different. They had a jovial way about them, where you immediately felt comfortable in their presence.

"Don't worry," Aunt Gardiner said, "we managed to store all of our luggage in these three bags, so we can leave immediately."

"Oh, thank god," Mom said, "nothing is more annoying that having to wait for the luggage to be unloaded from the plane. And with it being Christmas Eve, I want to stay at home as much as possible. Except for Mass. You won't mind going to the Christmas Eve service at St. Joseph's Church tonight, would you?"

"Of course not," Uncle Edward assured us. "We know that it's tradition."

"Promise me that you won't fall asleep during the service?" Jane whispered to Bingley, but I could hear it.

"Well, if you would only let me chew gum, that would help," Bingley replied. "Church sermons always lull me to sleep."

"Don't worry, the deacon is good at giving a sermon. He refuses to speak more than five minutes."

"Really?"

"Yeah. He even times himself."

"How enlightening."

We returned to Longbourn, where Lydia had a handle on the dinner, but we all opted to help her.

As I took the sourdough biscuits out of the oven, I got a text from Darcy:

Happy Christmas Eve

Cleaning my hands off, I wrote him the same thing back, and wrote to him about Bingley, and my aunt and uncle were there. He told me to say hi to Bingley for him.

I listed our events to him, and then wondered if he was lonely. Taking a risk, I asked him if he was interested in coming over. I know that he was supposed to come on Christmas day, but Christmas Eve/Christmas day… tomato *tomato*.

I informed everyone that we would have another mouth to feed.

"Whose mouth, is it?" Bingley asked.

"An acquaintance of yours," I said, "Darcy."

When hearing the name, Bingley's eyes widened.

"Now Christmas Eve is getting even more interesting."

"You both are so different," Mary said, "I always wonder how you became friends."

"Opposites attract," Lydia answered for Bingley, "and not just when it comes to romance. Men like Darcy need men like Bingley, to bring lightness to their heavy way of thinking, and men like Bingley enjoy other men who are good at being decisive."

"You knew that too?" Bingley asked, surprised that Lydia was aware of that. It was followed by Lydia giving him a look, which led to Bingley chuckling. "Silly me. Of course, you knew it."

"Is Darcy coming to church with us too?" Mama asked me.

"He has nothing else to do, so yes."

"Well," Lydia said, giving me a knowing look. "That's always the excuse people use when they really want to do something, but don't want to look eager about it."

I didn't even argue with her.

———

"Darcy!" Bingley cried. "Good god, man, you found your way to my family."

When Darcy arrived, holding a sausage, cheese, bread, and candy platter that he did order from the magazine I gave him, Bingley was the one to open the door.

The good thing about it was that it was interesting seeing Darcy respond to an old friend. Bingley always had a comfortable presence, but it had even more of a marked one on Darcy.

"Welcome back, Charlie," Darcy said. I had no idea Darcy ever called him that. "Back from Netherfield."

"Back from being on the other side of the world."

"You better have stories," Darcy announced.

"Always."

"Especially when it comes to close encounters with birds," I added, putting the biscuits on one of our potted dishes.

"Ah," Darcy said, looking between Bingley and me. "Birds coming at your plane?"

"It's like they have a crush on me," Bingley said, gesturing for Darcy to join him in the living room, where they could sit and talk, while watching sports games.

Naturally happy to see Bingley again, Darcy followed him. As he walked away, he turned and gave me the 'Happy Christmas Eve, and it's nice to see you' look. I returned it with one of my own and mouthed the words 'nice platter'. He responded by mouthing 'thank you' to it.

Smiling, I went back to helping set up the food while Bingley couldn't help but start eating Darcy's platter. Since he liked Bingley, Darcy clearly didn't have the heart to tell him to hold off till Christmas.

––––––

Once the dinner was all laid out on the dining room table, we all had to squeeze in to eat, because it was a table for ten people to eat, but we had a little more people than that. Actually, I liked it being a little cramped—we felt more like a family that way.

Bingley, Aunt and Uncle Gardiner dominated the dinner conversation. So, between praising Lydia for her expert cooking, we heard tales of life on the base, and of our aunt and uncle's children.

Conversation was still steering expertly away from my parents' love lives, so that was another good thing.

Somehow, the way things were arranged, Darcy didn't end up sitting near me, but on the other side of the table.

During the conversations, all we could do was steal glances at each other.

I liked it because our stolen glances spoke volumes. Sometimes, words aren't needed. Looks are enough.

After finishing the macaroni and cheese and ham on his plate, he began to eat his sourdough biscuit. Since Uncle Edward was amidst telling the story of when a fight broke out, at his job, because two men liked the same woman, I mouthed the words 'like it?' to Darcy.

I was speaking of the biscuit, but he didn't even look at it when he mouthed the words 'yes, I like it' back.

Dared I know what it meant?

––––––

We all went to St. Joseph's church for Christmas Eve mass, and the church was crowded.

"There are three times the people here than there usually are during the rest of the year," mom explained to Bingley and Darcy.

When filling the pews, Darcy and I were able to sit next to each other.

"Do you ever notice," Darcy whispered to me, "that people will go an entire year without stepping foot into any church, and then they rush to get here at Christmastime?"

"Oh yeah. Even the least devout still does it, simply out of habit. It seems to make sense to go to any place of worship at this time of year. It's to the point where I think it has nothing to do with feeling pressured, and more just a part of winter holidays. What about the end of the year that makes us all come together, for the sake of feeling like we all are drawn to one thing?"

"I think," Darcy explained, "it's because we're nearing the end of the year, and we're all so glad that we made it, that we are still here, and found our way to the right place to be, that we feel connected to each other."

I didn't look at Darcy, but I felt his words, and our shoulders were next to each other. So, I bumped my arm against his.

"Wise at Christmastime," I said, "how curious."

Out of the side of my eye, I saw Darcy's eyes grin.

———

Jane was correct. The deacon, who gave the sermon did speak for no more than five minutes. In fact, I think he really did have a timer placed somewhere in his pocket.

The service ended eventually, we returned home, and we proceeded to watch the animated short 'How the Grinch Stole Christmas', followed by a Christmas movie.

"I'm getting tired," Darcy said to me, and it was obvious that he was. "The dinner is now getting to me and I'm afraid of falling asleep. I should get home before I get too tired to move."

"If you're okay with it," I offered, "you can always spend the night here. I've got some long shirts, and Bingley can give you a pair of flannel pants."

Darcy shifted in his seat.

"You're okay with that?"

"Yeah. As you can see, our couch is very comfortable, because many people have slept on it before. Sorry that I can't offer you a bed, but I had to give mine to my aunt and uncle. I have to sleep on the floor."

"Well, as long as you are okay with it."

"Sure," I assured him. "I'll take you upstairs so that you can take a shower, and I'll get the pajamas for you."

I felt like Darcy's whole body gave a huge sigh. I don't think he felt like driving back to Richard's apartment.

While we were choosing what movie we would watch, I led Darcy upstairs, and got him a large thermal shirt, while stealing one of Bingley's pajama pants.

After he finished bathing, I tossed him the clothes through the door.

That gave me time to also slide into my nightgown and bathrobe.

By the time that we got back downstairs, they finally settled on a movie.

The movie was The Polar Express.

We turned the lights out, wished that Kitty and Richard were there, and played the movie.

Sitting on the sofa, armchair, or anywhere else, we were all assembled as the movie began to play.

Darcy and I were sitting together, on cushions on the floor, with our backs up against the armchair that dad was sitting in, and I wrapped a blanket around us.

Without even thinking about it, this put us in the position of us leaning against each other, and me resting my shoulder against Darcy's chest.

I felt the warmth that came from being next to him, of the safety and security it entailed as well. I suppose between that, and the natural exhaustion that comes from a long day, Darcy's eyes drooped, and soon I felt the weight of his body as he fell asleep against me.

Due to the darkness, and the movie putting any viewer at ease, Josie and Killian had no choice but to fall asleep. As a result, Jane and Bingley had to carry them upstairs, and they disappeared.

Then Mary had to go upstairs, because her pregnancy was making her a little sick, and she worried about being too far from the bathroom.

Next, Uncle Edward began to get sleepy, so Aunt Miriam thought it a good time to take him upstairs.

Lydia took one look at Darcy and me and made a flimsy excuse that she had to go to bed.

With the family dispersing, mom and dad naturally didn't feel comfortable being alone, with just me awake as company.

"Don't worry," I whispered to them both, while gesturing to Darcy, "I'll take care of him."

"Works for me," Mom uttered, said goodnight to me, and then went to bed.

That only left Dad, who was looking at me, with worry.

"Don't worry," I assured him, "he's not going to cook and eat me. I'll get him to bed."

"I'm just remembering when he hurt you for all those years," Dad said, sincerely. "I don't know why I'm thinking about that now. I just didn't like what he put you through."

I felt my heart soften about my dad still being worried about me.

"Do you know," I whispered, "you are one of the best dads ever?"

My father didn't respond because it was just too much for him.

"Merry Christmas Eve, Dad," I said.

"You too."

Drowsy, he also went to bed.

That was only left for me to sit there, and finish the film, with Darcy resting on my shoulder.

For some reason, I was not tired at all but enjoyed the intimacy of being alone to see the ending of the movie, which did resonate with me.

But of course, the movie came to an end, and I didn't have the heart to wake Darcy up. Vainly, I thought that nothing could be better than this.

The idea of us laying in the same blanket, with our bodies rested against each other—and in that moment, I was resigned.

I liked Darcy. So very much.

And I could see myself falling in love with him. Because I had already started to.

Lydia was right.

Delores was right.

So many people were right, while I had been so blind.

And now, I knew myself.

I was falling in love with Darcy, and there was no turning back.

Since the movie was over, there was no sound and nothing to view. I was left to sit there, watching nothing, while also feeling everything.

As I was lost in my thoughts, time moved around me, as it does to everyone, and I was astonished to see the clock on the wall say midnight.

I gasped, accidentally shifted in my place and that woke Darcy up.

"Sorry," I whispered.

"What is it?" he said, rubbing his eyes. "Did I fall asleep?"

"Yes, sorry to wake you up, but it was an accident. It's midnight."

"Midnight?" Darcy asked, his eyes fully opening, with our faces only three inches away from each other. "Then that means…"

"Yes Darcy. Merry Christmas."

"Merry Christmas," he responded, looking boldly at me again.

Although, this time, the boldness was not one-sided. I returned it with a bravery that equaled his.

Now there was no turning back. Romance and love are not planned, or manufactured, but something that sneaks up on you. That finds you when you are not seeking it out.

It didn't seek me out, but it found me.

And now I was brave enough for anything and everything.

Within my eyes was an invitation.

Within his was acceptance.

I felt his beauty, and he felt me giving in as our faces touched, and in the darkness, our lips met.

We kissed.

And it was real.

No holding back…

End of Book II

# AFTERWORD

Hello, Reader. Thank you so much for opening your attention up to Book II of the 'Seasonal Situations' trilogy.

As you may have noticed, part two deals less in the imagination. This was done for a reason. Therefore, first, I will tackle the concept of Darcy: fiction now made fact.

When Elizabeth was avoiding Darcy, confronting him became a process of her subconscious. And the imagination that came along with it.

But now that Darcy has seen her, and met her, he no longer is a part of her imagination but is a fact. He's a reality now, so it no longer dwelled in dreams. Reality is now the order of the day. Which brings us to the next reason why I chose what I chose:

**Darcy, the Friend**

The love between Darcy and Elizabeth is one of literature's most romantic couples. If not *the* most romantic couple. So naturally, it seems natural that I would throw them into a romance as soon as they settled their differences.

However, my instincts told me that their history was so turbulent that, when they did try to make everything right, they would need time to develop a romance. And that would be from them establishing a friendship first.

As a result, this chapter focused on them becoming friends, which steadily led to them becoming attached to each other, by constant conversation and seeing each other. And it will blossom into a romance, but as Lydia so eloquently put it, this is part of the fairytale.

And that brings me to:

## Lydia, the Genius

Usually, I write Lydia precisely as she is written to be in the original story: foolish, rash, brazen, and downright obnoxious. But every now and then, I write a different kind of Lydia, and in this one, I wanted her to be Sherlockian and highly intuitive. Rarely do I ever have Lydia give the ultimate point of anything I write, where she gives the moral of the story. For some reason, my instincts went in that direction. I hope the change will amuse the reader.

Also, when it comes to my personal life, sometimes, I have a habit of falling away from humanity and retreating into my own life. It's to the point where I am set in my ways. Looking back at my life, I did, for lack of a better word, hide from romance. Also, since I made some big mistakes by choosing the wrong man to like, or getting serious too quickly, you could say that I was against the idea of falling in love or feeling anything deeply for anyone. It took me a long time to realize that our romantic misadventures are not a fact that we won't have the fairytale ending, but that our constant trials and errors, are a part of the fairytale—of the ultimate ending that we will find, in some way, shape or form. We're all supposed to be a part of the story of falling in love. Come what may. So, when we are scrounging around, feeling like we are constantly getting it wrong, so why do we try? Well, that's the point of this story. Those trials are a part of what makes us find out what true love is and prepares us for when it comes.

That's what Lydia meant.

And that's what Elizabeth went through.

That's the curiosity to this story.

I hope that you liked it.

## George Washington's Farewell Address

Within the story, I introduced a document written in 1796, which was President George Washington's address to the USA people when he stepped down as president and handed the position over to John Adams, who would become the Second President of the USA.

The Farewell Address was a document that I had been aware of for some time, and found it to be not only important, but also felt that it should be required reading in every High School in the United States of America. I thought so, because of how many lessons were beneficial. Although it also would give a basic understanding to teenagers of how a government, such as the USA's, ought to work, and always remain so. But after I had to accept that it would never happen, I just wanted to bring it to light, so that hopefully, someone would one day realize the importance of it. Perhaps it was wishful thinking.

Have a happy holiday, or whatever day that you read this story on. Remember, we're all made up of a series of misadventures. Why not let that be a part of what makes our tales great?

Ney Mitch

Don't miss out on your next favorite book!

Join the Satin Romance mailing list
www.satinromance.com/mail.html

———

**THANK YOU FOR READING**

Did you enjoy this book?

We invite you to leave a review at the website of your choice,
such as Goodreads, Amazon, Barnes & Noble, etc.

———

**DID YOU KNOW THAT LEAVING A REVIEW…**

- Helps other readers find books they may enjoy.
- Gives you a chance to let your voice be heard.
- Gives authors recognition for their hard work.
- Doesn't have to be long. A sentence or two about why you liked the book will do.

# ABOUT THE AUTHOR

**Ney Mitch** has been a long-standing Jane Austen enthusiast, having written forty novels that were inspired by her various works. Since stumbling on Miss Austen's books after graduating from college, she has always dabbled in Austen inspired literature, ranging from writing works for teens to adults. Originally, her desire was to adapt Jane Austen's writing in a way to help young adults connect with her, however over time, she has spread her aims to other genres and styles. Having received her BA Degree at Desales University, she is a writer, both literary and dramatic, as well as being a Historic Reenactor.

facebook.com/courtney.mitchell.589
x.com/CMMitchelPsyche
pinterest.com/shebaanna

## ALSO BY NEY MITCH

WITH SATIN ROMANCE

### *Austen Gaskell Series*

Curiosities & Contemplation

─────

### *Kitty Bennet Adventure Series*

Vanities and Vexations

Forms & Fashions

Romance & Recklessness

Nuance & Novelty

Doubts & Difficulties

─────

### *Romance & Revolution Saga*

The First Impression

─────

### *The Memory Series*

Moments of Moments Past

Moments of Moments Present

Moments of Moments Future

Moments of Moments Infinite

─────

### *Pride & Prejudice Reimaginings*

Rapture & Rebellion

Fortune & Misfortune

Desire & Destiny

Pride & Peace

Resolve & Revelations

Hope & Hopelessness

———

### *Chances Series*

Chances Are

Chances Come

Chances Fade

Chances End

———

### **Seasonal Situations**

Considerations Near Christmastime

Considerations at Christmastime

———

### *Novels*

The Tale of Mr. & Mrs. Bennet: A Pride & Prejudice Christmas Tale

The Wonderful Time of the Year: Pride & Prejudice Tale of A Christmas Carol